ATTEMPTED IMMORTALITY

ATTEMPTED IMMORTALITY

The Withrow Chronicles
Book IV

Michael G. Williams

Falstaff Books

Cover Design by Natania Barron

Print Formatting by Susan H. Roddey, Clicking Keys
www.clickingkeys.com

ISBN: 978-1-946926-12-8

For more information on this or other Falstaff Books publications, visit www.FalstaffBooks.com.

Published by Falstaff Books
Charlotte, North Carolina
Printed in U.S.A

To my many friends, always up for adventure.

Author's Introduction

This novel took longer to write than expected. There are a lot of reasons why but they would probably bore you: personal dramas and writer's block and day-job-related "work stuff."

It says a lot about the society we've constructed, that we can so readily and effectively summarize the obstacles between happiness and ourselves, at many moments of our lives, as "work stuff." That's a topic for a different book, though, and it isn't a problem to which I know the answers. I've got a mortgage like anybody else, and writing doesn't pay for it, and over the last year or so I've had to sacrifice a lot of my time at the altar of "work stuff." Such is life.

This was also a difficult novel to write because I wanted it to have elements of a spy thriller: a beach locale, secret operations, saboteurs and surprising violence and competing agendas. That sort of stuff is hard to write. It's plot-heavy, and plotting is not my strong point.

Ultimately, though, the hardest thing about this is that it kept making me ask two questions about Withrow and his cousin Roderick: why are they still alive, and why are they doing this?

In its way, this, the conflict between Withrow and the ancient elder vampires from before the industrial revolution, is not at all the answer. Withrow is alive because he doesn't know what else to be. He's alive because he doesn't give up. He's doing this because it's what's in front of him, and because it's a way to stick a finger in the eye of someone who wants to tell him what to do, and because people and places he loves are endangered. None of that is why he's hung around sixty—no, nearly seventy now—years as a vampire living as quiet a life as possible while haunting the artistic career he could have had. The reason for that is a lot more complicated, and I'm not sure Withrow himself could explain it. For most of us, the reasons we stay alive are obvious or easily determined: people who need us, a desire for another serving of what's good in our lives, a driving passion, a focus of obsession, even simple momentum. For many of us, the answer to why we're alive might well be, "Why not?" That's fine, too. None of us needs to justify our ongoing existence.

For vampires, it's not so simple. Vampires are people, sure, but they're people who decided their lives are worth more than ours. Period. We can dress them up in frilly shirts and give them hot accents and eternal abs all we want, but they are still ultimately people who have decided the lives of the rest of us are a price worth paying for their own continued living. Maybe for some of them the answer is also, "Why not?" That isn't good enough for me, though. As a writer, I find Withrow and Roderick very compelling characters. Every project, no matter how unrelated, at some point has to pass through the Withrow/Roderick gates to see if there's a place for them. I'm not sure why, but I love them. I love their banter. I love their affection for one another. I love their vastly different ways of living. I love the energy between them. I love watching the sophisticated strategist in Roderick peek out from behind the mask of harmless insanity. I love seeing Withrow stumble when he realizes he actually likes people (well… some of them).

I like them so much I got tattoos representative of each of them.

For the rest of you, though, making them compelling is the whole point of the books. If you're going to sit through five novels about these two, I have to make you like them. They don't have to be perfect, they don't have to be nice, but they do have to be people you'd like to see succeed. And I can't let you forget they're monsters, either.

That's a pretty tough tab to pay off.

(The funny thing is, I don't think I have to do anything to make Jennifer compelling to you. She's the third member of my favorite trio, and readers universally seem to love her right out of the gate. She is probably the character of whom I'm proudest, of all the characters I've created, because for me she is a combination of several of my favorite real-life people and I think I did a pretty good job of reflecting those persons' curiosity and tenacity and seriousness and humanity. If you secretly hate Jennifer, please never tell me. Or, go ahead, tell me, but I'll think you're wrong.)

I don't think I did all that in this novel. I don't think I've ever done all that. Never, when I read these, do I think I've managed to put on the page what was in my head at the beginning. I don't think I ever will. Every writer feels that way, and so does every painter, every sculptor, every sketchbook beginner down at the coffee shop, every maestro, every soloist, every composer, and every other person who tries to take an idea and give it a form they can use to present it to another.

I do, however, think this novel is finished. I think I put all the pieces in place for the fifth and final novel of The Withrow Chronicles, titled *Nobody Gets Out Alive*. I know how it's going to be structured, and I know the main points of the plot, and I have a lot of character ideas, and you'll finally get to meet some people who've been named but never shown, and you'll get to see some familiar faces again. I spent most of the last year and a half dreading Saturday afternoons spent working on *Attempted Immortality* because it was such a struggle, and because those persistent questions kept nagging at me, and because work stuff drained me of so much mental energy and personal drama drained me of so much emotional energy. Those are over now, though, and this book is finally ready, and I have so many ideas for *Nobody Gets Out Alive* that I'm kind of scared of it.

I felt scared of *Perishables* when I wrote it, too. I consider those butterflies in my stomach to be a good sign.

Please enjoy *Attempted Immortality*. If you're familiar with Sunset Beach, please also forgive the mild liberties I've taken with its geography. (It's a real place, of course. All my settings are. Even Mr. Ares is a real place, with a real college. It just has a slightly different name.) I'm due to be there next week with my friends. We go every year to kick off summer and celebrate a friend's birthday and it's probably my favorite week of the whole year. It's going to feel good to go to the real one, not the one in this book, but I'll tell you this: when I'm there, I always wind up going for walks in the middle of the night. I go out to the beach and walk up and down the shore, out of town, into the nature preserve, and back again. When I do, when all is drowned out by the roaring wind, when the ocean looks like it's sucked in its breath and is getting ready to scream, I'll look back up the beach towards the town and wonder for just a second in which Sunset Beach I've found myself. It happened a time or two last year, for sure, and the year before that.

It never seems to happen anywhere else.

--MGW

A Bit of Background

If you haven't read *Perishables, Tooth & Nail,* or *Deal with the Devil,* it might help to know that Withrow Surrett is a vampire lord who lives in suburbia. He's asserted personal authority over the vampires of North Carolina but spends his nights trying to go unnoticed by the state's many mortals. In *Perishables* Withrow battles a highly localized zombie apocalypse twice: once at a meeting of his neighborhood association and again six years later at a discount store. In the latter instance Withrow allies himself with an exceptionally resourceful human named Jennifer McCordy who is a fellow veteran of what the Internet calls "Z Day": the brief, highly localized occurrences of zombie outbreaks the larger society has tried hard to forget.

Tooth & Nail features Withrow investigating a bunch of redneck vampires in his native Asheville, North Carolina. With the assistance of Roderick, his psychopathic cousin and fellow vampire, Withrow learns that there was a vampire conflict in the past though he doesn't know when or why. Withrow also develops his Last Gasp, an ability each vampire manifests upon "second death": when there is no one left in the mortal population who knew that vampire when they were alive. This is both a superpower and a coming of age as a vampire. Withrow's Last Gasp ability is referred to as hindsight: the power to pick out one topic from a victim's life and learn everything there is to know about that topic. Unfortunately, it requires the victim's death.

Deal with the Devil sees Withrow, Roderick and Jennifer working together in pursuit of a hidden vampire, a mortal super villain, and the first vigilante superhero of Durham, North Carolina. Along the way, Withrow learns the vampire conflict in the past was a vast rebellion in 1893 by the youngest vampires of that time. Almost all the elders—ancient and monstrous, incapable of viewing mortal society as anything other than snacks on the hoof—were wiped out by their slightly more human and humane offspring. The elders turned to dark magic, summoning demons and discovering a way to call back a dead vampire from beyond the veil. The chief side effect is the summoning back of random humans, too. These reanimated souls became the mindless zombies with which Withrow and Jennifer are so unfortunately familiar.

Better yet, why not read *Perishables*, *Tooth & Nail* and *Deal with the Devil* yourself?

Chapter 1

I still need the sun.
I still need the chemicals.
--Antarctica, "Absence"

My old black trench coat billowed behind me in another gust of salt-soaked ocean wind as I leapt from the roof of one house, cleared thirty feet of open air, and came down running across the roof next door. The geezer in front of me didn't bother to look back. He clamped one veined, liver-spotted hand around an exhaust pipe jutting out between shingles and used it to swing himself in a graceful arc, feet forward, toes pointed like an Olympic gymnast. With flawless grace and speed to match my own he arced out of sight beyond the gutter like a salmon slipping over the top of a dam: a glint of belt buckle and pale skin in the starlight and he was gone.

I was too smart to fall for that, flipping a couple of unlikely somersaults—given my, uh, generous proportions—and digging in my heels to skid into a parallel run along the edge of the roof rather than going over. A complete set of deck furniture shot through the air where I would have been had I followed him: four chairs, a glass-top table, and one of those big umbrellas hurled like a spear. I let myself laugh once, just a clapping yelp of defiance, something to let him know I was still in the game and having a great time.

There was a great crash of shattering glass below so I did a neat pirouette into open air, came down on the deck, and smashed headlong through the other half of the sliding glass door the guy had just shattered. He was ahead of me by a few yards and this was one of those beach houses with multiple decks, multiple sliding glass doors, so he smashed right through the one opposite. A blast of frigid Atlantic air blew through the ink-dark room. Rental property checklists and tourism brochures spun through the air on the funneling wind as I bounded over the couch and coffee table. Thank the Devil the place was empty in the off-season: the closest thing to human habitation in the place was a pile of dirty laundry someone left behind. I didn't envy the cleaning crew who had to get this place ready for summer, either. The whole house stank of dinner someone must have left out last autumn. I threw the right lapel of my coat over my face and crossed the room so fast I passed through the cloud of glittering glass shards before they had time to hit the ground.

I heard my target's footfalls, light as a feather, as he ran across the deck and bounded up onto one corner of the railing. I drew back the lapel of my coat to see where he went and was just in time to watch as he took a leap so long and so high it looked like he might be about to take flight.

If I were going to follow him I had to go *now* but it was going to be a hell of a jump, even with my strength. I shouted as I shot into the air after him, pedaling my legs like the air itself were a bicycle. I waved my arms in big circles, watching with jealousy as he nimbly landed on the tips of his toes, up a flight and across the street. Scrabbling to make it, knowing I wouldn't, and without an inch to spare, I arced upwards through the night, over the street, toward the other house, and slammed chest-first into the gutter he'd so ably cleared. Before gravity could grab me I dug my fingers into the wood under the shingled roof and held on for dear life.

The senior-citizen-looking motherfucker I was chasing took his chance to laugh in turn at me, throwing my own earlier guffaw back in my face. He was so distracted by his moment of triumph he didn't hear my mad cousin Roderick shout from nearby, "*Wabbit season!*" It took me a split second to remember that was his way, a la the old Bugs Bunny cartoon, of yelling, "Duck!"

Out of the darkness came a dozen aluminum softball bats, thrown like they were on a truck when it fell over. They weren't going to hurt a vampire, of course, but they sure as hell surprised him. Tripping over his own feet, the old guy went ass overhead and face planted, then rolled and tried to right himself. Roderick was already on him, knocking him down and holding him there, black plastic go-go boots digging into the guy's thighs and my cousin's spidery little hand pressing the guy's jaw into the roof of his own mouth while the other boxed him in one ear.

"Stop hanging around and get over here, Cousin," Roderick said through gritted teeth. "This one wishes to escape."

I hauled myself up and over the lip of the roof with a horrible, straining groan—no matter how strong I was, the angle was terrible and gravity has always worked against my apple-shaped frame—and rolled into a crouch to walk over. "Do we recognize him? Is he on the list?"

Roderick twisted the guy's face back and forth and shook his own head. "I don't know. You tell me."

I stepped around and stared at the guy. His fangs were out and his eyes were wide and rolling around in his head like crazy. He had huge bags under them, the drooping and flabby skin of one who aged before the era of Botox or even Oil of Olay. He looked vaguely familiar to me but he wasn't for certain one of the ones the Interloper—an elder vampire who tried to set up shop in my back yard a year ago—had seen before. I'd drained the Interloper of all his blood and, with it, his memories about the conflict between ancient vampires of yore and the modern vampires of *our* time: the here and *now*. Taking people's memories when I kill them is my thing, but I don't do it often. It isn't the killing that bothers me: it's the memories. I may be trying to live forever but there are still some things I'm willing to respect about the dead— and some things I just don't need to know in intimate, mystical detail.

"I... *maybe*," I finally said. "I don't get, like, an encyclopedia. I get flashes and... it's like I watch it all go past really quick and it all sticks but that isn't the same as *knowing*." I shrugged and made a disgusted noise. In truth, I could get a better understanding than that, but it took practice. The Interloper wasn't my *first* but he was pretty close. Back then, when all this was happening, I was a lot less certain of myself and of my powers.

Roderick gave me a look of mild frustration, like I was trying to tell him about a movie but couldn't remember its name: you know, that one, with that guy, who does that thing. "Oh, Cousin," he said, "Just eat him to be sure. See if he knows anything. If nothing else, he is a trespasser in your declared territory."

I smacked my lips a couple of times and tried to think of a way to do this—to do exactly what Roderick suggested—without also having it be an assertion of my authority. I was the self-declared boss of all the vampires of North Carolina, sure, but that didn't mean I wanted to *act* like a dictator.

The guy looked maybe ninety, spindly, shrunken with age when they turned him, and he was dressed in a canary yellow golf shirt and plaid pants so loud you could hear them on a bad connection in the middle of a hurricane. He screwed up his face and hissed out a few words. "My people will avenge me," he whispered between clenched teeth. "Kill me and they will make your death worse by a thousand fold! *We will finish what we started!*"

"Oh, fuck *you*," I growled. I hadn't wanted to kill the guy to prove I was in charge but I sure as hell didn't mind doing it if it was going to piss off my enemies. I twisted him out of Roderick's grasp, flipped him over, and planted a knee in his back. "Got any last words, asshole?" He sucked air between his fangs to speak but I cut him off. "Just kidding. Nobody cares."

He screamed when I sank my fangs into his throat, and I couldn't help thinking what a wimp of a vampire he was. There's raging against the dying of the light, sure, but there's also dignity.

It turned out his memories were plenty useful, too. That was how we found out about the Italian restaurant, and, from that, how we wound up in the enormous mess the sleepy little town of Sunset Beach would turn into by the time the month of March was over.

An hour later I was standing in the dark, beside Roderick, on a slightly elevated platform in a restaurant called *Cacciatore*—Italian for "hunter," Roderick told me. We'd gone right away to the site of the only clue I'd gleaned from the old guy's memory: that this was his base of operations, and that he shared it with another vampire and their human blood bag. We didn't want to waste time, and we didn't want to give his companions the chance to realize he'd been chased down and bumped off.

Out of sight behind a huge red curtain, I reflected on the possibility there is nothing lonelier than a beach town in the off-season. Waves crashed audibly against the sand outside, in an old and simple song: one about oblivion and distance and how in the end we're always alone under cold and careless stars. Each pounding breaker invited anyone in earshot to step off into that endless expanse of moonlit high tide, if only to see what happens to those freed of the cares of the living.

I wasn't being all melancholy as hell for my own sake, mind you. Mostly I was wondering about these sorts of things because I figured the next poor sap I aimed to murder probably *wasn't*.

I think that sort of thing is why vampires love and hate these off-season tourist trap towns in equal measure. Sure, we can be exquisitely alone under a jillion tiny stars, normally lost in the light pollution back home, but we are never closer to the gulf of mortality we think we've outrun—and believe me, we're running from death just like anybody. We just hopped a ride halfway through to get way out in front.

Any person, viewed from the appropriate angle, can be described as the sum of every fear they've tried to escape over their life. A vampire is no different. Chief among those fears, always, for every single one of us, is death. And the best way to overcome that fear, we eventually find, is to become the agent delivering it unto others. We tell ourselves the world is all kill or be killed, and we choose the former every time. It can be enjoyable, or it can be a burden, or it can be just another night at the office. Sometimes we kill just to give the universe the bird. Sometimes we do it to pass the time when we're bored. But sometimes, and more often than most of us would admit, we do it to prove we can, to tell ourselves we've still got it going on. We score a few points just to show we can still make the shot.

Sunset Beach is a tiny little vacation sandbar perched on the Tar Heel side of the line between the Carolinas. Roderick and I were not there on vacation. We were in search of vampires. The town, if you could call it a town, mostly consists of a couple of gas stations, a grocery store, a Tex-Mex restaurant, *Cacciatore*, and a few other places. There's an old planetarium doing laser light matinees to progressive rock soundtracks and, in good weather, letting audiences view the actual stars through its huge glass domed roof. There are the offices of a chiropractor who wandered in from somewhere and the orthodontist he married. There's a golf course lined with townhomes owned by rich snowbirds with Florida plates.

There are houses, too: lots of houses, *hundreds* of houses, but they're investment properties rented out by the week and don't quite make the cut for being *homes*. Most of Sunset Beach is on an island separated from the mainland by a long, tall bridge over the Intercoastal Waterway. Beach houses there scrunch together, densely packed across two thirds of the real estate. Each is raised up on tall stilts in case of inundation by flooding from a hurricane tide. Most of the rental properties have borderline criminal names based on dad-joke-level puns: things like "Shore Enough" and "Dune Time". In any given warm weather week they would be rented out to sprawling families or giggling co-eds but it was the end of winter and that time of year they mostly sit idle. A handful of them are actually occupied by the owners: those few who chose to pass the cold months getting sandblasted by the Atlantic's whipping off-season winds. The rest sit dark, empty as a new grave, dust gathering in the corners.

The disused houses are unattended from October to May and, not to put too fine a point on it, easily compromised. I've known more than one vampire who goes every winter to a town just like Sunset Beach—silent, barely inhabited, utterly unaware of the vampire's presence—to spend a couple of nights listening to the waves murmur that oblivion song. On the short winter days between, with certain death high in the cold sky, any such bloodsucker simply crashes in the pitch-dark laundry room of an unoccupied rental. Why not? It isn't like anyone will notice them. Hell, even another vampire couldn't find them in that place: the winter wind carries off our predatory stench along with all the other trash it picks up.

I figured all that was why Sunset Beach was where my enemies had holed up: plenty of anonymity, oodles of available real estate, and endless opportunities to hide.

A year before, when we took out the Interloper, we found out the ancients had resurrected one of their own: immensely powerful, destructive beyond belief and dumb as buying a secondhand toothbrush. Whatever they got back from that resurrection ritual, it wasn't a vampire with any agency or force of will. It was more like an appetite with super powers. Roderick and I knew they were hiding it somewhere, trying to figure out what to do with it. We even knew it was somewhere Down East, the southeastern corner of the state of North Carolina. It's all swamps and beaches and legends of ghostly leopards. That was a lot of ground to cover, though. I could spend eternity combing tobacco fields and get absolutely nowhere. Then Roderick pulled a name out of a hat: Marty Macintosh.

A couple of years ago Marty was the very first vampire to tell me there was more going on in our history—and our present—than I'd ever known. He showed me a map he'd made of disappearances in the Asheville area. It led me to a hidden vampire lord in the mountains: the Transylvanian, a redneck old bastard with a bunch of spawn of his own. Marty had been brainwashed out of being able to tell me directly what he knew, but he strained at those bonds, sweat bullets the whole time, to get me to connect the dots.

After that, I sort of gave Asheville to my cousin to keep an eye on things for me. I was more than just a little surprised to find out Marty was still alive after my cousin moved there. I figured Roderick would probably hunt him down and kill him for being too smart.

Marty ran a bunch of numbers on our current question—where are the elders?—and coughed up Sunset Beach as the answer. I don't even really know how he came up with it, but Roderick said his methodology and results were, and I quote, "almost clairvoyant in nature". Roderick was impressed, and nothing *ever* impresses Roderick. He's been too cool for school since the 1960's.

Marty's a counter, which happens sometimes with vampires. We've all got our quirks. Mine appears to be getting dragged into the deep end of the vampire political pool when what I really want is to stay home and watch something interesting on the tube. Roderick's main quirk seems to be giving everyone the ever-loving heebie-geebies. Marty's thing is math and pattern recognition. It's like he's got a sixth sense for the stuff. Just don't spill any race in his path if you want him to do anything useful for the rest of the night.

"This is absolutely ridiculous," I whispered to Roderick in the darkness. "This is never going to work."

Smiles stood by my side, alert as ever, his nose twitching up and down as he sniffed in the direction of the curtain.

Roderick didn't respond to that. Instead, he whispered, "So have you been back to Power Company? Or anywhere else?"

I sighed. "Now is not the time," I murmured. I was not interested in having a conversation with Roderick about whether I'd been hanging out at the gay bar he roped me into visiting back home.

"Alright," we heard someone say in the room beyond the curtain, from the restaurant's dining area. "Whenever you're ready to get started."

Roderick pulled out his phone and opened the camera app. "I want to preserve this for posterity," he said to me with a wink in the darkness. Roderick is just plain better at living in the modern world than I am. He speaks the language of *now*. He knows the landscape of its veins in a way I just can't seem to grasp. Watching him type on a phone is like watching a professional secretary on a Selectric II from back in the day.

We heard a knock on the front door, and someone stood up and started walking across the room. Like most restaurants in Sunset Beach, *Cacciatore* was officially closed for the off-season, but we knew the truth of it: the vampires who owned it and lived there were inside, doing what they spent all winter doing according to the memories of the one I'd killed: they were auditioning bands to play on their small stage during the summer months.

"Answer the question," Roderick said to me. He meant business. "Have you been to Power Company? Have you gone on a *date?*"

There was another knock at the door to the restaurant, more insistent this time.

"Yes," I finally hissed. "I've been to Power Company, goddamn it. Once or twice." I frowned at him in the dark. "Okay, a few times."

Roderick smiled and half-closed his eyes. "And did you meet any nice boys?"

The curtain started to rise.

"You are holding the bass guitar in an incorrect manner, Cousin," Roderick whispered. "Also, you should smile."

The lights went on.

Roderick and I were standing on a stage, wearing guitars. Smiles was crouching next to me, a growl rising in the depths of his chest. Roderick took a picture with his phone and shoved it back in his pocket. I wasn't even sure the curtain was out of the way. Sometimes he gets excited and jumps the gun like that.

Dog—Roderick's massive St. Bernard—was seated on the stool behind the drums.

Roderick stomped on a pedal with one of his go-go boots and swung his arm in a huge arc, producing a chord like a chainsaw biting into a nail.

"*HELLO, SUNSET BEACH!*" Roderick screamed into the microphone. It was almost lost under a piercing squeal of feedback. "*AND HELLO ITALIAN-FOR-HUNTER! WE ARE JUST DANDY AND THE MOUNTAIN MAN AND WE ARE READY! TO! ROCK! YOUR! WORLD!*"

I could hear the front door open.

Even with the wind, I could hear an argument break out at the front of the restaurant.

There was no one in the audience watching us. Every seat at every table was empty. The vampire who was supposed to be auditioning summer acts was nowhere to be seen.

"I didn't order any fucking pizza. This is a fucking restaurant!" I heard that from the front of the place, out of sight around some latticework covered in fake vines. Fifteen very long seconds passed—normally time enough for Roderick to craft three one-line jokes and a dirty limerick, but he stood there, frozen, mid-guitar-riff, his face slowly falling in disappointment—and I heard someone make a sort of startled noise of surprise.

Smiles barked and I tore off the bass guitar to cast it aside. The light at the front of the restaurant shifted from the slightly blue flicker of fluorescents to the yellow flash of a sudden burst of flames, followed by the roaring *fwooshboom!* of a small explosion. A car alarm went off in the parking lot, and glass shattered somewhere inside. Roderick roared in frustration. I leapt fifteen feet forward from a standing start, my trench coat rippling behind me, to land on a four-top table and hop off onto the ground, Smiles bounding at my heels.

I thought for about the millionth time of The Bull's Eye, and her first night as a vigilante, and I wondered when I had crossed the line from half-assed dictator to action hero.

Beach restaurants like this are always decorated for the 1987 Southern Living summer special issue: smothering pastels and a bunch of wicker furniture with thin padding and tables held half-steady by an old matchbook under one leg.

They always feel just a little bit forgotten. The owners are trying to squeeze some kind of profit out of a million and a half bucks of investment so they cut corners where they can. Sure, they rake it in for four months out of the year, but the rest of the time they've got to pay property taxes and make mortgage payments and I doubt that leaves a ton of cash lying around to buy artisanal cheeses and humanely murdered beef. The places usually look a little more ÜberBargains than Belk Simpson and the food is a little bit fresher than cardboard.

The interior of *Cacciatore*'s lounge and bar was upholstered floor to ceiling in the floral prints of yesteryear, and maybe from the year before *that*, with a few sand dollars and a once-jaunty nautical birds theme turned sad. I hung the corner out of the lounge area of the restaurant and into the big, central dining room and saw two people there. The first was a young woman with at least a couple of addictions written in the dark circles under her eyes. She stood in front of the door to the kitchen, having just walked in from there, screaming with her mouth open and her teeth showing. She was completely frozen in a rictus of wide-eyed shock and horror. The second person was a kid who looked vaguely familiar for some reason: Latino, young, maybe 20, with the same expression of excited fear as a kid in the last moments of their virginity. He wore unseasonable blue board shorts and a white tank top and he was standing just to one side of the front door, outside it, peeking in around the edge. He looked down to examine a ring of smoldering linoleum just inside the door. In one of the kid's hands was a pizza box. In the other was a big flashlight that had a bunch of extra stuff tacked onto it: wires and electrical tape and what looked like colored gels from a stage theater's lighting rig.

I opened my mouth to yell at him, but he beat me to it: "What are *you* doing here?" He shouted it directly at me, over the screaming girl whose cry faded as she ran out of breath. Instead of speaking I made eye contact with the kid and I probably looked pretty stupid while I wondered who he was.

Of course, I finally thought. *Jennifer McCordy.* This kid was one of the technopagans from Durham, the people to whom Jennifer and The Bull's Eye had gone for help against El Diablo.

What are you doing here was supposed to be *my* line. I growled at him like a great beast, my fangs out, and pointed at his super flashlight. Whatever it did—and I had a decent guess—I didn't want it going off by accident. "Put that fucking thing away!" I shouted, and with my other hand gathered up my coat tails to throw them over the screaming woman when I tackled her from the side.

Roderick appeared beside the technopagan "pizza guy" and put one hand on the kid's forearm, swinging the flashlight down and out of the way. The kid tried to resist, but humans never get very far when they try to fight a vampire. Roderick nodded at me and spun the kid around so he was facing the other way.

My cousin knows I hate it when people watch me eat.

The screaming woman was just a regular human and she was in extraordinarily poor health. They hadn't been feeding her well—the vampires who'd enslaved her—but they'd kept her hopped up on her substances of choice. I could tell there had been plenty of meth, just from the way her blood tasted like burning paint thinner. She died in my arms and it took *maybe* six seconds. Her heart was beating like a hummingbird already, but a sick one that isn't sure how long it can stay in the air. The last of who she'd ever been flowed into me and, with it, the very little she knew about these vampires and what they'd been doing.

I set her corpse down on the floor as gently as I could once I was finished. Ramon—that was his name, I now remembered—Ramon was still holding the fancy flashlight but Roderick had his hand on it also. With a twist of his wrist, Roderick took the flashlight and threw it the whole length of the dining room and beyond, into the lounge, in one smooth movement. "We shall have no need of that," Roderick said in his very calm voice.

Ramon frowned and started to say something, but cocked his head slightly as if listening to some fourth person we couldn't see. He said aloud, "It was a Code Five, and he's gone, and so is his thrall. And those two from last year are here, too." He paused. "You know, Dan's ex-boyfriend and the big guy."

I spluttered. "*What?*" Dan was a queeny kid from Duke University and another member in the technopagan coven in Durham: lots of sass and attitude and he was really good at something involving computers.

Roderick sounded skeptical. "Well, now," he said to no one in particular, "I think the term 'boyfriend' is a tad strong."

"What in the *hell?*" I glared at him and said it with two syllables: *hay-ull.*

"Always keep tabs on interesting people," Roderick said to me. "Especially when they are adorable and flirtatious." He sniffed.

Ramon turned to me. "Jennifer says hello," he relayed. "She'll keep the bridge tied up for a few minutes while you..." He couldn't bring himself to speak even some euphemism about the corpse on the floor. I wasn't sure if he thought I was going to bury it or eat it with a fork and spoon. Neither seemed to make him very happy.

I pointed a fat sausage of a finger at him. "Jennifer? Why, I..." I worked my jaw in silence then growled at him, "Tell her I said..." I paused again as I struggled with how to express the combination I felt of nice-to-hear-from-you and get-the-hell-off-my-lawn. I liked Jennifer. I liked her too much to encourage her getting embroiled in shit like vampire turf battles, and I distinctly did *not* like the idea of her people becoming vampire hunters. I walked over, met Ramon's eyes with mine, and leaned close. "Tell her I said *see you soon.*"

Chapter 2

Jennifer puffed air across the top of a mug of coffee to cool it. Ramon had made it for her using whatever he scrounged up in these dead vampires' restaurant kitchen. "So anyway, when the cop pulled up I was standing beside my car with four shredded tires and my phone in my hand. I pretended to be talking to the motor club. I convinced him teenagers must've put tire spikes on the bridge as a prank." Jennifer chuckled slyly at me. "It's a pity to be out my last set of tire spikes but I guess I didn't buy them to keep them on display, you know?"

"Why were you carrying tire spikes in the first place?" I was just as baffled as I could possibly be by finding Jennifer and her cadre of computer witches here in Sunset Beach, trying to do my job for me. "How did you even know about this place?"

"All questions I could just as easily ask you." Jennifer was as cool a customer as I'd ever met in my life—and had been since the night I first met her. I knew I wasn't going to bluster her into spilling the goods. Jennifer took another sip of coffee and set the mug on a counter. It bore a few odds and ends already, the detritus of whatever life the addict had led as a slave to vampires, scrounged from her pockets. "I figured we were the only people on the trail of the old guard."

"I'm the boss," I said. "I hunt down problems. Specifically, I deal with *vampire* problems. Let me say that first word again: I. Not y'all. Jennifer, these people are *dangerous*. You shouldn't be drawing their attention."

Roderick stepped into the restaurant kitchen with a smile for Jennifer. "But it is good to see you," he said.

The two of them exchanged a friendly nod and my head spun with the possibility Jennifer and Roderick had struck up a friendship of their own while

I was busy trying very hard to keep her—and all the other curious humans I seemed to acquire—out of the affairs of my kind. More than once I rebuffed Jennifer's offers of friendship. She was the most capable mortal I had ever met but she just didn't get the fact vampires and humans are not meant to be buddies. The lion does not lie down with the lamb.

Roderick threw me a bemused glance. "Of course we keep up. It is the age of social media. Everyone keeps up with everyone they ever meet. There are no strangers anymore, Withrow. There are merely acquaintances you have not yet made."

I worked my jaw but I couldn't think of a thing in the world to say. Technopagans littered the restaurant, scattered around it like castoff shoes. Ramon and Dan were going over something on their smartphones out in the lounge. Sheila and Xi were seated under the small front awning, playing casual lookouts. The whole crew was here. What was supposed to be an extremely quiet operation known only to Roderick, my second-in-command in Raleigh named Seth, Marty, and myself had all of a sudden gotten really crowded. Eventually Jennifer stepped in and filled the silence.

"What did you find out from the thrall?"

They kept using that term: "thrall". They'd picked up *our* jargon for this stuff. They were studying us—vampires—from outside and understanding us as well as ourselves. Two types of people do that: scientists and hunters. I very much wanted to know which they were. I was frustrated by the needling voice in the back of my mind telling me I'd turned Jennifer into an enemy by refusing to make of her a close friend. I was frustrated by the technopagans being here. I was frustrated by the killing of a vampire *I* wanted to kill. I was frustrated by only finding two vampires after weeks of lurking in the shadows of this very small place. I was frustrated by not being home with my feet up and nothing on my mind. I'd come here thinking I'd spend a few nights ripping apart elder vampires and instead I'd spent it hanging around listening to the surf sing that old, sad song and not getting much else done.

Roderick cleared his throat. "Cousin?" Very innocently, he steered me back towards the here and now.

"She didn't know anything," I sighed. "She hadn't seen the Rhinemaiden and she didn't know here the elders are keeping it."

Jennifer arched one eyebrow. "Rhinemaiden?"

I smiled a little. "That's what we're calling the resurrected vampire the elders have somewhere. She's supposed to be mindless, unfathomably powerful, utterly destructive, and unable to be swayed by ideology or pleading or bribe."

"The title was my idea," Roderick beamed. "Positively Wagnerian. I could not be happier."

Jennifer shook her head. "Not my area of expertise, I'm afraid."

Roderick's eyes were half-lidded and he looked away, out one of the restaurant's explosion-shattered windows, as he spoke. "The Rhinemaidens are supernatural figures from Wagner's *Der Ring des Nibelungen*. All-powerful, perhaps driven by whim, perhaps motivated by a grand design too large for others to detect. They seem to be omnipotent and to come from some mysterious source left unidentified." Roderick held out a hand as he spoke, as though gesturing at something only he could see. He gazed into the distance, at the night, and beyond the night to the invisible sea. The smile slid off his face as his expression fell into the neutrality of the dead or the mad. "The opera is about a magic ring with the power to rule the world, passed from each possessor of it as they are slain by the next. Wagner was relentlessly an asshole as a person, but the composition is so great elements of it crop up in pop culture everywhere one looks: the One Ring of Tolkien, the wands of J.K. Rowling, the operatic mayhem of the Bugs Bunny cartoon." He smiled a little again, and his eyes swung back to Jennifer and then to me.

Jennifer and I snorted in unison at the Bugs Bunny reference, then looked at each other and laughed. Annoyed as I was to find Jennifer in the middle of all of this, standing here talking with her felt a little bit like putting the band back together.

"So maybe this Rhinemaiden isn't in Sunset Beach at all?" Jennifer shrugged, her mind always trying to get back to the practical matters.

I shook my head. "Our best intel says there's got to be either one very old vampire or a bunch of very hungry ones around here. The patterns of disappearances map a perfect arc about 20 to 30 minutes driving time from this town. Someone here is routinely driving somewhere *else* and gathering prey in what they think is a random pattern."

Jennifer nodded, immediately comprehending. "But in reality, they're constrained by their willingness or the time they can invest or some other factor and so, in actuality, 'random' is itself constrained to a very specific and limited set of options for where they can hunt on a regular basis."

Roderick smiled at her. "Precisely."

"How did you figure this out? Just out of curiosity?" Jennifer asked it in the most innocent voice I'd ever heard: two choir boys and a troupe of mewling kittens couldn't have sounded more pure-hearted if they'd been singing *All Things Bright And Beautiful* in four-part harmony.

I chuckled derisively. "As if. Hand to the gods, I will keep *some* secrets from you, and you can bet your last nickel one of them will be how to find vampires on demand." I drew a breath. "Except it doesn't seem like you *need* that one, does it?"

Jennifer let one corner of her mouth twist up for just a second. She'd taken it in the multilayered spirit I'd intended it: we all liked each other here but we all had to be careful we didn't push our luck with each other, too. "So what now?" Jennifer wasn't going to comment, and she wasn't going to ask too many questions. She hadn't so much as mentioned the human addict. She knew I killed the girl to rob her of her memories. Either Jennifer didn't care at all or she didn't care enough.

I've only done that sort of thing a few times, ever, because cracking open someone's life out of idle curiosity is both too tempting and also too far into Definitely Confirmed Monster territory, even for a devoted monster such as myself. I did it to that girl, that night, because I needed information and I needed it bad. I was tired of waiting for something to happen and I was tired of having no idea how to make something happen on my own. That girl's slim potential to know something useful had been worth more to me than what little was left of her pitiful life. Not all of me was entirely comfortable with that, but not all of me was entirely upset about it, either.

"You tell us what y'all're doing here," I said. "That's what's next. Then you cut out and leave this to the creatures of the night."

Jennifer quirked up both her eyebrows for a second, a look that said *oh is that so* in the blink of an eye. "I'm here to find a war to fight," she said. "Same as you."

I shook my head. "I'm not here to start any wars. I'm here to prevent one, or maybe to finish the one that started a long time ago. However you want to put it, I'm here to prevent these bastards from coming back in a big way. I'm here to stop things getting worse."

"Well good luck with that," Jennifer sighed. "But on behalf of the rest of the natural resources you're fighting over, it looks like you're a little late to the peace process."

I knit my brow together and said, "What do you mean?"

Jennifer gave me a look. "Don't, Withrow. Dumb's not a good look on anybody." She met my eyes, and her face softened a little. Now she was the Jennifer who wanted to be my friend—perhaps already considered herself so—and I realized this was the version of Jennifer I had in my mind whenever I thought of her. "Why do you think vampires are fighting? Why do you think the rebellion happened?"

I sniffed. "Freedom," I said, stupid in my easy answer. "Freedom to live how we want to live. The freedom to be a part of a larger society to some degree or another instead of imprisoned within our own plantation house."

Roderick looked a little surprised by something in that statement, but Jennifer nodded. "I hadn't quite imagined putting it that way," she slowly said, "Do you *believe* that?"

"Sure," I said, being not at all.

"Okay, Withrow. I'll take it at face value if you say that's what you believe." Jennifer said. "I wish I could agree with you, but I can't. You make it sound like your ideals are in the right place. The bad news is, nobody ever fights a war over ideals. You—vampires, I mean—are fighting over blood: my blood and the blood of every other human on the planet. You can tell yourself it's over something more complicated if it makes you feel better. I'll happily give you credit for being complex enough creatures to have more than one reason to do a thing, just like anybody else. But the elders are fighting to be able to reassert direct and *extremely violent* control over the blood they consume to live. They want to run the whole ranch, just like the old days, and 'young' vampires like you are fighting for the right to invite the cattle inside for a chat before they fire up the grill." She shrugged. "I think it's that simple."

We watched each other for a moment, Roderick watching both of us, and I changed the subject. "What's the story on the super-flashlight? It burned him like sunlight."

"That's because it creates sunlight." Jennifer smiled just a little and didn't even stumble over the shift in topics. I didn't know if the pride was in inventiveness on her part or that of one of her new minions. It was clear Jennifer was the boss of the technopagans but she hadn't bothered to explain how or why. "Well, technically it *releases* sunlight, but same diff."

"So you're using some sort of full-spectrum bulb on ultra-bright? Something like that?"

"No," Jennifer said. She didn't laugh, and I knew it was generous of her. "It's *sunlight*. It's just that simple: a tube of daylight waiting to happen. Press the button and it comes out in a directed beam." She shrugged a little. "These guys are very good at what they do. They invent the best toys." With that she nodded around the place at her cabal. Dan, the one from Duke, mimed a short curtsey of insolent appreciation for the recognition. He and Roderick exchanged the glance of people with a past. The air between them just about shot sparks.

I shook my head. "Magic? Hardly seems your style. You're a technologist: nuts and bolts and baseball bats." Jennifer had been a professional computer whiz before she found out the monsters in humanity's anxiety closet are real. That's too short a summary and it doesn't do her biography justice, but I've already written all that down once before.

"Magic is just a way of getting the job done. You do a thing and you get the result you want. Sounds a lot like technology to me." She shifted her weight to the other leg. Events had unfolded in Jennifer's life to change her in big ways, but then, in whose don't they? Vampires' lives, I supposed, or so I'd always liked to think.

"I respect your initiative," I said, but whatever warning I was about to give her—whatever tired platitude I was going to retread and stick back out on the road of our pseudo-friendship for the hundredth time—was interrupted by three sounds from the front of the restaurant: a roaring engine, a scream from the lookout named Sheila and the thud of a dead body hitting the pavement.

We all ducked, waiting, and after a second Jennifer crept over to the front door of the place. Roderick and I followed. We found Xi dead on the sidewalk outside, an arrow through the very middle of his heart. His eyes were open but empty, the spark of him gone forever. Now all that was left was the meat he'd ridden around. Sheila was on her knees next to him, half to take cover behind the bench on which they'd been sitting and half to check to see if CPR would be worth it. As we crowded the doorjamb, the floor still giving off the faint stench of scorched wood and charred linoleum, she looked up and shook her head. Tears welled in her eyes but she didn't quite let herself shed them. I didn't know if they were all this tough or if being around Jennifer had made them that way. Jennifer had seen it all and done it all by the time these technopagans met her and she could be as steady as you like through the roughest of seas.

The arrow had a note attached, sort of: a USB stick poking out the back. It was tiny, wedged into a slot custom-made for it. I had no idea how the arrow flew straight. It had to have been made for that, weighted so the tiny little chip of computer memory would balance it rather than throw it off.

Jennifer squatted beside Xi's corpse, ran fingers over his hair, felt for a pulse and then closed his eyes for him. She stood back up, archers be damned, to remove the memory stick from the arrow, then turned to the remaining others in her group: Sheila, Dan and Ramon. "We need to move him," she said to them. "Low-key, somewhere safe. We can mourn him later. Dan, you're on. Get to work."

He paused a moment, staring at Xi's form, and nodded his head. "I'll go get the car," he whispered before he stepped gingerly over the body, around us, and took off running across the parking lot on the awful errand Jennifer had just assigned him.

Jennifer turned to me and pointed at Xi. "See? Your war's here. And one of my people is a casualty. That means it's *my* war."

"You have to leave," I said, shaking my head. "This is way outside your bailiwick, Jennifer. These are not just bad people. These are *monsters*. These are the creatures your and my ancestors made up fairy tales to warn us about. They are going to do all the terrible things you can think of and then a few more just to keep you on your toes. They are not going to hesitate from a fit of morality. They are going to relish every second. This was just a warm up. This was to get your attention, not hurt you. Whatever is on that doohickey is probably just more of the same. Killing a random human is so meaningless to them, so trivial, they'll do it to deliver a note and not say one new thing in it." I shook my head at her, cutting off her attempt to cut off me. "Do what they're obviously saying you should do: quit now, while you still have people left." I pointed my finger in a wide arc to take in the others. "If they wanted all of y'all dead they would have just firebombed the place and picked each of y'all off as you escaped. They'd have to clean it up after, though, and it would be big and obvious. This is them saying you have to leave and you have to take your mess with you."

Jennifer stood there and stared at Xi for a moment, then shook her head. "We *do* have to go deal with him, and we have to do it together. For… reasons." She sighed. "They want to control our circumstances so we behave in a way they find amenable. But I don't want to give them the satisfaction. Not long-term."

"But you're going to leave anyway, right? Even though it pains you?" I asked it but I knew I wouldn't like the answer.

After a long five seconds, and through gritted teeth, she surprised me. "I am," she said. "But only because I *must* do it. There are… things we have to do now, and we have to do them fast. But you talk about the ancients like they already hold all the cards, pull all the strings. That's not true, Withrow, and if you act like it is you're already giving in. Try to remember this was at least in part actually a gamble for them. They don't know for sure whether we'll come back here after we deal with Xi. They're betting we won't. We will. Already, they've bet wrongly."

"Why?" I asked it as gently as I could. They had targeted one of her underlings to get her off their case and done so in a way they knew would perfectly constrain her choices. They would do it again and again if they had to and they would make it more painful every time. They had no compunction against making life pure hell, whether for one mortal or for a thousand, purely as a political tactic. Hell, look at the meth head slave they'd had. They did this shit for *light entertainment*. They always had. These were the guys in the castle on the hill, looking down at the villagers with their pitchforks and their torches, who smiled to themselves in the firelight of a peasant uprising because now they had an excuse to cull the human herd.

Jennifer fumed, silent, for just a moment. I wondered if a little of her anger were at me for challenging her in front of her people. "For the same reason you're here," she said, her voice low. "You can talk all you want about your duties as boss or whatever, but you're here for one reason alone: revenge. They killed your friend back in Kills River and now you want to make every last one of them pay." She looked me right in the eye as she said it. "And either you're going to let me in on that action or you're going to have to race me to take your shot, because they have just turned my high-minded little quest to defend humanity from monopolistic predation into a desire for some extremely personal revenge."

We held each other's gaze for a long few seconds and then I nodded. "Now *that* is a reason I can respect," I said.

What neither of us asked was how the elder vampires had known the technopagans were there at all. They must have, of course, if they had been prepared to kill one in order to send a message to the others. It wasn't just a message for the technopagans, either. It was at least a little bit a message for me, too: care about humans, get involved with them, and we will make them suffer. The ancients knew about *all* of us and were willing to sacrifice a couple of worthless assets in order to send us a message.

Dan backed into the drive in a small SUV and the back hatch popped open. Roderick walked out onto the porch and helped the others lift Xi, very gently, and carry him down the steps to set him inside. They carried him like a sleeping friend they didn't want to awaken, never looking away from his face. Roderick and the technopagans cradled Xi like a child they all had loved. Something important occurred to me as I watched them move their friend with my cousin's help: Roderick could have just carried Xi for them, but he didn't. Roderick assisted, but he still let have the experience of caring for their dead friend. He was a part of the situation without dominating it. They set Xi in the back of the little black SUV, stepped back, and closed the hatch with all the somber ceremony of sealing a casket.

"Let us deal with his body," I said to Jennifer. Yes, I was missing my own point there, with the whole *part of the situation without dominating it* thing, but I felt like if they were going to get killed in vampire business then I owed them something and it was what occurred to me in the moment. Jennifer's eyebrows went up a little. I went on. "We'll do whatever you say, down to the letter, in terms of how we handle him. But fuck it. Fuck *them*, the assholes who did this. If they want to drag us both down together, let's fight them together." I couldn't believe the words coming out of my mouth, but I meant them with every part of my being. "If they're going to try to kill you, to kill your people, then goddamn it, let's make them wish they'd left you out of things altogether instead. Last I checked, we're pretty fucking good when we fight back to back."

Jennifer blinked at me, decided I was serious, and held out her hand. "Deal."

I shook. She had the textbook perfect grip: firm but not strangling. Jennifer was born to lead. There was a time when I reflected on how dangerous The Bull's Eye would have been had she become a vampire. Jennifer, I realized as we clasped hands and pumped twice, then held it for a second to seal our shared sincerity, would be *ten times* more formidable were she granted eternal life. Before I let go of the shake, I nodded and echoed her response: "Deal."

"But I can't actually let you handle his body." Jennifer rocked her head back and forth. "We've got that part. We're not just burying him. We're… trying something. But it would be damned nice to know whether anyone follows us, or comes in here after we're gone, or anything like that."

Ten minutes later, Roderick and I were sitting two blocks away in my Firebird. We were waiting for Jennifer and the technopagans to drive off in their SUV so we could see what happened next. Roderick was sketching in a small notepad beside me, but every time I glanced over he closed it so I let it go. We sat in silence for a few minutes. I wanted to listen to the radio, but another vampire might have heard that, even over the distant, sing-song waves, so I made do with listening to them instead.

"It is always possible," Roderick said without preamble, "That the elders thought Xi to be a vampire. A wooden arrow through the heart? It is a tad, as they say, 'on the nose,' and at the same time it would work on either human or vampire. It is a hedged bet. From the street they perhaps could not tell one way or the other."

"It's ambiguous," I grumbled out the side of my mouth. "But I think these guys know what they're doing. Any ambiguity in their actions is probably intentional. I'd bet they have dossiers on all of us—us and *them*, the technopagans—and they want to leave us standing around second-guessing each other rather than chasing them down the street. They killed that poor bastard to thin out the opposition on hand and keep the rest of us busy, and if you ask me…" I turned a little to look sidelong at Roderick again. "That means they're about to do something big."

"Such as?" Roderick was staring into the distance, down the long, shadowed street.

"Such as moving the Rhinemaiden."

"Or taking her out for a test drive." Roderick licked his lower lip very slowly, once, from left to right.

I dug around in the pocket of my trench coat before remembering I didn't smoke anymore. "Yeah. Or that."

Roderick swiveled his eyes my direction without actually looking at me. "Good," he said. "I grow restless with waiting."

I nodded. We were both going stir-crazy. At least a demonstration of violence would give us something to do.

"I know I said it was dumb," I said to Roderick while watching the street, "But I really liked the whole sneak-in-and-pretend-to-be-the-auditioning-band thing."

Roderick smiled at the night. "Thank you, Cousin."

"Too bad about the actual band, I guess." I shrugged. They would eventually manage to escape their bonds, it turned out, which was pretty awkward when I saw them on stage in Raleigh a month later.

"What will you do when Jennifer returns?" Roderick smiled very faintly when he asked it and I couldn't tell why or what was in his head.

"I'll hope like hell she doesn't get herself killed," I said. I tried to shrug it off, but I couldn't. Roderick wouldn't have bought it anyway. I felt protective of Jennifer and I knew it. That was a part of why I'd tried to keep her out of our business: I didn't need to worry about her on top of everything else. I had siblings, long ago and far away: siblings whose names I remember but whose faces are lost to time. Jennifer was the closest thing I'd had to a human friend in a while but she was the closest thing I'd had to a sister since I was *alive*. I needed to avoid letting that be used against me, though. This was the start of a war between monsters and a part of me knew the winner, likely as not, would be the baddest monster around.

Roderick was silent for a moment, still staring into the distance, and then blinked. I turned my eyes in the direction his own were pointed. "There," he whispered. "In the darkness."

There was someone hiding behind a nearby palm tree, looking in the direction of the restaurant, and for just a moment I saw the stars reflect in the glass of their binoculars.

It was so dark where they stood I couldn't even see them with a vampire's eyes. Well, I could see them, but I couldn't make out any significant details. I couldn't tell whether it was a man or a woman, or a mortal or a vampire. It occurred to me that a vampire with a pair of binoculars would be a little like taping a magnifying glass to a telescope. There's no such thing as a vampire with bad eyesight. The big flush fixes all that sort of stuff. We're predators. Our eyes are special. I've met vampires who keep their superfluous old spectacles around, from mortal days, as a reminder of what they gained in return for what they gave up.

"Mortal," I whispered, but I realized Roderick had spoken at the same time:

"Vampire," he said.

We looked at each other for a moment and we both grinned. We'd have fun figuring out which of us was right. I yanked the knob for the headlights so that I flooded the street with the brightest lights you can get installed on an old car like mine without melting the wiring or breaking the law. The figure was thrown into sharp relief: it was—or appeared to be—a young man, military cut, narrow frame, and he would have dropped the binoculars if they weren't on a string around his neck. The look of surprise on his face was priceless, and I gave out a guffaw of victory: clearly he was a human.

The kid didn't freeze on us as I'd figured he would, though. Instead, he ran: spun on a dime and leapt in a single bound over a fence between two of those elevated beach houses and was gone. Roderick clapped his hands in glee and pulled out the fancy flashlight the technopagans had used before. "Now to try *my* light," he said.

I was already cranking up the time dilation my blood afforded me, my foot on the pedal and my hands turning the wheel to guide us into the street in the somewhat float-y feeling you get when you drive a vehicle moving at normal speed but all your observations and reactions are spun up to turbo. I looked at the flashlight in my cousin's hands. "Wait, that's the…" I gulped. I felt like the guy who pulled the pin on a grenade and was trying to remember which number comes after two. "Holy shit, Roderick!"

He waved to dismiss my worry. "Yes, it is their sunlamp. Please put me within flashlight range of that vampire." He paused and giggled. "I wonder what flashlight range *is?*"

I swung the Firebird's tail around a curve like a drift of molasses and gunned it, pushing us forward on a great surge from the roaring engine. Roderick rolled the window down and leaned out as we started catching up to the guy. That surprised me: the Firebird is fast, but many vampires can run just as fast as any car.

In a few long moments we were almost up to the kid and Roderick's fingers started fiddling with the many buttons and switches on the flashlight. Throwing my left arm over my own face and eyes, I held the wheel steady as he finally found the on/off switch on the sunlamp. That vampires were using something like that—a tube of instant electro-magical death for anyone such as ourselves—seemed insane, but that made it so perfectly *Roderick* I couldn't have imagined him coming up with anything else for us to do. Of *course* Roderick went back in there and found the flashlight after he took it away from Ramon. Of course he hung onto it. Of course he managed to hide it on his spindly frame in some way even though it was the size of one of his own arms.

I heard the switch click again and Roderick said, "It is safe, Cousin! Probably!" I looked, and the kid was running alongside the car. He wasn't a pile of dissipating ash and flame, so he must have been a human being. He was damned fast, though, and this close I could smell something like the stench of a vampire I didn't know. He was being fed the blood of a vampire, then. It's what I do with my dog, sure, and we can do it to a human to make them stronger, or to heal them, but it makes them crazy. I don't mean *eventually* crazy, either. I mean they go crazy in a few weeks—maybe months if they're lucky—and they never come back down.

I started to swerve the car to try to hit the guy, but he stopped and spun and did a switchback behind us, across some yards, and as I came to a screeching halt I saw him run around the front corner of the only seedy little beach bar on the island of Sunset Beach. It was a half-assed shack with a beer sign out front and a big placard with its name: To Kill A Sunrise. Say it fast and groan at the pun.

The guy was seeking safety in numbers, of course. He went where vampires could not chase him and do him any immediate harm without drawing a *lot* of attention.

Roderick made a noise of frustration as I dropped out of super-speed and slowed the car to take a turn going the other direction. It was time to consider our options and we –

There was a person crossing the street in front of us.

The thoughts turning in my head tripped over their own shoelaces and tumbled into a heap as I slammed on the brakes to avoid hitting the gray silhouette in the road. I couldn't imagine where they came from—there wasn't anyone there the moment before—and I'll be goddamned if I knew what they were thinking. We were in a speeding sports car tearing ass down a narrow street in a mostly residential neighborhood. They had to see us. They had to hear us.

But there she was, in a long gray dress, cinched at the waist, her dark hair flowing in the winter wind. She stared straight ahead as she moseyed—that's the only word for it—across the street at a snail's pace. At the last second she started to turn but never got to look right at us. I saw her face in three-quarter view, the gray-white of an old handkerchief, the eyes dark in the dim light of streetlights and the stars. My heavy old Firebird's tires cried out to heaven, and the brakes sang, but we rolled right over her anyway.

There was no thud.

There was no bump.

The Firebird skidded, slightly askew, and Smiles and Dog fell halfway into the front row between us from their perches in the back. I saw Roderick's eyes narrow as he dug his fingers into the dashboard. Tires shrieking, we came to a rest.

I hung my head out the open driver's window to look behind us, but there was no body lying in the road. There was no dent in the front hood, no smell of blood splashed around, no nothing.

"Cousin," Roderick said after a moment, but I put a hand on his forearm, very lightly, just the heel of my palm, to stop him there.

"No." I pointed a finger at the road behind us. "Not right now. We have other things to think about than the possibility of a ghost wandering around."

"I would say it is rather more than a possibility," Roderick replied. His eyebrows were arched high and he looked a little bemused. "By all appearances, the classic 'gray lady' type of apparition described in so much beach lore and certainly not unique to any one tow-"

"*Not* right now," I snapped. The street behind us just stayed empty no matter how I willed it to manifest a corpse. "Just... not right now."

I drove us around the block a few times, to buy us a few minutes. I wanted the thrall we'd chased to have the chance to convince himself we were gone. I wanted him to relax, assuming he was early enough for that to be an option in the cycle of paranoia and confusion they always sooner or later develop. When prey relaxes is when prey gets sloppy. There's a point in the crazy when a thrall just isn't capable of relaxing anymore.

That it gave me a few minutes to come down off of driving right through a person who wasn't there was of course mere coincidence.

Roderick spent that time expounding on his observations of the elders we were chasing and the strategy he felt we should follow. "So far they have created one circumstance after another and forced us to react. They murdered your friend Clyde to put you off-balance. That your reaction was other than they expected was a happy fact of your character. They sent an expendable thug to Durham to test your defenses and you responded by eliminating that vampire *and* everything he influenced while there. They killed one of Jennifer's friends to restrict the options available to her and she immediately behaved as they hoped, at least thus far. In each example, they have been the ones to create the crisis and they have done so on their own timetable. We must create circumstances of our own. We must think of what we wish they would do and then create circumstances to force *their* hands for once. And at the same time," and here he pointed one finger, not directly at me but at the world at large, at our situation in general, "We must create in them the impression we are doing something *else*. We must let them think they are still playing their game, and playing it well, while we draw a slow circle around the options available to them so those options are more favorable to us than they know."

"Roderick," I sighed, "Can you give me the short version?"

"We must fool them." He smiled a little. "We must make them think they are in control and we must use that to hang them."

"Do you have any suggestions on how to do so?"

"Yes," Roderick said. "I believe so. But you will not like them."

I furrowed my brow with undisguised prejudice. "Go on."

"We are going to need help," Roderick said. "We will need all the vampires of Raleigh, except for one. No, *two*. We must engage the enemy in a battle of wits. In modern parlance, what I propose we do is labeled 'social engineering'. This will also require the technopagans' participation."

I put up a hand to pause him and looked sidelong. "OK, so what's the story on you dating one of the technopagans?"

Roderick rolled his eyes. "Dan? I would hardly call what we did 'dating', but OK. We had some fun. We went out a couple of times. Nothing serious." He shot me a look of something like disappointment from under the stringy blond hair flopped over his face. I noticed—not for the first time, but it was easy to forget—how old his eyes looked. Roderick was turned when he was nineteen years old, underfed, sunken-chested, strung out. He still looked that way. Just walking down the street, he looked like the misspent youth of any of a number of decades. In his eyes, though, were *all* those decades. "You do not think I am turning into some sentimental fool, do you? The technopagans are useful. I want to maintain relations with them. Just befriending Jennifer is not enough to guarantee that. Dan has been a member for much longer. He wanted more than I did, and so I have tried to maintain a friendship. I believe in the long run it will be advantageous to have… associated with him."

"Associated," I parroted. "And you got to have some fun, as you say."

"And there is nothing wrong with that, Cousin. That we were born in a less permissive age does not mean we live there still. I signed up for this life in order to see the future, not to remain in the past." Roderick clucked his tongue at me. "Now, do you want to hear my plan or not?"

I didn't ask how long he had been cooking up this idea he so readily wanted to give the appearance had just come into being, spontaneously, as though from nowhere. I was tired of waiting. I was ready to make a thing happen. "Okay, Cousin," I said with a little smile. "Tell me your clever plan."

He did. As Roderick told me his plan—and it was clever—one thing became clear to me above all: if the Bull's Eye would have been a dangerous vampire, and Jennifer would have been even more so, Roderick was the trickiest son of a bitch I've ever met, and then some, and he was already over the wall and on my side of immortality. I had to wonder just whose idea that had been, and why.

CHAPTER 3

"The blood runs hot before it's cold."
--HEALTH, FLESH WORLD (UK)

We ended up circling back to *Cacciatore*. The lights were still on, the front door still hanging wide open, and there were no cops or fire trucks despite the smell of burnt plastic and wood that wafted nearby. Maybe nobody much was around, so nobody had called the cops or the fire department. Sure, *maybe*. On the other hand, maybe it meant the cops and the fire department knew better than to respond. If the elders had started feeding their blood to the locals, why spend it on piss-ant townies? If you want to take over a place, you *take over*.

Roderick texted Jennifer to let her know there didn't seem to be any activity around—no obvious motorcade chasing after her or prowling in the dark.

A couple of minutes later she responded: DON'T SEEM TO HAVE BEEN FOLLOWED, EITHER. I WONDER WHERE THEY ARE?

"You were right," I said to Roderick. "They must be moving the Rhinemaiden, or doing something with her, and we don't have any idea what or where. They were just getting us out of the way."

"We have but one lead, Cousin. We should pursue it."

I nodded. It had been twenty minutes or so since we chased Captain Crew Cut through the dark streets of Sunset Beach. That was plenty of time for him to decide we weren't brave enough to barge into To Kill A Sunrise looking for him. It was getting late by mortal standards—nearly 11:00 at night, anyway—but last call wouldn't happen for hours. It was the off-season, so the place probably wasn't very busy, either. Roderick wanted to play the elders' game, put *them* in crisis mode for once, and I was all for that notion. We drove right up to the bar, parked on the street outside, and walked up to the front door.

It was hard not to notice the two cruisers with SHERIFF down the side. Fun times: this place probably got to stay open as late as it wanted as long as it kept serving the cops.

The bar was in a run down little brick building—correction, faux-brick paper siding—between an ice cream shop and Island Market, the mini-mart that passes for a grocery store on the island proper. The ice cream joint stayed boarded up until the first week of May, so that night it was shut tight. Island Market had locked up hours earlier. To Kill A Sunrise was tucked between them, narrow but long, with maybe more room inside than one might imagine driving past. Lots of people would drive past it, too: it was just across the street from the city lot and the only public pier. That night, the only thing in the city lot was a beat-up red pickup truck someone had parked there. By day, however, hundreds of people a day would drive right by this boozy little shotgun barrel with its horribly punny sign. They'd pay two bucks to park as long as they wanted and go watch the kids make sand castles while they drank a warm beer. Sunset Beach doesn't have a lot in the way of a commercial district. Almost all shops on the island itself are clustered together in easy flip-flopping distance for the benefit of beachgoers' wallets.

The bar's door was shut, but I could hear what sounded like honky-tonk music coming from inside.

"Rednecks," Roderick murmured. "How delightful."

"Aw, Cousin," I chided. "Rednecks are some of the most delightfully direct people I've ever met."

Roderick raised both eyebrows and gestured. "Then lead the way, Cousin."

I grinned and opened the green metal door. Light spilled out and behind it came a wave of Hank Williams–Junior, the shitty one. "Ugh," I said aloud. "Fuck *that*."

"How delightfully direct of you." I could hear Roderick smiling as he said it.

"Get inside," I growled.

The interior of To Kill A Sunrise was every bit as run down as the outside: a bare wood floor that badly needed a new finish, an old wooden bar top that stank of lemon-scented spray-polish and watery beer, ancient Formica tables with mismatched plastic chairs, and green cement block walls like the waiting room of a hospital where people only ever go to die. There was a jukebox playing and a few old coots holding hands of cards at a table to one side. The bar ran down the long side of the room, towards the back, and there was a barkeep staring into her phone behind the long handled beer taps. Neon signs advertised brands of beer I wasn't sure still existed. Do beer brands go out of business? You wouldn't think so, but not a single one of the logos looked familiar to me. I guess maybe it's been a while since I spent serious time on the beer aisle at the grocery store.

The card players looked up to glance at us, then back down to their cards, then back up. We were strangers, and this wasn't the sort of place strangers went. Not in the off-season, anyway. Not now, when most of the houses were empty.

"Liminal states," Roderick said aloud. He was looking at the card players, who were looking at us. He was dressed in a pink tee shirt that had a superhero logo on it with a big JD, the superhero identity Roderick worked out for himself, what he was hollering about when the curtain went up at *Cacciatore*: Just Dandy. He was otherwise dressed in black tight-fitting vinyl trousers and the go-go boots with a little bit of a lift to them.

"What?" I blinked at him.

"That is what I would name a bar," Roderick said, still looking at the card players, who were now openly staring at him. He smiled. "'Liminal States.'"

"What does that even mean?"

"It is from anthropology," Roderick said. He was still holding the card players' gaze, and now the barkeep—young, bored looking, maybe in her late 20's, very dark skin and frizzy hair—had looked over, too. "It is the moment in a ritual when initiates stand on the threshold between two distinct and recognized states of being. They are not initiated and yet they have advanced beyond the wholly unaffiliated. Imagine a child being presented her Girl Scouts badge for Science & Technology. She is, say, a Chemistry enthusiast and has earned said recognition for it. The moment she stands before the troop to be given the badge, but before she has been given it: that is the liminal stage of that ritual. Another would be, for instance, if she were in the process of taking her driving test." He raised his eyebrows. "Or if she became a vampire."

I blinked at him. Where in the hell did stuff like that come from? "Which are things that do not exist," I said aloud for the rest of the bar's benefit, because I'm smooth like that. "And you would name a bar that?"

"Of course," Roderick said. "A place where persons become intoxicated…"

"But aren't yet passed out," I said, finishing the thought. "That's… not bad."

I looked around the room again and confirmed what seemed to be the case upon first entering: there were people in here, sure, but none of them was Crew Cut, which was what I'd started calling the guy in my head. So where had he gone?

"If you ever open it," the bartender said, having now officially seen and heard it all, "Let me know if you're hiring. Anyway, you fellas want something to drink or are you here for the meeting?"

I looked back at her and met her eyes. "Meeting?"

"The historical society thing," she said. With her thumb she indicated farther along the shotgun building, where there was a door. "Back in the Celebration Lounge." The way her lips crinkled when she said it made it clear just how celebratory she thought the lounge to be.

"Oh, y'all rent out a room in the back for events?"

"Yep. Best rates in town." She looked back at her phone. "*Only* rates in town. Anyway, it's back there."

"Thanks," I said, and I put a hand on Roderick's elbow. "C'mon, Cousin."

He and the card players were still staring at one another and now I noticed his smile was affixed as firmly as possible, unmoving, with closed lips, but his eyes were very focused. He wasn't just looking at the card players. He was examining them.

For their parts, all three had gone slack jawed. I saw a little bubble of saliva in the corner of one's lips and their eyelids were heavy. They looked like they might be about to fall asleep.

Roderick licked his lower lip, very slowly.

I squeezed his elbow. "Cousin," I said. "Let's go." I tugged on his arm, and he blinked, very slowly, so slowly it made me realize he hadn't yet blinked since he started staring at them.

When he did, so did they, and as he turned to look at me they all seemed to awaken from a slightly somnambulistic state. They didn't do it all at once. Instead, they swam to the surface of the here and now from far below, with

Roderick in the lead but not by much. "Cousin?" He asked it as though he were surprised to see me there.

"Liminal states," I said. I guess I said it to myself as much as I did to him.

"That would be a good name for a bar," Roderick murmured. "I should endeavor to remember that." He smiled a little but his eyes had lost most of their focus.

"Let's go in back," I murmured. "I think Crew Cut must have gone that way."

The bartender had wandered over, looking back and forth between Roderick and the old white guys playing cards. I guess she heard me, because she said, "You mean Bobby? Yeah, he's back there."

Roderick's eyes snapped into focus. "Bobby," he breathed, and looked over at the bartender. "Thank you. Yes. Celebration Lounge." He looked back at me, sharp as a knife. "Yes. For what are we waiting?"

I rolled my eyes and let out a long, lip-fluttering breath as I turned towards the back.

The Celebration Lounge was a meeting room and event space with cheap carpet over a cement floor and no windows. I made note of that, because a vampire is always hyper-alert for places where you don't run much risk of sunburn, but it also occurred to me it was probably because they wouldn't have looked out on anything other than the unadorned backs and sides of the ice cream shop and the convenience store.

The carpet was that kind that's brown and green and beige and white and black, but all in flecks piled on top of swirling, random patterns. A million toddlers could puke their heads off in a room like this and the carpet would never look stained because it was already ruined the day it was made. The walls were beige-painted cinder blocks with a couple of fake potted trees leaned against them to draw the eye. Twinkling white Christmas lights were draped over the fake trees to try to cheer them up a little. The fluorescent lights were way too bright and I'd have bet a nickel one of them blinked at random intervals between seven seconds and a minute and a half.

There were ten people seated scattershot across three times as many folding chairs. They crowded the room, which was bigger than one expected of a chintzy place like this, but not as big as most people probably wished after they'd put down the deposit. At the front of the room was a guy with the damp forehead and upholstery pattern tie of a salesman. Most of the people in the chairs were significantly older than Crew Cut—Bobby—had seemed. But there, in the back, tantalizingly close to us, was Bobby. He was sitting next to a young woman and whispering in her ear, but nothing else about their body language was intimate. They were having a conversation but it was more business than pleasure.

The salesman at the front was in the middle of trying to answer a question, apparently. "Um, well, first, let me say that's an excellent question." I rolled my eyes, and I could practically hear the people in the audience do the same. "Yes, the XD model comes with a separate identifier module. It makes an independent determination of what you're detecting, which decreases the odds of you picking up trash and being told it's buried treasure." Then he laughed, but it was like he had to stamp out each one: "Ha. Ha. Ha." This guy was bombing, and he knew it, and I knew it, and if I'd been paying attention I could have smelled it from outside.

What surprised me was that the audience didn't seem to care. "And how deep does the twelve inch coil detect?"

"That depends on the metal, of course, and the size of the object. If you're talking about a coin, that's going to depend on whether it's flat facing or on its edge, and the alloys involved." The guy hesitated, and I noted it because a person who's a professional in sales usually presses hard with the best-case scenario in order to seal the deal. This guy wasn't pressing hard. He wasn't pressing at all. Hell, he was leaning *back*. He looked a little intimidated. That only happens when a salesperson who maybe isn't as knowledgeable as they should be encounters a prospect who's done their homework. "In the best-case scenario, I'm going to say… three feet? For something that size, I mean. The size of a coin." He hesitated again, and his body language was all huddled together. He wasn't talking with his hands the way a lot of professional pushers do—rather, he was, but he was also folded up like Godzilla had wrapped a hand around his chest and this guy was waving each hand at the wrists to signal for help.

"And the fifteen inch coil?" This came from an older woman with short white hair and a completely sincere sweater vest. "I've read claims it can find large deposits as deep as fifteen or twenty feet."

"Yeeeeeees," the salesman said, and I could tell now the rip tide had him. He wasn't going to be able to swim back to shore on this one. "That's true, but that's for very large deposits. The sort of things you'd find washing up on a beach like this are not going to register on a coil that large. Not from *any* distance, no matter how close." The salesman tried to escape this line of questioning by looking at Roderick and me. "I see we have a couple of latecomers." He tried a smile, but it was having trouble getting out of bed. "No problem, please, have a seat. Tell me your names?"

Everyone—including Bobby Crew Cut and his partner in their game of whispers—looked up and around at us. The locals other than Bobby and his friend gave us a look that surprised me in how consciously appraising it was. They didn't just shrug us off as people they didn't know who'd wandered into the wrong room. They looked at us to size us up. They wanted to know who we were and they wanted to know why we were there. A couple of them whispered to each other as they looked at us.

It's not in my nature to back down from a challenge. I shifted my weight and crossed my arms. "What're you looking at?" I said it aloud, right to the guy sitting closest to me. He was in his 70's, beer gut, thin hair worn long, but behind that easy-going beach bum look was the hardened, narrow-lidded gaze and sharp eyes of a tiger about to strike.

"I wish I knew," he said back, and he didn't look away.

That caught me by surprise. Mostly people back down when I come on strong. It's one of the reasons I do it. I frowned at the corners of my mouth and said, "Well then, let me tell you." I don't know what I was about to say— something generically insulting, something boastful, I don't know, but I was of course *not* about to say *the vampire boss of North Carolina, so screw you and the hearse you'll ride out in.*

Whatever I was about to say, Roderick put his hand on my arm this time. "My Cousin and I," he said, with the slightest smile on his pretty little twink face, in his harmless pink tee shirt, "Are here for the time-share seminar. Is this the time-share seminar? We were told there would be a gift bag for attendees.

We are interested in property development." Roderick took his hand from my arm and folded his hands in front of himself to await his answer.

I looked around at their reactions and noticed that Bobby Crew Cut had gone completely tense. I mean that every muscle in his body was as taut as a guitar string. He could have leapt from the chair and run out the door in two steps with no warning. A big bead of flop sweat burst out on his forehead and after a moment the smell reached me: it was the stench of another vampire, but it was very, very, very faint.

Well, well, well, I thought to myself. *So they* are *making thralls, and he's sweating it out. Madness.*

I cleared my throat and stuck my thumb in Roderick's direction. "Exactly," I said, turning to the guy who'd been a dick to me. "We're here for time shares and real estate. Family business. We're looking to flip some of these old busted-ass beach houses." I jutted my chin out at him. The houses on the island were of all kinds of sizes and ages, and a handful of them were pretty much still standing out of habit. "You got a problem with that?" I couldn't help get in a glance at Bobby Crew Cut, though, and he had balled up his fists just in case it was a fight rather than a flight kind of situation.

The geezer with the big mouth stood—with a little effort, and I realized he was probably younger than I, but I spent the night chasing people across rooftops and diving through plate glass doors, and this guy had to strain to get out of the barcalounger—and turned to me. "This is a private event for the historical society."

"The *North* Carolina society," said the woman sitting next to him—the one who'd asked about the fifteen-inch coils. "Nice try, *cocks*. Now get the hell out before Herman kicks you across the line himself."

The part of me that rose to his challenge before, that part of me absolutely leapt at the doors of its cage with its teeth snapping. It didn't matter that this guy was nothing compared to me. It didn't matter that he was just some wheezing old man trying to feel big one last time. It didn't matter that I could have flipped him ass over teakettle with one pinky finger. That part of us—of vampires—is always looking for a fight to pick. That part of us is always ready to bite. I drew a deep breath through my nose, let most of it out through my teeth, and said, "Sorry to interrupt." I worked my jaw. "Maybe the time share seminar is *tomorrow.*"

"Or maybe it's in *South* Carolina," said another one of the blue hairs perched on a folding chair. "You know, where *you* belong."

"We shall go now," Roderick said. His voice was very smooth. His eyes swept the room to make contact with each individual person. "Our apologies. Clearly there is something going on, of which we are not a part, and we do not wish to impose further upon you fine people." He started to back us out of the room, and I followed, and at the door he paused. Very slowly, as if he weren't sure he was doing it right but he was going to give it a solid try, Roderick said, "Go… *Heels.*" They're the mascot for UNC. Roderick nodded after he said it, and decided to say it again. "Yes. Go Heels." He raised one fist in a small pumping action.

Seconds later we were back in the bar, and the bartender was there, and the old guys in the corner were telling each other a story about one time when they were all out boating together, but they were all telling it at the same time as though none of the others were speaking.

"Oh, did you guys talk to Bobby?" The bartender looked up from her phone and then shrugged as she corrected herself. "I mean, Deputy Rudyard?"

I looked at her, opened my mouth, then shut it again.

"Have a pleasant night," Roderick murmured as we walked past, down the long, narrow room with all the beer signs I didn't recognize, and out the front door into the night. The island was still and quiet at this hour, no cars moving, no sounds but the surf on the other side of the dunes and the creak of an occasional rocking chair somewhere far away, far enough down one or another street that only one of us could have heard it. I could hear a little dog yapping away. Smiles and Dog were sitting on the sidewalk out front of the bar, waiting for us, and Roderick reached down to give each of them a friendly ruffle behind the ears.

I turned to Roderick to say something, but the door burst open behind us. It was Crew Cut—Deputy Bobby Rudyard.

"I'm not afraid of you," he said. He was looking between Roderick and me, back and forth, and I could have told you from a half mile upwind that he was lying. He was afraid—no, he was *terrified.* His voice was low, though, like it took a lot of work to get out from under all that fear and anger. "I know what you are," he whispered. "*And I am not afraid.*" He licked his lips. "But you should be."

Roderick didn't move towards him, but he did cock his head to one side and narrow his eyes, and there was something in Crew Cut's face that told me he had been looked at like that before—examined, the way Roderick had *examined* those card players inside—and he didn't like it one bit.

"Then what are we?" I asked it, but I tried to ask it as gently as I could. I didn't want to scare the guy into starting a fight right here. I might talk tough in the undertaker's waiting room in there, but I know better than to pick fights with the law—in public, anyway. My voice was soft and I used all the body language of relaxation and of opening up.

"You're vampires," he said. He whispered it, and it shook him right down to his guts to say that word aloud. "We won't let you take us back." He started to back away as he spoke, and then to arc around us, and I realized he was going for his car. I thought for a moment he was going to attack us, but to my surprise he was trying to escape. "We're never going back. And we'll never live like that again. And we will find as many of you as we can and stop you from hurting anyone else."

"I don't know what you're talking about, son," I said. The look on his face told me that had been dumb, and I put up my hands in a calming gesture. "I mean, I *do*, but I don't know *whom*. I don't know who did what to you, or how you know what you know, but hand to the heavens, I don't know for a fact that I have any quarrel with you."

"You always talk sweet," Crew Cut said. He looked so bitter when he said it. I'll never forget how much pain, how much plain old heartache, was written on his features when he said that to me. Later, when it was all over—*all* of it—I painted as close as I could get to a perfect reproduction of just his eyes from that specific moment. I have it hanging in my studio, in the basement of my house in Raleigh, and I look at it any time I want to be reminded what suffering looks like. A vampire sees terror all the time, and all the other delicious flavors of fear, but it isn't often we see the anguish of great personal difficulty. "Y'all always sound so calm, so measured, like the whole world's just a big old set of dominos you've put in place and you're ready to knock them over. But it's always a lie." Crew Cut opened the door to his car, climbed in, turned it on, and waited.

"Cousin," I said. Crew Cut was just sitting there in his car looking at us, engine idling, and we were just standing there looking back at him. "Cousin," I said again, "What the fuck is going on here?"

"We must wait for the other one to come out, and we must let them leave," Roderick said. He said it like there was no other answer, like I'd just asked what two plus two would equal and the answer was obviously seventeen. He was right, but it had been a long time—and by that, I mean, my whole life plus my whole *unlife*—since someone had walked up to me, called me out as a vampire, and then threatened me.

Right on cue, the woman with whom he'd been whispering walked out. She climbed into the other Sheriff cruiser, and the two of them backed out. With her in front, they drove away.

I turned to Roderick. "I don't even know which questions to ask first."

"Then start listing them in no special order." He smiled a little, but he was still looking in the direction the deputies had driven: towards the bridge, off the island, back to the mainland. The island was very quiet now, in their absence. It was the sort of quiet that sounds like people waiting for something.

"Okay," I said, "What would vampires want with buried treasure?"

Roderick nodded once, eyes still on the dark horizon. "So we have arrived at the same idea."

I went on. "The ghost thing—we're bookmarking that. We'll come back to it." It isn't that I didn't believe in ghosts. I'm a vampire, we run into a lot of weird shit, but on top of that I'm from the South. We've got more restless dead than relations. It was more like I would rather deal with one thing at a time. It bothered me that there might be a ghost getting around, of course, but that's an old fear I'd put away a long time ago. Every vampire with a lick of sense spends the first few months or years of their new existence scared shitless of ghosts. You can't help but kill a few people—probably more like a *lot*—when you're a vampire, and there's that part of you that says if ghosts are real then you're damn near guaranteed to get haunted as *fuck*. I mean, it makes a kind of sense.

You spend your whole life hearing spooky stories of the vengeful dead. Then you wake up one day and remember it's *night*, not *day*, and tonight you're going to have to go out and probably kill someone if you want to eat. You're still shitty at it, and you don't quite know how to keep them alive every time no matter how hard you try. Sooner or later you figure you'll rack up quite a score on the whole vengeful dead thing. You're a stranger in the land of the weird, and you can't help but wonder if you're going to find out the hard way that ghosts are as real as you thought vampires *weren't*.

When it doesn't happen and you become more accustomed to you yourself being one of the things that goes bump in the night, well… the fear of ghosts kind of fades into the background. I was realizing as Roderick and I stood there that it never quite goes away. "And why do their cars say Mecklenburg County?"

"Why does that matter?" Roderick didn't grow up here, and he doesn't know the whole state. He knows a couple of very specific parts of it.

"It's the county where the city of Charlotte is located. Couple hours inland," I said. "Charlotte is…" My voice caught in my throat, and I struggled to speak, and I didn't even know why—hell, I didn't even *consider* why. "It's a place we absolutely *do not go*."

Roderick arched his eyebrows and turned finally to look at me. His eyes met mine and held them, and I don't know… it isn't exactly that I felt like my mind was *invaded* but Roderick has a way of looking at you that makes you feel like his consciousness is, if not intruding on your own, at least pressed against the glass. "I wonder why that is?" Roderick mused on it, and appraised me, and I felt like we were standing in a crowded elevator. His mind had its elbow in my gut and it *hurt*. "How are your relations," Roderick murmured, "With the vampires of the state of South Carolina?"

I shrugged. "I've never met them. Not a one of them. I wouldn't even know whom to call down there."

Roderick nodded. "Exactly."

I wasn't sure what that meant, but it sounded as ominous as hell.

Roderick rocked back on his heels. All of a sudden the pressure receded. He was just my little boy of a cousin again, smiling sweetly with the devil's dentures

"Next question," I said, "Is what the fuck are you drawing all the time?"

"A weapon. But we are not yet ready to discuss it." Roderick smiled. I knew there was no point even pushing on that. I gave him a look, sure: one that said *this had better not come back to bite me.*

Roderick shrugged, as innocent as a choirboy holding a can of gasoline and a box of kitchen matches. "And now," he said, "We should check in with the technopagans."

"One thing," I said, holding up a finger.

I stepped back into the bar, and the bartender looked up.

"You guys get to talk to Bobby?" she asked.

I stepped closer and looked deep into her eyes and latched on with the hoodoo. Whereas Roderick has a way of inspecting people, I have a way of giving them orders. I felt her mind yield to me and I said, "Tell me where Deputy Rudyard stays." It was a command, and it reached deep into her mind and flipped all the switches it could find. Hell, her mind was easier than most people's.

I should have known something was up from that, but I didn't. Not until later.

The bartender's eyes wavered slightly, not because she was fighting me but because she was flipping through her own memory in an attempt to comply by providing what she knew. It felt like waiting for the computer to search its databanks for an answer on *Star Trek*. "The Surf Sound Inn," she said. Her voice was robotic, a little dreamy, coming from a long way away. She was digging deep for this one. "He mentioned it on the phone one time when he was here. I wasn't supposed to hear him, but I love to eavesdrop. I couldn't help it. Things have been especially slow this winter. No gossip."

I filed that way, too, and nodded. "Thank you." I felt my will detach from hers and she blinked rapidly a few times as she came back to the here and now. Roderick and I were back out the door before she'd even had a chance to say goodnight. The guys in the corner, with the card game, didn't bother to look up from their hands as they kept telling each other that story a dozen different ways.

Roderick and I went back to *Cacciatore* after that, to keep an eye on it, but nobody ever showed. Eventually we got a text from Jennifer that the technopagans were back from the errand of dealing with Xi's corpse and would be ready to debrief the next night. Roderick and I drove back to the motel an hour before sunrise, with Smiles and Dog piled in the back behind us, T-tops open, the early morning wind in our immortal hair.

Chapter 4

My friends had you figured out.
--Ella Henderson, "Ghost"

"Wait, OK, *record scratch*," Jennifer said to us. It was a couple of hours after sunset the next night. We were standing in the parking lot of a tiny coffee house that looked like it was closed for the season. "Café du Mar" was nestled in the shadow of the giant bridge connecting Sunset Beach to the rest of the world, on the mainland side, and we were standing between our cars talking in the dark. "You saw a ghost?"

"Sure," I said. "Why?"

Jennifer gave me the sort of look smart people give the very stupid. "You're not even a *little* curious to investigate it?"

I shrugged at her. "I mean… it's a ghost. What do you want? To ask it if it's seen any vampires?"

Jennifer knit her eyebrows together. "Yes. Exactly that."

I waved the idea off entirely. "Ghosts are hard to pin down. Late night television is full of people failing to get ghosts to cooperate with them. I'm here to find the distinctly corporeal dead, not to get jerked around by lost spirits wandering the same staircase for eternity."

Jennifer's look didn't change. "You've got a crew of magic users who are also a paranormal investigations team. We can make a ghost talk to us, and ghosts see *everything*."

I started to say something—*so far all you've done is make a ghost out of Xi and kill the vampire I wanted to "interview"*—but I bit it back. That wasn't the place to take this. Not right now. "Then feel free to pursue it," I said. "But the vampiric concern here is vampires." After a second I said, "Wait, y'all are a paranormal investigations team? Like the ones on TV?"

Jennifer tried not to smile. "Well, you know, a coven's got to make a living somehow. I used to be in one a lot more like the ones on TV. It turns out they weren't very good at finding the supernatural. These guys are way better."

"Huh," I said. "And you, what, sell your services? Lone Pine Bed & Breakfast calls and says their guests are getting scared out of room 13 every Friday and they want you to find out why?"

Jennifer did not favor me with an answer. Instead, she looked at Roderick for a moment, then back at me. "Right. Vampires. And what's your plan for dealing with that?"

I let the paranormal investigations thing go. I realized I'd been a dick, but it's hard not to be sometimes. I'm not always the most socially skilled guy in the fight club. "That's… Roderick's department." I scratched my goatee and looked at him.

Roderick flirted with the idea of merely smiling but instead caved and gave her a great big shit-eating grin. "We do not have a complete plan. That is a *part of the plan*. We are going to initiate a few moves, see what they do, and react on the fly. That is our great strength. The elders are all consumed with convoluted plans within plans. We do not have that kind of time or perspective. We are young, though, and we have adaptability. They have demonstrated amply they do not. So, let us sow chaos among them. Let us behave unpredictably and cause them to reveal themselves through reaction. I would say we are already off to a decent start, but we could do more."

Jennifer blinked at him. "Your plan is…" I thought Jennifer was going to say something demeaning but she smiled instead. "Agile programming?"

Roderick's smile didn't move but the light went out in his eyes. "Sure," he finally said.

"Ha!" I smirked. "Mister Modern Era doesn't know what agile programming is, does he?"

Roderick swiveled his eyes like the sails of a ship: great and wide and slowly as though worked by many hands. "And you do, Cousin?"

"Shit no," I said, still smirking, "But nobody would expect me to. You're the one who's all Mister Here & Now." I clapped my hands together. "It's just satisfying *not* to hear you explain something for once."

Roderick gave me a cool smile under heavy-lidded eyes that said I would pay for this later in some unexpected way. The ties that bind, indeed.

Jennifer considered. "Tell me what my team's goal would be."

"Is that how this…" Roderick's lips squirmed for a moment. "Agile programming, you called it? Is that how this agile programming works?"

Jennifer shrugged. "More or less. Set a goal, a team gets to coding, problems and opportunities present themselves, collaborations arise as needed and the whole team moves the product forward in an organic fashion."

"Organic," Roderick said. He smacked his lips a little. "'Derived from life.' Yes. *Organic*." Something in that amused him terribly. "Your team's goal is to create some containable but unmistakable chaos. The violence we have thus far dispensed did not elicit an official response. I suggest we undertake an operation that cannot help but draw official notice. I wish to measure the degree to which mortal authorities do or do not extend special consideration to the ancient vampires hiding here."

Jennifer looked thoughtful for a moment and crossed her arms, leaning back against the small SUV Dan had been driving earlier, the one into which they loaded Xi's corpse. I didn't know where the rest of the technopagans were at the moment. It was just the three of us out there. "So you think they're running the town?"

Roderick shook his head. "No, I do not know whether they are running the town. There are a limited number of ways available to find out. This is one. It will be important for us to know. Their degree of control or lack thereof is one of the boundaries on the game board. We must know the limits of force we may deploy."

"But," I said, holding up a finger, "We don't want it to be obvious we're the ones behind it. That's part of the confusion factor. They know I'm here, I'm sure. They know we're looking for them. I want them to have some reason to doubt *we* are the ones doing what you're doing, though. I want to leave some room in their wicked imaginations for whatever crazy-ass theories they might come up with about it *not* being vampires this time. Let their paranoia do some of our work for us."

"Some sort of hit, but not obviously vampires." Jennifer nodded. "OK. I'm open to suggestion. No unconditional pledge to participate, though."

I smiled at her. "That's just what I told him you'd say. Hell, that's what I said myself."

"That is why it is your team's task," Roderick said. "I leave it to you to determine your own willingness to act, and the degree to which you are willing. I am proposing an alliance, not issuing you orders. You are free to be as creative as you are comfortable being—within the bounds we have asked of you."

Jennifer thought about it and nodded. "OK. I can live with that. What's off-limits other than making it seem like vampires are doing it?"

"I may be in a fight with these assholes," I said, "But I'm not ready for *everyone* to know there's a vampire turf war happening in Happy-Time Vacation Village. So, don't do anything that directly engages their... *vampireness*. No running around with wreathes of garlic around your necks and a tee shirt that reads, I dunno, hashtag-team-living. You know. Discretion." I touched my index finger to the side of my nose and nodded.

Roderick raised his eyebrows a little.

Jennifer looked between us. "I think we can somehow avoid declaring ourselves to be vampire hunters, sure. Now what's the *long*-term goal?"

"My plan takes a three-pronged approach: we will make the enemy nervous by testing their holdings; we will cause them to break cover so we may directly engage them; and we will force them to deploy the Rhinemaiden before it can be used to produce *maximum harm*." That was exactly the phrase he used when he described it to me the first time as we sat in my car: maximum harm. Roderick's face was deadly serious and still when he said it and—even knowing him as well as I did, for all that was worth, and as suspicious as I was of his predilections—I had to pause a moment and wonder if his participation in the fight against the elder vampires was purely self-serving. It sounded to me like there was a grain of compassion—or even guilt—inside him somewhere: a sense of responsibility for the mortal masses who would surely suffer in any scenario in which ancient vampires released their supernatural nuke on the world just to get at him and me.

Jennifer let the gears spin for a second. "I'm in," she said. "It'll be a good chance to test out Xi 2.0 anyway."

I blinked. "Excuse me?"

"You'll see," she said. "Let me call in the others."

Five minutes later, they pulled up in a mini-van being driven by the woman named Sheila.

Jennifer and the technopagans gathered in a circle in the empty lot. They ringed up around one of those toy helicopter things, a remote-controlled drone like you see on the Internet, made of lots of little rotors and with a bunch of stuff taped to it with glossy black electrical tape. Roderick called it a "quadcopter" which seemed to me like too stupid to be a real name.

Jennifer and the others turned their backs to Roderick and me, clasped hands around the drone, and hummed in unison, then harmony, and then unison again.

"Navigator!" Jennifer's voice was clear as a bell in the thick seaboard air. "Are the winds favorable?"

"They are," answered Ramon.

"Power management," Jennifer said to Sheila, "Release our brother that he may move again in the world of the living."

Sheila reached down and unplugged what looked like an electrical power supply from the side of the drone, flipping switches. The drone lit up, powering on, and a couple of glinting LEDs blinked into being. No one seemed to be controlling it but the drone whirred, its blades spinning in the abstract butterfly described by their plastic outer rings, and the thing lifted off to hover about four feet off the ground. It was bigger than some of the little ones, and seemed to have more heft to it, more power: it was able to stay still even in the constant wind of the coast.

Jennifer regarded it for a few seconds and then said, gently, "Xi? Do you hear us?"

A single red LED blinked on, then off again, then repeated a few times. Something itched at the back of my brain and then I realized—the memory rushing at me from a boyhood ended many decades ago—it was Morse Code. I had no idea what the drone said, but my guess was it was good: Jennifer let out a long breath.

"Can you see?"

The light blinked what looked—to me, anyway—to be the same pattern.

"How many of us are there? Switch to simple mode." Jennifer waved her hand, apparently tired of having to read Morse Code on the fly.

The light blinked six times—Sheila, Ramon, Dan, Jennifer, Roderick and me.

Dan whooped with excitement. Sheila and Ramon gave each other a high-five. I looked over at Roderick and said, "No *way*."

Roderick looked just as stunned as I felt but plunged ahead in an apparent inability to respond to what we appeared to have witnessed. "In the meantime," he said, "Cousin Withrow and I will be engaging with the locals." He smiled at all of us, stared at Xi 2.0 for a moment, and looked back at me. "I have a meeting with a client."

"A… client?" I hesitated even to ask. As far as I knew, Roderick was like a lot of us: wealthy enough to make it on residual income. It can be tough to find enough work to get by the first few decades after you get turned. Back in Asheville, for instance, I knew a vampire named Marty Macintosh who was scraping by in a small apartment doing medical transcription all night long. That was part of why we usually targeted people with enough wealth to make it without a day job.

"A client." Roderick nodded.

I looked at the remote control copter, still hovering in the air, and back at Roderick. "No way."

"Okay," I said to Roderick an hour later as we stood on the front steps of a beach house, waiting for a real estate agent to arrive. It was a jaunty yellow on the outside and had a sign with a cartoon mouse on it. Underneath it read THE HOUSEKETEERS. Smiles was by my side. Dog was sniffing around the bottom of the steps and the trash bin. "First of all, what the *shit* is up with that quadcopter. Second, tell me what *my* part in all this is. I can't imagine you've not thought of something special for me to do."

"I have no idea about the quadcopter," Roderick said. "It appears they have digitized Xi's personality and a decision-making matrix and loaded them into it after adding supplemental sensing software, such as an audio microphone." He paused, looked away for a moment, and looked back at me. "Ghosts. Ghosts made flesh. No, not flesh. Ghosts made into tools."

I waited. Roderick can be like that sometimes.

After a few seconds he blinked and looked back at me. "We *must* ask Sarah and her Greensboro cohort of vampires to maintain the appearance of vampiric activity in Raleigh," Roderick said to me. He looked me right in the face so I would know he was not kidding. "It is integral to phase one of the plan."

"No," I said. I was the boss of all the vampires in the state but Sarah was the boss of one town in it. OK, maybe two or three towns, but they were clustered together and I didn't much care about them anyway. She helped me get rid of the last boss, Bob the Third, and that had been our deal: she could have some turf of her own and I'd do my best to stay out of it. We weren't unfriendly, but not a lot of vampires are exactly *friends*, either. We kept in touch. Occasionally I went to see her and her crew. They were nice enough folks, *but*. "I'm not going to let another vampire move into my most..." I struggled. "Into my most personal territory and maintain it for me as a favor." Roderick—having done just that in Asheville at my request a couple or three years before—started to open his mouth but I put up a hand to silence him. "Your situation is different. You're there on my behalf and that isn't so much 'home' anymore. You're an extension of my..." I hesitated to say it. I hate having to talk out loud about being in charge. I hate the way it reminds me of The Bobs and what self-important pricks they were. Every last one of the Bobs was like that: everybody's pal when they needed something and then wondering what the fuck you were doing scuffing their carpet the second they had whatever it was. I didn't want to get into the habit of asking favors of Sarah and I knew my personal predilection would be to dismiss her when it was done—just plain get her the fuck out of my sight—before she could call one in of her own.

"Your authority," Roderick said. He smiled a little. "You can say it, you know."

I chewed my own distaste for a moment and shrugged. "Happily I didn't have to."

"So," Roderick waved it away. "You do not want to ask Sarah to mind the shop on your behalf because she might get too comfortable or be too eager to assert a favor owed or to expect to be treated as a peer rather than a vassal."

I worked my jaw again. The word "vassal" was particularly unpleasant to me. "I wouldn't say it exactly like that."

Roderick smiled more broadly this time. "I have already assumed you would say as much. Instead, we will engage two of her underlings on our behalf without her knowledge or permission. If it is discovered, you will appear to have subverted her rather than to have relied upon her. Being seen to make a move into her territory will, I assume, be an easier pill to swallow than to be seen as inviting her into your own. Two of her minions are interested. We have met socially."

I blinked. "You've already negotiated this with her crew? And they're willing to betray her?"

Roderick shrugged a little. "It is not a betrayal. It is side work. Negotiating from a cold start would be woefully inefficient. You needed agents in place. I did not know how you would need to use them but I had a strong intuition it would come to pass." *Yeah right*, I thought to myself as he spoke. "One does not open the box anew and complete the puzzle within the same moment. In the worst-case scenario we would never use them and I would quietly pay them a reduced rate to compensate them for their time and attention. Were we to find extra hands useful to us, they would already be available. I could find few reasons not to make the deal."

I arched an eyebrow, unclasped my hands and held them apart for a moment. "OK." I sighed. "And what is everyone else going to be doing?" Here I meant the other vampires of Raleigh. North Carolina is a few urban areas amidst vast swaths of rural land and small towns. There weren't many good places for a vampire to live. It was easy to know everyone by name.

"All other vampires in Raleigh—save one—will be relocated here for a period of anywhere from a few nights to a few weeks. Marty Macintosh will also be relocated to Sunset Beach for a small period of time."

I must have widened my eyes or something else to show my surprise because Roderick smiled just a little and nodded.

"I know," he said, "It will be a challenge for him, but it will also be beneficial. He must overcome his agoraphobia if he is to survive the coming changes in society."

I put up one finger. "Okay," I said, "We're bookmarking that one, too—'the coming changes in society'—because I want to come back to that topic and hear just what the fuck *that* is supposed to mean. Just not right this second."

Roderick's eyes twitched for a moment, looking elsewhere, as though he were recording that on the wax tablet of his memory using his eyes as the stylus. It occurred to me that was probably precisely what he was doing. "Yes," he said. "I will not forget your desire to discuss that further."

"Just to check," I said, not yet letting him pick back up just yet, "Are we talking vampire society or human society? With the, uh, 'coming changes,' I mean."

Roderick chuckled brightly out of nowhere and faded instantly to seriousness: a firework of amusement exploding and immediately forgotten. "Human, of course. They are the only society that matters. Ours is subject to their whims in every way and thus theirs is more important. Jennifer is not wrong when she says they are the natural resource on which we are dependent, you know. They are, and what happens to them affects each of us. I believe you have reflected on this yourself, in regards to the probability any smart vampire is also an environmentalist?"

I nodded. I had said that, true. "Okay. But how does all this *mean* anything to the ancient vampires? Are we just trying to camouflage ourselves being here?"

Roderick was right back to business. "Our agents will be unable to fool the enemy into believing we are all in Raleigh at all times, but that is not the goal: the goal is to give the enemy the impression of more vampires being involved than are. If we instill in them a concern there are more vampires closing in on their location than they, we may cause them to reveal themselves."

I leaned back against a railing and it creaked under me. From the position of the moon it was nearly 8:00. The real estate agent was running late: we'd said half-past 7:00, give or take. The house at which we waited was on the Intercoastal Waterway side of the island, with nothing but a few reeds between its back deck and the water. We could still hear the roar of the surf on the beach side, which was just a couple of hundred yards away. The wind was really tearing at the beach that night so the sound carried far and seemed closer than it was. I loved it there. I could have sat on that house's front porch for the rest of my life. Maybe when all this was over, I thought to myself, that was exactly what I'd do. "Seems complicated."

"It does take some things on…" but it was Roderick's turn to hesitate. He finally said the word in his head, but with something like irony playing across his sallow face. "Faith." Roderick cleared his throat as though that word tasted bad. "I have these ideas for how to start but am not so foolish as to believe we can plan what will happen after that. We must simply begin and then remain flexible. We must continually use our youth to our advantage. We are less than a century in age. We are accustomed to a fast-moving world. The enemy is not. They have shown at every turn a preference for turning to the past, to old ways, when confronted with a problem to solve. We must use the advantages we have, and those include the ability to go into something a little blind. They are so devoted to planning and strategy they have literally sold their souls—so they believe—in pursuit of power so great it might be regarded as *inevitable*. They are risk-averse, and they seek predictability." Roderick cocked his head and cupped a hand to his ear. "But enough. My client arrives." I, too, could hear a car's engine, but it was many blocks away. There were times I thought maybe that was why I liked spending time with Roderick: we could react to the things we perceived of the world, with our better-than-human senses, rather than having to pretend we'd heard nothing.

"And what the fuck is *that* about? What kind of client is this real estate agent?" I tried not to sound annoyed. Roderick had told me earlier that he would explain it all in due time. I had been patient an hour earlier but now time was up. I wanted to know what the hell I was walking into.

Roderick curled up one corner of his lip. "I am a private investigator."

I looked at him like he'd just farted in the middle of Thanksgiving dinner. "Bull. Fucking. Shit."

He produced his wallet and, from it, a little identification card. "It is true."

I didn't even look at the card. "No it isn't. The requirements for that in this state are stringent to say the very damn least. There is no way you met them. I know because *I* looked into getting licensed maybe thirty years ago. Every vampire does." Being a private eye is one of that variety of stories we tell ourselves about how to wile away eternity. Ultimately I think most of us try to live out every childhood fantasy and television trope and narrative stereotype we can think of until we decide to die of boredom. I wasn't sure which one I was on at that point. I'd done the Boo Radley thing, and the action hero thing, and the political intrigue thing—back when I knocked off Bob the Third—and for the last few years I'd kind of felt I was floating around waiting for my next starring role to find me.

Roderick looked mock offended. "Cousin, you wound me. Have you never heard of reciprocity laws? I was fully licensed in the state of Washington many years ago. North Carolina will honor a Washington State licensure with the appropriate paperwork and verifying documents." He batted his eyelashes at me.

"Okay," I said, waving that away, "Fine, whatever, still bullshit, but how have you gotten a *client*?"

Roderick brushed his white-blond hair back off of his forehead. He'd taken it out of the ponytail he wore much of the time and let it fall around his shoulders and over half his face. "Craigslist," he said as though explaining water was wet.

We saw a smart little import sedan with origami taillights and an unbuttoned collar of a sunroof glide up the dark street, cutting us off. It signaled just once before wheeling onto the pebbled drive. A woman of a certain age with hair as stiff as a board and a big gold sport coat climbed out from behind the driver's seat and gave us a friendly wave.

"Hello, gentlemen," she cooed at us as she walked up. She was wearing sandals to match the beach-town vibe but they were also heels in case we had money. We did, of course, like I explained before: we were vampires who survived our first couple of decades and now we were basically *set* within certain limits. In my case, Agatha, my maker, made sure my work was "discovered" after my "death" so it would be valuable—and that value was compounded by the assumption of limited availability of my body of art. I've been painting up small fortunes ever since. At the same time neither of us particularly dressed like we were walking moneybags. Roderick is more fashion-forward than I am, but also a little 1970's glam. Vintage may be expensive but it's also by nature *old*. A random person on the street would be just as likely to mistake us for a couple of low-rent club kids. From an uninformed perspective, we both looked like 20-somethings in secondhand chic.

The real estate agent kept talking as she walked up. "I *do* hope you haven't been waiting long. Thank you for answering my ad."

She looked between us, not sure which of us was the person she was here to meet. I started to ask what she meant by *her* ad, but Roderick cut me off.

"Good evening." Roderick's eyes were sly slits and he smiled just enough to let her know he was a little pissed off at her lateness but he would eventually forgive her. "I'm Roderick Surrett. This is my cousin Withrow."

"I'm Beatrice." She shook Roderick's hand, but pulled away too quickly to hide some small surprise. I figured it was his skin temperature. We're always colder than the living. It shook her sufficiently that she didn't even offer to shake my hand. "Do you mind if we speak inside?"

"Of course," Roderick replied. We stepped out of the way while she unlocked the door and led us into a dark beach house. Smiles and Dog followed us, silent the whole way. Beatrice didn't make any moves to pet them or acknowledge them, and they didn't bother to sniff or growl or bark. That put me at ease right away. If they didn't think she was a threat, she wasn't.

The inside of this house was almost angrily forceful in its good cheer. There were pastels as far as the eye could see, with stairs up to a roof deck and three bedrooms off a central living area. The overstuffed couches probably weren't as comfortable as they looked and they appeared to have had a litter: at least a dozen throw pillows were lined up perfectly on each, all brightly shaded, absolutely none of them much bothering with matching any of the rest. It looked like a bowl of Fruit Loops had puked up a furniture store.

"Let's speak in the living room," Beatrice said, then put a finger to her lips to keep us quiet. In the living room, she flipped the power switch on a stereo mounted on the wall. Distant jazz began trickling through speakers mounted around the room. Beatrice pointed around the room and held a hand to her ear to mime listening. Then she pointed at the radio and gave us the thumbs up. "We should keep our voices down," she said. Hers was very quiet. I could hear it fine, of course, but a human would have had real trouble. I arched one eyebrow, but I didn't say anything.

We settled into our seats and Roderick gave her a comforting smile. "So," he said. "Tell us the problem. You said in your ad you needed to engage someone to investigate something particularly unusual and you required an investigator with an open mind. I like to think," and here he pressed one hand to the center of his chest, "I have a more open mind than any other private investigator you can find."

Beatrice looked around as though checking the corners for eavesdropping shadows. "It's a client," she said. "Actually, a set of clients. They've rented under the name of a corporation. They rent longer-term, a few weeks at a time, even a month or two, and they pay cash up front. No one complains about them from nearby. No one even knows they're around. They aren't just quiet: they're silent. They're practically *ghosts*. They're ideal in a lot of ways, and this has been an even tougher winter than normal so I don't want to complain. But…"

Roderick nodded at her, and his eyes took on that half-lidded, half-glazed look. I could feel his mind reach out to analyze hers. "Go on," he said.

"They're weird," Beatrice said. The words came out fast, pushing each other out of the way. "I think maybe they're perverts."

"Why?" It wasn't my job, but I couldn't help sticking my nose in. "They leavin', like, slings and shit when they go?"

"Something like that," Beatrice said. Tears welled up in her eyes all of a sudden and that caught me by surprise. The cast iron hairdo and the gold sport jacket and the wicker chair heels told me she was all business all the time. I could practically hear the competing emotions tumbling around inside her guts, though. She was really torn up. It reminded me immediately of someone I'd seen just like this, a year before. He'd had a twin brother. They crossed paths with a vampire, and a few weeks later they died from it, but before that happened they had plenty of opportunity to realize just how completely fucked up their situation was. Beatrice went on. "But much worse." She drew a breath but it shook. "Much. Worse."

Roderick nodded. "And you wish me to…"

"Find out who they are," she said. "They sign the rental agreements with names, of course, but I suspect they're false even though we're able to run credit checks on them. Find out what they're doing when they come here and why. I'm…" Beatrice drew up some inner strength. "I'm scared of them. Find out what they *want*. If they're just coming here to do… what they do, well, perhaps someone can suggest another town. Perhaps they'll just go elsewhere. I just want to make sure they're not here doing something *bad*." She swallowed whatever surfaced alongside that word. "Oh, who am I kidding?" She laughed just once: *ha*. "They're doing something bad. Find out what, and find out some dirt I can use to get them to go away."

Roderick cocked his head. "What is it they do that has so upset you?"

Beatrice started to speak, but stopped herself. "I'd better just show you." She stood and walked to the front door. "We have to go down to the garage for this." I had the sense she was putting on a brave face for us. A pit was opening up in my stomach. I had a feeling we weren't just going to find someone's kinky playroom in the garage. I had a feeling it was going to be a whole lot more than that.

We walked down some steps and into a side door. We were in a single-car garage, but there should have been room enough in here for two or three. There were three garage doors on the front of the house at ground level. Beatrice gestured to the opposite wall. "The first bay has been preserved for automobile storage," she said, "But the other two have been walled in and given a concealed entrance. Originally there were similar spaces in a couple others of our properties. Mostly they were used for secure storage of personal goods: a place to put the furniture the owners didn't want renters to fuck all over." Her mouth twisted a little. "My apologies for the language. This is all rather stressful." She patted her hair as she apologized. Appearances, in her line of work, can be everything.

Roderick surprised me by reaching out and taking her hand, right there where they stood, and looking her in the eye—they were the same height— to say, "Do not apologize for speaking the truth to us. Research has shown persons who curse are more reliably honest. When you let slip the façade of propriety, you begin to tell me what I need to know." Again, I felt his mind reach out for hers and do whatever it is he does. She relaxed a little, and she gripped his hand in return. He murmured, his voice distant, "What did you discover inside this one?"

Beatrice was a lot more at ease than she had been, but she still struggled to tell us. "Hinson's people seem to have made some modifications."

Hinson? That was the first time I'd heard that name. Roderick and I exchanged a glance.

"Have you spoken to Hinson about this property?" Roderick's question was asked in the most neutral tone available to him: polite inquiry, like he was asking directions.

"No," she said. "I'm afraid to mention it. This is just one of the ones on their list."

Their list. I found myself wishing I had a notepad to write this down.

"Anyway," she said, and her mind snapped back to itself like a rubber band, "Let's get this over with." Her hand went to the back of a standing utility shelf set just a fraction of an inch from the wall. A manicured nail swept over something just out of view behind it and a click sounded. The shelf and the segment of wall to which it was attached swung inward, hinged, just a fraction of an inch. The smell of dust and a little mold wafted out. Behind it was the smell of dried blood. Any vampire would recognize that smell. It was strong, and old, and it stank. Beatrice's features stiffened. Reaching into the darkness behind the hidden door she found a switch and flipped it. Fluorescents flickered to life.

I looked in over her shoulder. It was a big room with the same concrete floor as the rest of the garage but it also had half a dozen twin beds, all stripped of linens. It was hard to imagine a bunch of elders, so spoiled, so accustomed to mastery over those around them, also bunking up here.

In the center of the room was a rough circle. It had been chalked, first, then drawn and redrawn in candle wax and blood and what looked like tufts of hair or maybe fur. There were bones in the middle, piled haphazardly, and all over the floor and the walls were pools and splashes of what was unmistakably dried blood, some old and some less so. Whoever or whatever bled all over that room had done so with a lot of violence, torn limb from limb, ripped open by ravenous teeth and claws. The bones were too small to be human—or at least, too small to belong to an *adult*. Maybe they had belonged to animals, but my money was on *not*. There had been rituals in the circle—lots of them. The vampires staying here kept the room sealed up from the sunlight and when the day came they snuffed out their candles and went to sleep in squalor before getting up and doing it all over again. If Hinson was a corporate account, with multiple houses rented, I wondered how many of them there were. Were they using all the houses at once? How many elders were there? And where had *these* gone?

On one of the walls was a giant map of North Carolina, like the kind you'd see in a rest stop on the highway: all the major roads marked, and a bunch of local attractions set around it like a frame. Blood had been sprayed all over it in the course of the murders these fuckers had committed.

On the wall opposite was a giant map of Sunset Beach, hand drawn but recognizable, and it, too, had been painted in the blood of victims. It stuck in my craw, how arrogant these bastards had been: going to the trouble and risk of finding victims only to rip them to shreds in their *own den*, with no respect for themselves or for their own space, and then on top of all that they wasted that much blood? The sheer ostentation of it—the conspicuous consumption—just ate at what was left of my heart. I fucking *hated* these assholes.

Beatrice was very carefully staying composed and not looking into the room. Instead she was looking at a spot on the opposite wall. I thought again of those twins back in Durham—the ones who were the victims time and again of a vampire who loved to make them suffer. They seemed strong in the face of such abuse, but Beatrice was making them look like total wimps. She barely showed any emotion. Either she was already half-crazy just from knowing this or she was made of solid steel. I wondered how long it had been since she finally consciously admitted to herself she was, in her capacity as a real estate agent in a happy little beach town, actively assisting some boogeyman and his buddies as they turned her town into a patch of terrified hell one secret-passage garage bay at a time.

We aren't supposed to cozy up to the world of the living and negotiate a long-term lease. They're supposed to be afraid of us. We're supposed to make them stay away.

Roderick stepped into the room and I followed. While he picked up the mattresses of the twin beds—old mattresses, bare metal frames, like a stripped cabin from Camp Kills-a-Lot—I stepped into the circle and started examining the pile of bones. I wasn't any sort of expert. I had no idea where they came from, other than they were too big to be a chicken and too small to be a man. It occurred to me the technopagans might be able to do something with them, though.

I crouched there, looking around at the circle, my trench coat spread out around me. Smiles and Dog had followed us downstairs in perfect silence and now sat in the dark garage, looking in: two sets of eyes reflecting red from the lights in the room. When I picked up one of the bones, Smiles produced a noise somewhere between a growl and a whine: a grating little wince. I thought about putting the bone back, because that could not possibly mean anything good, but then, what did I expect? We knew we were dealing with ancient vampires who turned to some kind of twisted blood magic to try to gain the upper hand in a war they lost over a century ago.

When I slipped the bone into my inner coat pocket, Smiles actually barked.

I snapped my fingers and he was silent, but he wasn't happy about it: one paw raised, stroking the air, his head ducked down. I watched his reaction as I reached down and picked up a second bone. He sniffed the air and worked his mouth open and shut but didn't whine. He knew to stay quiet when I told him to stay quiet but whatever was left of his instincts—the ones he had as a *pet*, not the ones he'd developed as a supernatural monster maintained by my blood—were telling him to object anyway. I had never seen Smiles struggle to obey like this, not once, since the first year I had him.

That was 1967.

I reached down and gathered all the bones in the little pile into one of my big, fat hands, and when I picked them up Smiles threw his head back and howled like a hound out of a Hammer film. The sound shook the bare sheetrock walls and rattled the garage doors. Beatrice hadn't been ready for that. She threw her head back at the same angle and screamed until her lungs were emptied of all the fear she felt and all the madness she suppressed since figuring out her town had been invaded by things that go bump in the night.

I put the bones in an ÜberBargains bag I found back in the kitchen, then washed my hands. Roderick got on his hands and knees and checked the undersides of every bed frame. Then he and I went around the plywood nailed up over the garage doors. There were no garage door openers, and the doors themselves were jammed closed with spikes. The plywood over them had a rubberized seal affixed to the edge. No sunlight was getting in that way, for sure. On the one hand, it was a rough and tumble job of securing the place, but on the other it reflected forethought and planning. The average human neighbor was not going to overcome that sort of setup.

When we were done looking the place over, Roderick pulled out his notebook and tore a few pages from it. He used a glue stick to post some of his sketches around the room. I stepped up and looked at them: every single one was a crude drawing of Ross, the demon the elders summoned up, the demon who tempted me a year before by awakening all the lusts and passions I thought I buried forever when I became a vampire seventy years ago.

One was of Ross being shot in the face with a bottle of seltzer water, like an old cartoon.

One was of Ross being fired from a cannon.

One was of Ross being stepped on by a giant shoe.

"What the fuck?" I laughed, I couldn't help it, and looked at Roderick.

"Weapons," Roderick said. "As I told you, Cousin."

"Weapons."

"One of several I wish to try."

I opened my mouth to ask him how that worked, but Roderick closed the door on that by walking quickly over to the real estate agent. "Thank you," he said. "We will require copies of their paperwork."

"Sure," she said. The scream had scared her worse than ever. She stood in silence the whole time we searched the room, not even looking at us.

We walked upstairs and sat back down. Beatrice sipped from a glass of water. Smiles behaved right again as soon as I was out of the circle of wax and blood and fur in the middle of that room. The bones didn't seem to bother him anymore once I took them out of that space—or the blood had finally asserted itself over whatever part of him was still a dog.

I couldn't help speaking up. "You know, these are probably not people who are likely to fall for blackmail." I tried to shrug a little, out of an uncharacteristic desire to be nice. Beatrice's scream had reminded me she was a person from outside the dark forest of the strange the rest of us get so accustomed to traversing. "I mean…" I shook the bag of bones so they rattled. Beatrice winced. "You're not going to scare them off with, like, the news they did something naughty once."

Roderick frowned a little. I was butting in. To Beatrice, he said, "Ignore my cousin. We shall do our best to find something that will give you leverage with them."

"So you two are cousins? Do you mean, like, *real* cousins?" Beatrice looked between us as she latched onto a distraction. "I mean, the two of you could not look more different if you tried."

"Oh yes," Roderick cooed, "Blood relations." His voice abruptly took a dangerous turn of tone I wondered if only I could detect. I pondered the possibility he meant to kill her off right here and now, to eliminate someone who maybe had seen too much.

"Come, Cousin," I said to Roderick. "I believe we've accomplished our mission?"

"Almost," he said to me, then back to the client as he withdrew a slip of paper and a pen. "Standard contract, Beatrice. I will require a small retainer. A personal check will do, but I can also accept a card." There was a little plastic magnetic swipe thing in his hand and he plugged it into his cell phone when she handed over a gold card.

Wonders never cease.

When we walked outside, Roderick's eyes unfocused for a long moment as he looked at the sky. I followed his gaze for a few seconds, then looked back at him. His eyes closed, then opened, then focused, but slowly, and he licked his lips. "All I want," he murmured under his breath, assumedly to me but so softly it was as though he were speaking to himself, "Is to destroy everything they have. I want every slave, every coin, every book, every journal, every photograph, every stitch of clothing: every component atom of the dead world they insist on dragging forward with them into our future. I want to pile it together and set it aflame so I might watch it burn to ash. I want to stand so close to those purifying, *corrective* flames, I singe myself just a little. I want to reach into the world they occupy and bathe it in a great wave of hate and destruction and chaos." His eyes were very wide, and his lips very pale.

I licked my own lips now. "Why?" I mean, sure, I was on board, but Roderick's intensity was something I didn't often see on open display like that.

He turned halfway towards me, but not to look at me: Roderick looked instead at the closed door of the one garage bay left as it originally was, then turned again to put his eyes on Beatrice as she got in her car and drove away. "Because," he breathed, pausing before he went on, "Because they think the world is still theirs, like we never came along, like we deserve no inheritance of our own, like it should never be *our* turn to rule." He took a shallow breath. "And because I can. Because they are *there*." He looked at me now, but his eyes still didn't look right. Whatever was speaking to me was Roderick, to be sure, but it was one of his faces I don't often see. "Because we are vampires and we *take*, Cousin. Because this world is full of life and I wish to taste it long, and fully, and at *my* whim and no other's. I did not survive my making so I could trade one set of masters for another. I did not wait for a more interesting future to arrive so I could surrender it to someone incapable of understanding even one *iota* of the possibilities it presents. They do not just fail to comprehend. They misapprehend at every turn. They think the world can be turned back into something they understood some night long ago. They are like some half-wit dolt who thinks the smoke can be run back through a fire and turned into *wood*. They do not see the proper use of this gift of immortality. It is not the world that must change. It is we who have the responsibility—the *duty*—of learning to change with it."

Roderick blinked a few times and now he was fully back, returned from whatever vision of flame and blood had held him for a hot minute. He spoke like a philosopher but in those eyes, while those words tumbled out in a low murmur, I saw nothing but hate. Roderick's fangs were out, but he didn't lisp like I do. For a long time I had thought of Roderick as a vampire on whom I should take some measure of pity for being, frankly, fucking nuts. It was in that moment I realized Roderick was the one of us who was by far the better vampire. I don't mean in a moral sense. I mean that, crazy or not, Roderick was simply better at every part of being a monster.

He locked eyes with me and leaned close, speaking low while the wind howled around us. "Do you not see, Cousin? Do you not understand why I try so hard to have you join me in the *now*? The world is changing and is going to change even more. I do not mean the normal tidal forces of time and entropy: I mean the world is discovering we are here. Take Beatrice: when she discovered obvious blood sacrifice, what did she do? She hired a private investigator. *She did not run away and she did not submit to being a victim.* When human society fully awakens to our presence, how shall we present ourselves? Shall we appear to them as sufficiently similar to be tolerated, perhaps even embraced? Or shall we appear so off putting, so demanding, so *childishly* insistent on some impossible return to a past that never was, the massed living blot us out with a sweep of their giant, crowd-sourced hand?"

I blinked at him. "This is what you meant by the coming changes in human society? When they realize vampires are real?"

"Of course, Cousin," Roderick said. Now he sounded a little angry, though not with me. No, not angry: fervent. He had the gleam of a true believer in his mad, dark eyes. "When humanity becomes aware of us they will, en masse, lash out at the vampires who try to overrule them. The only chance we will have—we, you and I, the vampires we know, our allies, our *friends* if you will permit the use of so light a term—will be found in having allied ourselves early with as many charismatic and relatable supernatural *mortals* as we can. One of the changes it is our burden to accept is that one night you and I, and all we wish to survive beside us, must be seen as one shade on a spectrum of the impossible. Humankind becomes better and better at accepting, even valuing, a diversity of identity and experience but they have *never* permitted the survival of a single, identifiable, and entirely opposed *Other*."

"Permitted?" The word leapt out of that last sentence like a jump scare on a carnival ride.

"Permitted, Cousin. We will one night require their *permission* to survive. Accept that now, or walk into the sunlight tomorrow. There are no other ways forward."

I blinked at him. I didn't have the first clue where to start with a response.

Roderick didn't give me the chance to respond. He put one hand on one sleeve of my big black trench coat and twisted it as he spoke. "When they discover us they will also inevitably gain awareness of their own supernatural kin: the technopagans, the Book People, the Squared Circle, Blue Dawn, Winter Wheat, the Cat Ladies, shape shifters, spirits, and all the others of us and them who haunt their darkest dreams. The strangest of us will frighten them. The most alike to them will fascinate them: all the little pockets of their *own* kind who bleed—yes, I like that word—who *bleed* over into this world of magic and mayhem we occupy. What *those* humans—the ones like Jennifer or like Dan—think of us, and how we relate to *them*, will determine a great deal about how the rest of humankind react. In a world in which long-distance telephone service was the only available form of instant global communication, it was still possible for us to stay hidden. Cousin, that day is over. Remember what I told you about feeding on a college campus, of having a photo go viral, of leaving a record no one ever *can* delete. That same degree of connectedness, of *permanence* is here, now, forever—or at least for a little while. They—the mortals—are a little bit afraid of that, in part because it is no longer possible for them to take a secret to their grave." Roderick shook his head. "Their feelings about the permanence of electronic memory are a version of the envy with which they will regard us. Ultimately this is a fear of death and the grave: there has previously at least been the assurance of any individual's narrative finding its natural denouement and conclusion. Now, their image persists in perfect digital reproduction. Their Twitter accounts sit idle but able to be followed. Their friends write eulogies on their Facebook wall as though they were still alive. That photograph of them doing something stupid *lingers* phantom-like in online albums and reposted memories. The grave has become a hollow promise. The immortality now available to them is one they still ultimately must miss. I think that drives them mad, just a little, when they consider it.

"Imagine what they will think of we who aim to have no graves at all? If we are to survive their discovery of our immortality, Cousin, we must make sure to seem very mortal, very *now*, when they do. That will be the difference they perceive between us and those monsters who revel in their monstrosity; between themselves and the sort of immortal experience they often wish to have but cannot. It is important you realize something about our habit of hiding ourselves: the secrecy under which you and I have thrived as vampires was not the elders' idea. They would have humankind fear the beast in that iconic castle on the hill for all time. No, our precious secrecy is the notion of the rebels who made *us* after they overthrew the *ancients*: the generation inclusive of Agatha, your maker. They see living in secret as the safest and most humane solution in a world of newly illuminated night. They read the newspapers of their day and knew humanity would never again abide a tyrant who never dies."

"Come on," I said, still parsing what Roderick had just spilled out of some dark place in his own mind. "We need to jet." Together we walked up to Roderick's car, having brought his big gold Cadillac this time. He slid into the driver's seat and I took shotgun. Roderick glided out of the driveway and up the street. That same beat-up red pickup truck sat in the parking lot by the town's only pier, and I felt like it was staring at me. *Cacciatore*'s front doors were still open: no crime scene tape, no sign of any official attention. The streets were more desolate than normal that night, too: houses were dark and no cars were out. To borrow Roderick's imagery, the villagers were already wary of activity in the castle on the hill. Neon lights were on in the windows of To

Kill a Sunrise but no cars were parked out front. Roderick was right. Humanity notices more now, and they react to what they notice. Maybe at first they hide or they look the other way, but it wouldn't last forever.

One phone call later, the rest of the vampires of Raleigh—all except Seth, of whom I had not asked it because he was a reformed elder the ancients didn't know survived, and thus was explicitly included from Roderick's plan—were on their way down to Sunset Beach. That didn't amount to much, actually: just Beth and Old Shoe and whatever pocket change they had between them, I guessed. They were both young and both lived pretty close to the edge but they agreed to help with Roderick's crazy-ass plan.

As my cousin drove in silence I started replaying back to myself the things he'd just said. I thought of his friendship with Jennifer and wondered how much of it was genuine and how much of it was to use her as a bridge between their society and ours in case an apocalypse of awareness broke out on the human side. I didn't buy they would find out all about us, but ten years ago I never would have guessed *anyone* in my neighborhood would learn of me. I wiped the memories of those who did, and at the time I thought I put the genie back in the bottle. Jennifer proved me wrong; then the Bull's Eye; then the technopagans. Roderick mentioned the Book People. I liked to tell myself they thought I was a demon or some other type of dark spirit, but what if they knew? What if they realized exactly what I was and were just being *polite* about it?

What if my crazy-ass cousin was exactly right about the coming changes in human society?

Roderick's phone buzzed and he glanced at the face of it. "Jennifer is working on their first action," he said. "They begin tomorrow. And Beatrice emailed me everything she has on this 'Hinson.'"

Chapter 5

Did you exchange a walk-on part in a war for a lead role in a cage?
- Pink Floyd, "Wish You Were Here"

Jennifer was standing behind a dead gas station a couple of miles inland wearing rubber kitchen gloves when she picked up the receiver on what had to be the last payphone in the North American wilderness. It was the following day. The sun was out. It was one of those days in April when Spring reminds you summer is on its way: bright spots are warm, but the shadows still feel like the winter that's just passed.

"911 Emergency," said a voice that sounded professional in the way of people everywhere whose work task is to sit through long periods of exhausted boredom waiting for something to demand their highly trained skill sets: a little resentful, a little sleepy, a little surprised. "What is the nature of your emergency?"

Jennifer pitched her voice up and deployed a thick rural drawl she had never used unironically even once in her life. "I think there's a fire at 425 Main in Sunset Beach it's a gray two-story rental unit with no cars in the driveway next to a beach access there's a big cactus in the yard at the corner by the mailbox the mailbox is silver," she said, all in one go with no pauses for breath lest she be asked questions. Jennifer had gotten pretty far in life by being almost entirely honest with people and it had served her well. As an engineer and a technician, honesty had been a requirement of the successful completion of any task. Sometimes it had harmed her. For instance, she could never disguise when she was utterly disgusted with someone and that happened a lot at ÜberBargains. Overall, though, it had worked out way more times than it had not and that made it very hard to lie.

"Is that location currently burning?" The professionalism in the voice of the operator was surprisingly crisp now and Jennifer found it gratifying to know people still cared somewhere.

"Yeah," she said, really amping up the drawl, "I'm pretty sure it's aflame right this second." Jennifer glanced at the watch her technopagan coven had given her with assurances it would stay synchronized to all others in the same group. Right this second was in fact when they were supposed to take the first step in their plan.

"So there is an active fire at this time?"

Jennifer grasped at air for a second and said, "I think 't'is," she said, and then she hung up. Ramon was sitting in the passenger seat of her car and looked up expectantly as she slammed the phone receiver down and jumped into the driver's seat.

"So they're on their way?" His voice was full of fear. This operation wasn't just a step up from their usual. It was like *ten*.

"Yes," Jennifer said, "At least, I have to assume so."

Ramon pulled out his phone and started texting a simple message to Sheila: GO. Jennifer did the same, but sent to Dan.

The two of them sat in the dark and waited.

Sheila's phone buzzed and she glanced down. She didn't need to read it. She knew in her gut it was a go across the board. The wind was with them. She could just feel it deep inside. All the tools felt right in her hand as she lifted the match, whispered an invocation to a god of bright light and searing heat—technically, she noted in some part of her mind, an atavistic construct made of previously deconstructed belief systems dissected on the altars of hegemonic faiths, but that was just the sort of noodling around she and all the other technopagans had going at any one time—and set flame to a two-minute measure of timed fuse.

The fuse was in turn taped to one of the landing legs of a four-bladed remote control helicopter. Watching through her phone, she guided it into the air from behind one of the many empty homes, one with empty houses on either side to minimize possible witnesses. The copter was also carrying what looked like a badly deflated water balloon. It was, in fact, an only barely inflated water balloon carrying a half-pound or so of homemade napalm. The other end of the fuse was taped against it.

Sheila was no expert in flying these things but she'd practiced a little that morning, out on the beach, way out on the end towards the nature preserve so no one would see her. The whipping Atlantic wind made it no easy feat but she brought the helicopter up between the dark, scrubby trees to hover high over the houses, where no one would see it. Counting backwards from one hundred twenty the whole time, she piloted it across the street, to one side, and across another street so that by the time she reached *eight* she was hovering directly over the chimney of the target house. The camera on the copter couldn't afford her enough of a view to know whether the flue on the chimney was open or closed, but she bet nobody much thought about them. Open was probably a pretty safe bet.

At zero, with the copter angled just so, she crashed it into the inner corner of the chimney as the flame of the fuse kissed the flesh of the napalm balloon. One perfectly banked ball of fire struck the edge of the brick and wood siding so that some of the flaming gel sprayed across the roof and some spattered against the pile of pristine, desiccated driftwood decorating the fireplace below.

Even three houses away, she could hear the soft sound of a *fwoosh*.

In the far distance, across the marshy width of the Intercoastal Waterway, Sheila heard sirens. She smiled to herself as she ducked back under the house, into her car and off up the street. In part Sheila smiled because the sirens had, themselves, been the signals for Dan to start his part.

Swagbot, as Dan called his creation, was not truly *his* creation. It was a bunch of open source code and off-the-shelf parts he'd enhanced with code of his own and then brought to life the first time in a ritual he designed with the rest of the technopagans.

"Brought to life" is probably too strong a phrase as it had no mind, no animus, but it was how Dan thought of the thing. All his creations were like children to him. He thought of them as extensions of himself, of his own will and potential, more than he thought of them as offspring per se, but that's the thing: so do *most* parents, though they don't like when you tell them that.

Swagbot was maybe four feet tall, on a set of treads that could swivel in any direction. Its base was weighted so its center of gravity was low. It had four arms with different kind of grips and connectors. It held them all partly aloft as it moved, elbows crooked, "hands" held out flat to the side. It looked like a hat rack sticking out of the top of a tank. Dan said it sashayed like it was walking the runway, like it was showing off for everyone else every time it rolled into a room, and thus its name.

The part of it most impressive, he told people, was its ability to hold and use tools otherwise made for human hands.

That morning, the sun high in the sky as noon approached, Swagbot was in the driveway of a random beach house on Sunset. It was a modest home, bright blue with white accents, but there was a two car garage on the ground floor. Dan was four doors up, alternately bouncing back and forth between the tablet computer in his hands and looking at the robot itself. The tablet displayed the view from a camera mounted just over the central ring of shoulder joints for Swagbot's various arms. Dan was wearing head-mounted binoculars, an expensive piece of hunting gear he'd picked up at a going-out-of-business sale for an online outfitter during the last tech bust. When everyone else is yelling *sell sell sell* is usually a great time to buy.

The hole saw in Swagbot's hands was a pistol-gripped maw of metal teeth in two rows, the blades made so they could cut through wood like butter and through metal like wood. The plastic dust shield between the bearer and the blades—like the round bell-shaped guard on a sword—was a hilarious touch of propriety on a machine designed to look like a gun that cut six-inch holes in whatever needed a tidy but gaping wound.

Dan used the controls on the tablet's screen to nudge Swagbot forward and raised the saw. Very gently, he pressed the shield to the garage door. Xi 2.0 hovered nearby and blinked his green LED at Dan. Swagbot pulled the trigger on the saw at Dan's direction, and dust and sparks filled the plastic guard like a snow globe version of Hell.

Twenty seconds later, the blade plunged through the door and Dan backed up to switch arms. The one that swung to the front held a long plastic tube up to the "eye" atop Swagbot, the other end inserted into the hole in the garage door. Dan tapped the tablet screen and flipped to night vision mode.

In the darkness were several people. Three were lying on beds with their arms folded across their chests like vampires from an old Hammer film. Did anyone actually bury their dead like that? Would any self-respecting creature actually sleep that way? Surely these assholes had watched a movie before. Surely they knew how ridiculous that must look.

There was a fourth person who was sitting in the dark. It looked like the sawing had startled her awake, as she was blinking in the general direction of the door and rubbing her face. Dan supposed this was the thrall, enslaved and forced to be their guard during the day. She realized where she was, and what was happening, and she stood up and staggered over to the garage door to see what was going on.

She blinked sleepily into the black plastic tube, like a peep hole in reverse, and then stood up again. Dan guessed she finally awoke enough to start processing what was going on because she screamed: not the long, sustained scream of mortal horror he imagined most people produced when one of these monsters grabbed them and dragged them off to die, but rather the short, sharp scream of shock of someone who has just realized there's a fire in their trash can.

"Shit!" He heard her say it through the tube, then over and over again as she ran away from the tube and over to one of the sleeping forms. "Shit shit shit shit *shiiiiiit*," she yelled. Tugging on the arms of the first vampire did nothing; same for the second; same for the third. Dan almost felt sorry for her. She was already gone, though. Jennifer had explained it to them. Once a human was addicted to vampire blood they were beyond help. It wasn't like heroin, or meth, or anything else. It changed them forever. It was the worst sort of magic: the kind that can't be unwound.

The woman started slapping the faces of the vampires, trying to get them awake. It did no good. They weren't going to awaken. Jennifer had told Dan that, too: the sun puts these fucks to sleep *hard*. Dynamite wouldn't wake them. One junkie smacking them on their withered old cheek wasn't even going to show up in a *dream*.

Dan backed Swagbot up and raised the arm with a pneumatic battering ram held in it. It wasn't big, but with a hole already made in the door, it was enough to start caving in the door *around* the hole, widening it and letting in the sun. The woman started screaming at the top of her lungs, the mindless shriek of someone who sees her death coming down the train tracks towards her.

Xi 2.0 had already started to hover backwards, slowly retreating while keeping his cameras aimed at the house.

Dan raised the mirror to the hole and panned it around in a slow arc for one second, two—surely he'd hit a vampire with the rays of the sun sooner or later, right—then a third and then—

The garage door exploded outwards in a fireball.

Windows upstairs in the house shattered.

Windows in the house across the street blew inward.

There was a tremor in the earth.

At least three car alarms went off.

Smoke washed out over Swagbot, obscuring his camera and Dan's view of Xi 2.0. After five excruciating seconds, Xi 2.0 emerged from the smoke and started flying *fast* towards Dan. In Morse, he blinked: *we need to get the fuck out of here.*

Dan smiled. It looked like they had managed to preserve at least *some* of Xi's personality.

The smoke cleared after a moment and Dan used Swagbot's still-working arms to right it, then backed it up the street at high speed towards their position. This was going to provide *lots* of good data.

The sirens from across the Waterway came blaring over the top of the bridge, from the mainland, and barreled down the other side into town.

Jennifer and Ramon moved the car a half-mile to get away from the phone booth, then hauled out the laptops and candles. While Ramon murmured and flipped the switches on the bottom of a set of LED "7-day" saint candles—in honor of Saints Dorothy, Sophia, Rose, and Blanche—Jennifer set up the satellite modem. Expensive as hell, but when you needed connectivity anywhere, it worked.

She had spent the day researching what she wanted to do but never tried it in the wild. It didn't seem especially complex, but the candles certainly made her *feel* better about it. As the satellite connection established she fired off a script. Through an obfuscating chain of other sites and servers, long enough to make it very hard to track her down, she broke into the monitoring infrastructure for Henrietta Industrial Insurance Worldwide.

There were plenty of stories in the tech media about people having figured out how to hack cars via the onboard monitoring and roadside assistance systems installed on them. Think for a moment about the sort of feature where you can, in addition to asking directions, maybe also get your car's manufacturer to find out where your stolen sedan was taken and lock its engine so it can't be driven anywhere. If the manufacturer can do that, so can anyone who hacks that system. Remote control is only an Internet connection away.

The same sorts of systems are installed on heavy equipment. In that case, they aren't to get directions. They're *only* to track them in case of theft. A brand new backhoe can cost many tens of thousands of dollars. Insurance rates for businesses can be through the roof. The insurance company may cut them a deal if they install a tracking device on all the bulldozers and backhoes and other equipment someone could literally drive off with in the middle of the night.

Or, Jennifer thought, *Drive it off in the middle of the day.*

Systems like that check in regularly with their controller rather than maintaining a steady connection. All it took was a little patience and *ping* Jennifer had one call home. It was a hydraulic excavator: a long arm with a toothed bucket, an enclosed cabin, and giant tank treads. Jennifer smiled. It would do the job just fine. While her scripts ran to take control of the excavator, she checked the position and registry: it was among the equipment owned by a particular construction company there in Sunset Beach, where there was a house going up on an empty lot. Ramon's *Golden Girls* candles were worth it: the coordinates looked good. The excavator was maybe a two-minute drive from her target.

The guy inside—if there was one—probably wasn't going to enjoy the ride very much, but she was going to do her level best to keep him safe.

Jennifer didn't have long to get her part done. The driver would pull out his cell phone and call 911 the moment it drove off with him in it. She had to get it there and attack the house, blind save for the directions Ramon would feed her based on the view from a weather conditions webcam Ramon had already hacked. It was like driving a remote control car on a track you can't see while someone in another room shouts directions.

The script finished. The indicator on her custom-written application turned green.

Go-time.

As Jennifer started to drive, two fire trucks blew past.

Sheila screeched to a halt in front of Dan and Xi 2.0 and hit the button to pop the hatch on her minivan. That's the funny thing about minivans: they often handle way better than you'd think just looking at once. Sometimes I think that's supposed to be a balm to the ego of whoever is stuck toting their kids around: it may look like a shoebox but at least it drives okay.

Dan yanked out the plank they were using as a makeshift ramp and drove Swagbot up it and into the back. Xi 2.0 flew in and set down on the bench in the middle, his battery light blinking. Sheila plugged him in and Dan climbed into the passenger seat.

"Sounds like we were both successful," he said with a grin.

The sirens went up in resolution as the trucks came around a corner and roared past at the end of the street.

"C'mon," Sheila said, "We've got to get over the bridge and back to the hotel before the camouflage wears off."

Dan whistled as four cop cars blew past the *other* end of the street.

"I wonder if that's for Jennifer?"

Sheila sucked air through her clenched teeth. "Did you strap down Swagbot?"

"No," Dan replied.

"Then get back there and hold it down. We need to go."

Jennifer's hijacked excavator was careening—there was no other word for it—down the street. "Careening" takes on a different meaning when the vehicle's top speed is 21 miles per hour, but 21 can look pretty damned fast when it's a machine the size of four or five cars piled on top of one another, with a giant arm sticking off the front. A couple of degrees off at the point of the cabin could put the arm many yards to one side or the other. At least Ramon's webcams had confirmed the cabin was empty.

"That was… another mailbox." Ramon winced. "Oh, Jesus, Jennifer. This is *ugly*."

"That's what insurance is for, kid." Jennifer gritted her teeth and tried to adjust the steering a hair's breadth this way and a hair's breadth that.

Ramon clapped one hand over his face, but didn't block his own view all the way. "Right… right more… more no *left a little*… OK, *now*."

Jennifer rammed the accelerator control and the excavator spun on its center axis, the treads ripping up asphalt and leaving a long, rippled impression like feet in the sand. The target was dead ahead on her map, and Ramon held up one thumb to signal she was good to go. The arm of the excavator extended before her, held aloft, like a battering ram or the jousting lance of a charging knight. In her mind, she could hear the engine revving up, redlining, chugging its heart out, and she hoped to powers above and below no one chose this moment to back out of their driveway.

"Well, *shit*," Ramon said, and Jennifer leaned over to look at his screen since her own controls were set.

Two police cars skidded to a halt in front of the excavator and their occupants dove out and ran to the side. *The whole police force in a town like this,* Jennifer thought to herself. The cops seemed to be shouting at the empty excavator as it charged them from two blocks away. They lifted their guns and started firing. The one frame-per-second video was jerky, to say the least, but she could see the sparks of bullets ricocheting off the bright yellow excavator. At the last moment the cops ran from the path and watched as their cruisers were crushed flat beneath the excavator's ridiculous treads. It rode over them with the barest wobbling rise and fall, charged up the driveway at the end of the street, and rammed its bucketed arm through the center of the modest beige beach house at the back of the lot.

Jennifer looked back at her screen, wiggled the controls for the bucket arm to angle it down like a cat pawing at the edge of a counter over which it can't see, and then hit reverse.

On the webcam, the excavator seemed to be sitting still. The cops stepped back into view and were aiming their pistols at it, but seemed uncertain: half-crouched, half-standing, guns only half-lifted.

Abruptly the excavator ripped free of whatever had held it in place. The treads spun, then bit, and it pulled half the house out from under itself like a tablecloth yanked out from under the place settings in a magic trick.

The house crumpled like a tin can. Junk started falling out of the bottom: a great cascade of furniture gushing out as it sagged and split open down the middle. Each half fell away when the excavator's bucket split a support beam or two on its way out, and the house opened like an apple split in two.

The light of the sun struck sleeping vampires, Jennifer guessed, because the next frame showed a burst of light from three places, like incendiaries going off in a Polaroid.

The next second, the image was nothing but white light, brighter than the sun.

The next second, the image was of the cops being knocked flat, the excavator rocking to one side by the blast.

The next second the excavator swayed the other way, its arm a ten-ton pendulum. Smoke billowed out of the house. Debris flew at the camera.

The next second, the house's shattered husk was consumed by flames.

"Oh, *shit*," Ramon said.

Jennifer already had the car in gear. She shoved the laptop at Ramon and said, "Wipe my trail, and *don't turn off those saint candles until you're done.*"

So, Jennifer thought to herself as she drove. *They definitely won't think* that *was the work of another vampire.* The Hinson list Roderick sent her had seven addresses on it. They had just singlehandedly assaulted three of them during broad daylight with no witnesses and no fingerprints left behind. If this didn't make the ancients jump, nothing would. She just hoped they didn't decide to run away and hide.

CHAPTER 6

I snapped awake in my hotel bathroom the next night as the last of the sun dropped below the horizon. I walked out into the bedroom, turned on the television, and while it warmed up I ran my hands through my hair: I needed a shower, and a set of un-rumpled clothes, and it was probably time to think about taking that trench coat to the cleaners. The chatterbox was set to one of the news networks—vampires are always addicted to the news—and I paused to admire the reporter. He was an absolutely drop dead gorgeous guy and he looked *very* excited.

"But authorities say this was a gas leak explosion and *not* an act of terrorism. Later, Janine Savage will have footage from today's scene of destruction in Sunset Beach, North Carolina."

I blinked as the channel went to commercial. The fade-out showed an inset map of the North Carolina coastline with an arrow pointing directly at the town in which I stood. I threw my head back and bellowed Roderick's name so loud I heard the thump when he dropped whatever he was holding in the next room over.

"Cousin," Roderick said, but he stopped there. He was sitting demurely on the edge of the other bed in my room, his legs crossed, a mug of something hot in his hands.

"And what in the fuck are you doing with a cup of coffee, anyway? And what the fuck is going on with a gas explosion in Sunset Beach?" I pointed a fat finger at the mug. "You don't eat, that's *my thing*."

Roderick gave me a sympathetic look. "I am not trying to steal your 'thing' from you. I merely wish to warm my hands. It is not real coffee or tea. It is simply hot water. I thought it would feel interesting in my hands." He paused, considered the mug for a moment, and looked back at me. "You will perhaps be pleased to know it *does* feel quite good."

I glowered at him. "Have you heard from Jennifer? Is this what they were doing today?"

Roderick smiled more softly. "Yes. She is fine. As are the rest of her crew."

"That isn't what I was asking," I said.

"But it *is* what you were wondering." His smile deepened. "Cousin, admit it, you like them. They have grown on you. Stop being such a stick in the mud."

I shook a fist at him and made a growling sound, then stood up and paced back and forth. "Tell me what happened."

He proceeded to read me an email from Jennifer, with his phone in his hand, and I made exactly the sorts of angry sounds you might expect.

I will be the first to tell you, though, I laughed when she said she ran over the cop cars. I tried to cover it, but I couldn't. The humor overwhelmed my annoyance for a moment.

"See?" Roderick asked. "This is what I mean by agility. You and I would not have predicted such action, and we could not have executed it. The elders built defenses against the sun but had no means of preventing those defenses from being torn down around them while they slept. Now we must try something different. They are certainly on alert at this time, doubly so since they will of course know this was not the work of a vampire."

I waved that off. "It could have been the work of thralls, or of people we'd mind-controlled into it."

Roderick pondered it and then shook his head. "No. It is too… public. In the past, when you have killed vampires, what have you done?"

I pondered, arms crossed, pacing stopped. "I went to where they were, barged in, and murdered the bastards."

"Exactly." Roderick nodded. "You fought them yourself. You were direct in your approach. You did not command slaves. You did not hide behind others. They will not know who did this, or why. They are very likely to engage in missteps at this point. We must act again as quickly as possible."

I looked at him for a moment. "I've got shit to do," I said.

Roderick blinked.

"Sorry, Cousin." I shrugged. "There's a great honking loose end I need to tie up before we do anything else. If we've got agents in the field, pieces on the board, whatever you want to call it, so do they. We need to know about one of them in particular."

"The deputy," Roderick said. He stood then, slipping his phone deftly into an inner pocket of his white pleather jacket.

I nodded. "The deputy."

"Might I join you?" He straightened his jacket.

I hesitated, then: "No. Roderick, this is something I need to sort out on my own." I worried I would need to defend myself, or that he would accuse me of cutting him out of the action on something, but he nodded with perfect diplomacy.

"Then I shall work one of my angles while you are occupied. I will be available via mobile device." He curtseyed at me and walked out.

I spent a stark thirty seconds wondering what the hell Roderick was up to.

I parked my Firebird at the Surf Sound Inn, where the bartender told me Deputy Crew Cut was staying. *Rudyard*, I said to myself. *Not Crew Cut.*

Getting the desk attendant to tell me the Deputy's room number was trivial—vampire hoodoo, blah blah—and two minutes later I knocked three times on the guy's door. This wasn't exactly the most subtle approach to the guy, I knew, but I was banking on a few specific things: one, this guy would, as a law enforcement officer elsewhere, not be hugely likely to start shooting up the place since he knew how many questions that would raise with the local cops. I was also assuming he would know shooting at me with a gun probably wouldn't do him any good anyway. Finally, I was hoping he was up on the news, too, and wondering what the hell was going on with the vampires in Sunset Beach. If I just walked up and knocked on the door surely he would realize that meant I wasn't here to try to kill him.

The light shining through the peephole went dark for a moment and stayed that way.

I stared right into it and said, as quietly as I could while being confident he would hear me, "Deputy Rudyard, it's me. We, uh, met earlier."

I let my vampire senses wash out across the door, and under it, and all around me. Sounds started filtering in I'd previously been unconsciously filtering *out*: bugs in the spring air, bats flapping in some scrub trees nearby, water lapping at the shore of the Waterway a mile from here. I could hear Crew Cut breathing on the other side of the door. He was taking short, shallow breaths, the kind taken by a frightened person in the dark.

I could also hear—and smell—what smelled like a barnyard kept in a shoebox under a bed. There were the accumulated and varied stenches of a dozen different animals in a place that needed some serious airing out.

I leaned close to the door, knowing how people are: he would have his ear pressed against it. "Deputy," I murmured. "I am not here to try to harm you. If I wished to do so, I would remove the door, kill you, and get it over with. I want to *talk*."

The silence continued, but I heard him hold his breath for a couple of heartbeats.

"Believe it or not," I said, "I think maybe we have the same enemies. Please. I am…" I sighed. "I am *begging* you. Open the door and let me in. I'll swear on a stack of bibles I'm not here to do anything else. Right now, I promise, I will not use my powers to sway you."

A few more heartbeats.

"I want to help you." I paused. "At least, I *think* I do." I hesitated again but plunged ahead. "And let's be honest, if I wanted to use my powers I already would've done so."

Another few seconds of indecision passed.

"C'mon, man, I want to know why none of us goes to Charlotte." I licked my lips. "I want to know what's hiding there. And I think you know, because that's where you got mixed up in all this. That's where you were the last time your life seemed *normal*."

The deadbolt slid back and the security chain was removed from its hook. They were meaningless to me, of course, but mama raised me to knock first when it's an option. Crew Cut opened the door and looked me right in the eye. "I know what you are," he said.

"I know," I replied. "You told me that already."

"What do you know about Charlotte?" The way he asked it, it sounded like a challenge, like he wanted a password or like he already didn't believe my answer.

Behind him, in the room, I saw the walls of the cheap motel were covered, stacked to the ceiling, with metal wire cages containing animals: chickens, lizards, at least a couple of rabbits, a snake in a glass aquarium with magic marker writing all over it, a puppy. The wires of the cages were not the perfect grid patterns one would expect. They were haphazardly bent into patterns even I could recognize as being of occult significance, all obviously done by hand and in a hurry. They had the look of something done on the fly, in desperation, out of fear. Of all the animals jammed into that room, the roosters in particular were arranged in a geometric pattern and their cages were like starbursts of wire and gold paint. The hens were in another pattern, in cages in a complex, curving configuration that made them look like the wire itself was captured in a motion blur. The snake's aquarium had astrological symbols all over it like you see on cheap jewelry at that store in the mall that sells all the teeny-bopper goth stuff. There was also English writing on it, but it was backwards, as though for the snake itself to read.

The rabbit cages were painted bright red and sky blue, and there were crystals hanging from them by long strands of regular old brown twine.

In the second I had to look, I kicked in the super speed so I could take in more, and to my growing horror I realized not a single one of the animals in these cages looked healthy. The rabbits were all foaming at the mouth and twitching. The snake's scales were dull and mottled in patches here and there. The chickens were missing feathers. The cat was one of that kind born with two faces.

The puppy had six legs: two of them were vestigial and stuck out at odd angles to the rest.

A bunch of the poor things were hooked up to intravenous fluid drips and looked like they were knocked out on drugs. Not a one of them looked *happy*. They were at best catatonic. At worst they were shivering in fear. This wasn't a barnyard; it was the veterinary equivalent of a hospice ward. My first thought on seeing them was to wonder how no one complained about the sound. Now I realized none of these animals were healthy enough to make noise.

In the middle of the wall, with the dozens of animal cages arranged to frame rather than to obscure it, was a map of Sunset Beach. There was a grid pattern drawn over it and in front of the whole thing was the biggest aquarium I've ever seen outside an episode of *Lifestyles of the Rich and Famous*. Unlike the animals in the cages, the fish and plants in the aquarium were absolutely thriving.

I snapped back to normal speed so I could talk to the Deputy but my eyes stayed on the aquarium for another couple of seconds. There were huge streaks of vividly colored algae or moss or bacteria or *something*. Whatever it was, it looked like a strep throat test gone horribly wrong. Emerging from the base of the tank was a giant coral growing—maybe groomed—into roughly the same dimensions as the map of Sunset Beach and there were at least a dozen kinds of fish swimming rapidly backward and forward. I wondered what had them so agitated, as they looked like they weren't sure whether they were chasing something or running away. Some were tiny, some were slightly bigger, and all were colors I could only call *violent*: bright yellows, vicious reds, with spots of neon blue and purple and stripes of black. They formed a living kaleidoscope. As a school of tiny ones swam past the bottom like tiny jets in formation, I saw something flat and ugly pop out of the mud and sand along the bottom. It snatched one of the tiny blue fish with its flat, ugly jaw. This didn't look like the sort of aquarium you want to sit in front of and meditate. It looked like a gladiatorial free for all.

For a second, all I could think of was that converted garage in the house the real estate agent had shown us, and I turned to look Crew Cut in the eye. "Life," I said.

"What?"

"Life magic. They're using death magic—ritual sacrifice and bones and blood and all that jazz—and you're using living things. You're trying to keep them from finding you. Or—no, not *only* that. Am I right?"

He blinked. I shouldn't have gone straight to the heart of things like that, but something about it jumped out at me and I couldn't stop myself from saying it as soon as the idea entered my head.

I put my hand against the door when he tried to close it again and changed subject back to the reason why I was there. "No, I'm sorry. You asked a question.

What do I know about Charlotte? Damned little. Nothing, to be honest, except it hurts my head to think on it too long." I tried to give him a sincere shrug. "Really, I'm not here to do anything to you. You're after the ancients. And so am I. I'm one of the young vampires: the modern ones. I don't want to rule the world. I want to be ignored by it." I tried harder to look sincere, which is the hardest thing in the world to do when one is actually entirely genuine. "Look, I don't believe in gods or Jesus or any of that shit, but I will swear on anything you put in front of me that I am opposed to the same vampires as you and I think we will get a lot further down the road if we work together instead of apart." I took my hand from the door and held it out to him, offering it to shake. "My name is Withrow."

Deputy Rudyard stared at my hand like it was a fish on a stick.

"I know people who can help you with this stuff," I said. I gestured beyond him, at his room, with a nod of my head and a glance of my eyes. "We can help each other. I *think the* ancients are what's in Charlotte: like, that's their base of power, at least in these parts. I think Charlotte is their actual *den*."

Deputy Rudyard still didn't shake, but he did look at me. "They've made some of you stay away," he said. "They're afraid of what will happen if some of you go there." He twitched a finger. "I mean, anyone who knows about them."

I nodded. "Please, Deputy, this is the stuff I need to know. I want to stop them, just like you do. And I know people who would want to help you protect yourself. I would want to help you protect yourself. Please, man, let me in. Let's share what we know."

His eyes narrowed at me and his grip tightened on the edge of the door. "I don't believe you," he said. "I know better than to believe any goddamn one of you. I know just enough to know that. Even if what you said was true, and there were vampires who were against other vampires, what good would it do me to help *you*? Do you think you're the good guy? Do you think you're the *nice* vampires?" He smiled at me in a twisted, mocking way, showing the cruelty of someone already wounded. "There are no nice monsters. There is no middle ground, no gray area you can tell yourself you occupy in the least immoral way possible. And that's even *if* I believed you."

I started to get my hackles up and said, "Well, son, let's not rush to –" but he cut me off.

"This isn't a vegetarian giving someone a hard time about a hamburger." He looked at me with the coldest eyes I'd seen in a mortal in a *long* time. "You are a predator, and I spent most of my life as one of the prey, and I am turning the tables on every last one of you, one dead vampire at a time. You're all in it together in the end, and you're together against *me*. At least I have the decency to be honest about things."

He tried to force the door past my grip, but he was the irresistible force and my foot was the immovable object. It splintered and caved in at the bottom corner. We both looked down at it for a moment and then I looked back up at him.

"Tell me who made you a thrall, Deputy," I murmured, "And let's go kill them together."

He looked back at me. "I'm going to have to repair that now. Just *leave*."

The two-faced cat almost—*almost*—stirred in its medically induced slumber, and that was too much for me. This guy could be a dumb asshole all he wanted as long as it was on his own dime, but the critters in the cages were a bridge too far. I wanted to pop this asshole's head off and then call a vet's office. How dare he stand there and lecture me about the cruelty of thinking being while he kept dozens of souls in cages around his own goddamned bed?

I couldn't just murder him on the spot, though. Too many people might have seen me. I could hoodoo deskman downstairs but I didn't have time to mind-fry the whole motel. Besides, one of the first rules of being a vampire is, don't murder a cop. The Transylvanian had ignored that at his own peril, even if I was the instrument of karma in that particular situation.

I stepped back. Crew Cut closed the door.

I walked back to my car and climbed in.

For just a second, when I glanced in the rear view mirror, I thought I saw a woman in a gray dress behind my car. When I turned around to make sure she moved before I backed out of the space, there was no one there.

I breathed in once and out again, fast, through my nose: a sound of frustration and annoyance. I was not going to get drawn into some half-assed ghost story when my plate was already this full.

Okay, so Crew Cut had his own set of prejudices and no special reason to believe me. I started wondering whom he *would* believe, as I realized immediately he had information I needed. That setup he had in there, and the fact he was still alive, told me he had figured out a way to stand opposed to the ancients without getting waxed by them. I even had a theory cooking on where he got that thrall strength. If I couldn't convince him with a friendly visit, though, I either had to work without him or I had to find someone who could convince him in my place.

As I drove off, I started trying to run down the list of allies available to me. There was Roderick, of course, and there were Jennifer and the technopagans. I was trying not to think overlong on whether they were a little too tight, because that's the kind of suspicion that can gnaw at a good thing and I know myself well enough to realize I run a surplus of suspicion anyway.

There were the vampires of Raleigh, whom Roderick had already decided we had to have. They were no use to me in convincing Deputy Crew Cut to help out, but they might be useful against the elders if it came down to a bare-knuckle fight. The last time I'd fought one it had taken two vampires and two humans to take him out and it had still been a close thing.

I knew better than to ask Seth to help us, much as I wanted him on the team. He was my second in command (I guessed—I wondered if Roderick being around so much had put a dent in that) but a year earlier I'd found out he was one of the elders, too. Rather than join their mad plunge into the darkest heresies they could gin up in hopes of surviving the rebellion of their own offspring, Seth used his access to that same power to be forgotten by his peers. He disappeared into the ranks of the young vampires who otherwise would have wanted him dead and adopted a life of quiet anonymity in Raleigh, a small city in a not-especially-special state. When I told him I knew, he made his priorities very plain: if the elders ever brought their fight to his doorstep so he was forced to choose, he would simply walk away. To call him up and ask him to come here would be to send him as far away as he could possibly get.

I didn't want that, for any number of reasons, not least of which is my general agreement with the notion a body ought to be left alone if they want. Seth made it clear he was no threat to me, no threat to the others in the city, and had no interest in picking any fights nor even in finishing them. After all the trouble with the Transylvanian up in Asheville and then with Dmitri and El Diablo in Durham the year before, it was kind of refreshing to hear of a vampire who knew of the old conflict between young and old, ancient and modern, whose reaction was a hearty *no thanks*.

Beth and Old Shoe, however, were potentials. It was a little unfair of me, perhaps, to call in Beth because she and Seth are some degree of an item—vampire relationships are complicated and rare and hard to characterize—but she owed me and I wasn't above calling in a favor when I needed it. Beth had washed up in Raleigh fifteen years earlier, not entirely sure what she was and maybe not entirely sure *who* she was. I've never known who her maker was, as she or he seemed to have abandoned her on my doorstep immediately after I took power. I'd wondered at the time if that meant she was the pet of my predecessor, the last boss, the one whom I murdered myself after laying a trap. It wouldn't have been beyond him by any stretch. He took great pleasure in trapping others and seeing what they thought of their cage. It would have been just like Bob The Third (that was how he signed things, written out like that: "Bob The Third," he was *such a bastard*) to ensnare someone—anyone who took his fancy for five minutes—and leave no provision for them in the case of his own demise. Hell, it wouldn't have been beyond him to load her up with hypnotic triggers so she'd forget everything, burning off her original identity like a self-cleaning oven, just to play one last cruel prank on whoever came after him. There are urban legends of that, among vampires: of bosses who use the hoodoo to booby trap the place they run so everyone is afraid to knock them off for fear of whatever mindfucked mortals will come out of the woodwork.

It's plain that Beth was a dancer. I don't know if she worked in a ballet or a strip club or both but she has the grace and balance of someone trained to that sort of performance. The time I got Seth and Beth to join me at a ballet performance, the night I first encountered El Diablo, Beth sat in silent, hypnotized fascination as the dancers moved in slow arcs. Beth gets by now as the owner of a club on the outskirts of Raleigh. It's a strip club, yes, and she has a silent partner whose name is on everything—and is probably purely a legal construct, as are most of our identities on paper—but she runs the place, takes care of her dancers, and has the sort of reputation one only hears about in whispers. Rather than be regarded as someone low on the totem pole of our increasingly vocally misogynistic society, denigrated for using her body exactly the way the woman-hating men who run most things seem to *want* her to do, she's seen as an artist whose work and humanity make people a little bit afraid. Guys go to her club expecting to have a dirty good time, to feel a little guilty and also a little smug about not feeling *too* guilty. Instead they experience awe and the shock of discovering they still *can* experience that awe. I don't know why, but patrons of Beth's club leave feeling more in touch with humanity than before and they don't quite know what to think about that. According to Old Shoe, they sure as hell *do* go back.

Old Shoe wasn't that dissimilar, in terms of his situation when he arrived in Raleigh, but at least he knew who made him and why. He lived in Wilmington when he was turned into a vampire. A college kid, just some random John Doe, he wandered drunkenly into traffic one night. A vampire ran him over. Apparently she felt guilty as hell and turned him to "save" him. Can you hear me making quotes around that? Christ alive, he looks like last week's hamburger left out in the sun. The front of that leech's car chewed him up like a shredder and the blood trapped him that way for eternity. In theory I imagine he could heal all those wounds—push the blood to them and make the bones knit, the skin close up all pink and new—but ultimately we get trapped in the bodies we had at the moment we were turned. That much damage, he'd be famished when he was done. He'd have to drain at least one mortal, maybe two, or go crazy from the hunger. The real kicker is he'd wake up the next night looking just like he did when he awoke the night before. The damage would all be back, the bones jutting out through shredded skin, half his insides on the outside again. I asked him once how he gets around and he said every night he wakes up and without even thinking about it heals just enough to be able to move under his own power. It's a reflex. If he didn't, he'd be an invalid.

Now Old Shoe haunted the sewers under Raleigh. He was on the run from any chance of encountering the life he once knew. It wasn't that he thought someone there might recognize him—they would not, *could* not—it was that he didn't think he could handle contact with any part of who he once was. How could I turn him away? I forbade him walking the streets but I gladly gave him all the sewers he could ever want. Plenty for a vampire to eat down there, and if he wanted to turn himself into the resident bogeyman of a place here or there while he was at it, great, as long as he was mindful of staying out of the spotlight. He adapted well: a funny guy, eager to crack wise when the chance presented itself. There's something charming about a horror movie monster with a zinger up its sleeve. I always assumed he was someone charismatic when he was alive. Maybe he was a jock, maybe he was the class clown, maybe he was Mr. Nice Guy. As a vampire he became the ears and eyes of the darkness, the vampire who knew everything about everyone. He gathered more secrets hiding in the shadows than I'd ever be able to remember in the first place. I never asked him to reveal them to me, but he hinted here and there he has the dirt piled up like a dug grave. The only person I ever asked him about was Beth and he told me most of what I just said about her. When I heard enough to satisfy my curiosity I told him so and suggested if he ever decided to write any unauthorized biographies he might want to get *very* far away first. I think he got the point. He owed me, too, after all: a lot of bosses in other places would have killed him on sight. He appreciated being left to gather up the bits and bobs of others' dirty laundry. Old Shoe found a better deal in Raleigh than he could get just about anywhere else.

Sunset Beach is about an hour from Wilmington and at first I wondered if maybe that would be too close for comfort for Old Shoe. He said he wasn't worried, though. "You could stand me up next to a picture from my high school yearbook," he said, "And nobody would know it was me. They'd all be too busy puking." He laughed at that, over the phone, like it was a hilarious joke instead of a simple statement of fact. He once told me Old Shoe was his name because that's how he smelled first thing in the evening: like an old shoe, because he lives in the sewers. Again, he laughed at a statement of fact as though it were the highest humor. Sometimes I think vampires must be the weirdest people around.

Neither of them was going to get me anywhere with a guy who hated vampires, though.

If I was going to get through to Deputy Rudyard, I was going to need mortals he could learn to trust. They couldn't be thralls—I felt sure he would spot that. They had to seem like independent operators. That left me with the technopagans but I didn't like relying on that one card too much.

I was going to need the Book People.

In the meantime, I had Beth and Old Shoe to help me work the vampire angle. When I texted them to talk about them coming down here, it turned out Roderick had already been in touch. They were already on their way and they were bringing with them a surprise guest.

Beth left Raleigh in her little hatchback with Old Shoe and Marty Macintosh riding along, the latter having caught a ride to Raleigh from the "girlfriend"—translation: steady blood supply—he obtained against my advice. I mean, it's his life and everything, but I explained to him once already that he would ultimately suffer if he tried to restrict himself to a single source of blood. A vampire who does that either kills their donor or sentimentally starves until madness sets in. Either way, the end result is never pretty.

They hauled ass, Old Shoe texting me their progress, so that by 8:30 that night they were pulling up to the parking lot of a different little motel in the nearby town of Calabash: not the Surf Sound Inn, but one that had at some point been called The Wetherby. Now it was just an abandoned property in which we were squatting. I didn't want a legit hotel and I didn't want to tip anyone off by buying this outright. I figured I could just hoodoo anybody who looked into what we were doing there. The Wetherby put us a few minutes away from Sunset Beach but there was only the one way onto or off of the island—the tall, long two-lane bridge—and we assumed the elders would be watching that closely for at least a night or two after all the antics with the garages and explosions and the hydraulic arm thing.

Jennifer and the technopagans had joined us there. We were all standing in the parking lot, in almost total darkness. Jennifer was talking to the quadcopter. "Xi, you have a mission. Fly across the waterway to Sunset Beach and observe it for the movements of vampires. Do you understand?"

The light blinked once.

"Good hunting, and welcome back to the land of the living." Jennifer's voice nearly caught, but she caught it first.

The drone—I still couldn't think of it as Xi—rose into the air to a height of 30 or 40 feet and then shot away. Everyone tracked it, heads turning, like we were all gawping at a UFO or a 747 about to crash. It was quiet and what little sound it made faded almost immediately but we all kept looking up as thought waiting for something. Finally I looked at Jennifer and spoke.

"Okay," I said. "There is no way—"

Jennifer turned and cut me off with a shrug. "It's what Xi wanted. He worked on it for months. He called it his 'cold spare.'" She made a sound like a single chuckle, a strangled little sound unsure where it was or what it should be expressing. "It isn't really Xi, of course, but it works based on a set of if/then statements he designed and recorded beforehand. If you read someone like Kurzweil, he breaks down artificial intelligence as nothing more than a set of decisions expressed as a mathematical formula. Take, say, the computer in a car. It decides when and how much fuel to inject into which cylinder at what time based on a formula describing all the decision trees related to that one task. That's how artificial 'intelligence' for automating any one task works: break that task into its component yes/no decisions and then design a program to run through them. Xi's theory was no A.I. he or we could build in a practical amount of time could reflect all the inner and outer workings of a human being. But maybe it *could* handle some social interaction and take orders if it had a big enough vocabulary and a set of priorities to go with them. He broke those down into a decision tree that isn't universal but does reflect his own thought processes for them and then described that tree in software. It's a way to give us a physical, mobile entity that will respond more or less the way Xi *might*. To him, that's as close to immortality as is…" She shrugged almost apologetically: sometimes one's word choices can be awkward with a vampire in the conversation. "It's as close to immortality as we *should* get. He looked down on all the other methods available. No offense."

I raised an eyebrow. Roderick chuckled. "None taken," I said. "But… I mean, isn't it kind of like saying he bred a dog that will bark when you say his name? Plus, there's…" I waffled on how to say it. "I feel like there's a way in which this doesn't have the, you know, the magical fireworks. It seems pretty mundane for y'all."

"Xi doesn't believe the social algorithms and some sensory processing are the end-game," Sheila said. "He thinks they're the beginning."

Ramon picked it up and went on. "Xi believed it was possible his spiritual essence would re-condense around the echo of himself still in the physical world. The more like Xi the 2.0 version acts, and the more we treat it like we treated Xi 1.0, the more it will draw to itself the essence of what was Xi 1.0. Like attracts like. It's intended to form a sympathetic bond with what was his soul."

"You are all speaking of it in varying degrees of past and present tense," Roderick murmured.

"We have differing opinions on how effective it may be." Dan shrugged. "The only way to find out if it will work is to try."

"So did Xi know he was going to die?" I was still trying to wrap my head around the whole concept.

"His personal divinations pointed to a change in memory state," Jennifer said. She waved a hand. "Explaining it more finely than that takes a while."

At that moment, Beth's car pulled up and she and three men got out: Seth, Beth, Marty Macintosh and a kid I didn't recognize. Beth was dressed in shorts, sandals and a hoodie top. Her hair was pulled back in a ponytail and she looked about as sane as I had ever seen her.

Seth had his long mohawk haircut dyed bright blue and falling down in front of his eyes. He was also wearing a hoodie with the hood up and he hunched a little, as though trying to hide. I was shocked to see him that close to some of his former peers, but his loyalty to Beth must have overridden even his fear of the elders.

Marty Macintosh looked sallow and unkempt even by the standard conjured by the phrase "vampire hermit" but he was there and that was what mattered. Marty was in baggy jeans and a stained button-up shirt. He had on a baseball cap with some meaningless corporate logo on it.

The final one, the young man I didn't know, was dressed in board shorts and a green polo shirt with a popped collar. He had on flip flops and a bracelet made of white coral and his brown hair was the bog standard frat cheese cut: close-cropped sides, parted and gelled so it hung just a little over his forehead. He could have stepped out of a Sears Wishbook catalogue from anytime in the last thirty years. He was Caucasian and his appearance was so ordinary as to be difficult to remember any longer than it took to look away.

Beth was saying something to him as they walked up. "And that's how I know my mother was born with no tonsils," she said.

"Fascinating," the new kid said with what was Old Shoe's voice minus all the scraping sounds and shredded bass notes. "Hey, boss. Did you know Beth's mom was born without tonsils? Fascinating stuff." He twirled his fingers next to his head, Bugs Bunny style. "Crazy, man."

"Old Shoe?" I blinked at him. I had never seen him fully healed from his nightly accident damage. I had never stopped to really think about it, but I had literally no idea what Old Shoe had looked like before and now I knew: he looked like everyone and no one. No wonder he wasn't worried about his family recognizing him. It wasn't just that he looked different when he wasn't injured. It's that he didn't look like anyone in particular at all. He looked like a composite of every conformist-minded college junior I've seen since the 1950's.

"That's me, boss." He stuck a hand in one pocket and with the other swept his hand up and down to indicate his body and face. "Feast your eyes on it while you can, assholes. Looking this good is thirsty work. I ain't gonna do it every day."

I introduced everyone around. Beth took it entirely in stride that we were working with humans. Old Shoe clammed up at first, socially awkward like he was being introduced to a set of stepsiblings he'd decided ahead of time he probably wouldn't like, but Jennifer was polite and Dan was outgoing and Old Shoe, for all he's one of the most off-centered vampires I've ever met, tends to get along with just about anybody like a house on fire. In a matter of minutes he and they had made each other laugh and everyone seemed to relax.

"Time for me to go," Seth said to Beth.

"Not sticking around?" I asked it as casually as I could, not wanting to pressure him but *damn* he was *there* and I could sure as shit use him.

He shook his head at me once. "I need to open the bar in a few minutes," he said.

"It takes more than a few minutes to drive back to Raleigh," I said.

Seth and Beth locked eyes, ignoring me, and Seth gave her just the barest hint of a smile. "I'll call when I get back," he said, and then he winked out of existence with a soft metal clang.

I mean it when I say he literally disappeared: he was there one second and gone the next, in the blink of an eye.

Beth's phone rang after a few seconds and she answered it. "Thanks," she said. "I'll be home soon." Then she hung up.

Of course, I thought: his Last Gasp. Seth calls it "borrowed time." He says he's never heard of anyone else having the same power. When he kills someone by drinking from them, he gains all the time they would have had left if they lived out their natural life. He adds that unspent lifespan to a pool of personal time. He can step between two moments of normal time, from his perspective causing everything around him to freeze, then go where he wants and unfreeze it. He simply froze time, walked back to Raleigh—a hundred fifty miles if it's an inch—and then restarted things.

"Jesus Christ," I said aloud to no one. "It really works."

Marty blinked at everything, standing close to Roderick and never quite participating in conversation. For a moment, my mind superimposed over them the images of Igor and Dr. Frankenstein from the old Universal Pictures version. It seemed clear Marty looked to Roderick for what to do and otherwise was completely incapable of participating in a situation involving this many persons all at once. All of a sudden, he turned to me and blurted out, "Roderick says you need to generate false evidence of many vampires being here at once."

I nodded at him, stepping a little closer to him and a little farther from the rest of the group as they chattered away. Old Shoe was telling the technopagans and Roderick a dirty joke and Beth was staring at the sky. Marty and I could have a moment to discus this ourselves. "Does he? I like that idea. I would love for them to be operating on the basis of bad data."

"Normally what I do is interpolate from data in the wild," he said. "I've never tried to seed a false impression."

"But you could tell us what would *look* like good data to them." I noticed the other conversation had ground to a halt and the technopagans were paying attention to us now.

"Did somebody say 'data' over here?" Sheila sidled closer to us. "I mean, hello, geek Batsignal."

Marty ignored her and the others and focused on me. I met his eye and put just a touch of the hoodoo into it when I said, "Ignore them. Tell me any ideas you've had on the drive here."

Marty reached into his pocket and produced an electronic device about the size of a standard postal envelope. It lit up in his hand and he started tapping and swiping away on it like a natural. Of course, Marty is so young this stuff isn't strange to him. He hasn't yet begun slipping into anachronism. A couple of years ago he was the key to me finding out about The Transylvanian. At the time I noticed a few things in his apartment pointing to the beginnings of being dated: VHS tapes, a computer monitor that's thick like an old TV instead of those thin little things they sell now down at ÜberBargains, that sort of thing. Marty is more capable than most of us of catching up, though, because he has to make up so little ground to do it.

"Is that the Matsuzaki TouchPane?" Dan's voice was dripping with a very specific admixture of admiration and envy.

"Y-yes," Marty said without looking away from the thing in his hands. "But I installed a custom version of Android."

Dan cooed, "That's my favorite phablet," whatever that meant. The technopagans threatened to crowd around but Jennifer and I stepped between them with a quick glance between us.

I cleared my throat to reassert the hoodoo. I didn't want to push Marty around, just keep him focused. He looked up and nodded.

"The available public data sources manifest vampires in three main ways: disappearances, aggravated assault and reported animal attacks. A vampire who stalks transient or ephemeral prey—either opportunistically or out of habit—either kills them, leave them grievously wounded, or injures them in a way that appears to medical professionals to be an attack by a carnivorous animal."

Jennifer's eyebrows shot up and she looked at me. "I don't remember anyone at ÜberBargains fitting any of those categories." The night we met, she saw me feed *kind of a lot*.

I shrugged at her. "What he's describing doesn't normally happen. Normally we make the person heal over before we let them go. If a vampire is stupid or cruel or in a hurry, though…"

Marty glanced at her for just a moment. "As Withrow says, these are exceptions. A mainstream contemporary vampire on her or his home turf leaves no lasting injury in the interest of going unnoticed. That also leaves nothing in the datasets available to an informed researcher. Elders out to make a point or cow the local population have no such incentive to behave. They could leave a statistical fingerprint. However, I have to interpolate—to come up with a measurement from the known data *around* what I seek—to form a conclusion. Looking at those statistics in this area, there are very, very few vampires suggested. I would have trouble making a case for there being more than one, if that. Compared to the behavior patterns of The Transylvanian and his brood in Asheville, for instance, the data in Sunset Beach would suggest there are three tenths of one vampire present."

I harrumphed. "And if you expand that out to, say, fifty miles?" I was thinking of what Roderick had been told about the patterns.

"Things get much more interesting. I would estimate six vampires."

I nodded. "But we already know there are more than that based just on the rental histories and the number we've killed ourselves in the last few days."

Marty nodded at me. "There just aren't enough meaningful data points to suggest a ton of elders. Either they brought donors with them or they have covered up their tracks. The strangest thing I can find in the data is a surge in exotic animal thefts and break-ins at veterinary clinics. At this point I'm wondering if they're even eating human blood or if they've gone vegetarian just to maintain a low profile."

I blinked at him. "Exotic animals?"

Marty shrugged at me. "Sorry, boss."

I waved it away, immediately having a guess who might have stolen a bunch of weird animals, but not yet ready to talk to everyone about my brief conversation with Deputy Rudyard. "Forget it. So let's flip it around: how do we shift those numbers to suggest as many as that, if not more, have rolled into town all of a sudden?"

Marty looked uncomfortable for a moment. "Well, that's the problem. What characterizes us—the population you want to suggest—is the absence of data. We *are* incentivized to cover our tracks. We can't fake the *absence* of data points. I could fake up a bunch of other elders being here, but not a bunch of successful modernists."

I scratched my beard for a second. "You said *successful*. What about unsuccessful ones?"

"How do you mean?"

I shrugged. "Sloppy modernists. Ones too young to hide themselves well. What if…" I paused and looked out into the darkness for a moment. I could see Roderick's eyes on me, glittering in the dim light of a parking lot down the street, and he smiled. He knew where I was going. "We've already acted once to suggest to them this isn't being driven by vampires at all. What if we try to confuse that, now, by suggesting there are vampires at work but not *us*? What if we make them think we drafted a ton of new vampires *and* mortals. I mean, a *ton*. What if we tried to make them think we've gone out and put the Big Flush on dozens of random people in order to bulk up our numbers. They're elitists. It wouldn't be hard to scare 'em by making them think we're trying to flood the streets with our own rabble."

"'Occupy Vampirism'?" Roderick asked.

I smiled and nodded once. "Exactly."

"Well," Marty said, but he stopped and cleared his throat. Roderick reached out to pat him on the elbow and that seemed to encourage him. He looked down at his fancy phone and punched numbers for a few seconds. "How many?"

"Let's say… three dozen." I shrugged. "Just grabbing a number out of the air."

Marty nodded and typed more before speaking. "I would say we need to wound one person every night, seriously maim one person every three nights and kill a person every week to suggest ten *young* vampires. Multiply accordingly for target numbers."

Jennifer blinked slowly. "Young vampires," she said. "So the elders are doing the same stuff, just getting away with it."

Marty shook his head. "They would be less likely to generate injuries, though they would generate *some*. We have to assume a significant percentage of their prey simply are disposed of when that happens and thus are not reflected in the data available to us."

"Except by things like…" Ramon trailed off in his question. "Like the red pickup truck?"

"What of it?" Roderick immediately twigged to the question.

Ramon shrugged. "There's a red pickup truck in the parking lot by the pier. It's just sitting there with the door ajar, keys in the ignition. We picked that up on the cameras during our operation earlier. It's like whoever put it there just got out and disappeared. And a couple of houses are sitting open but nobody's home."

"Disappeared," I said, flat. "But no one reports it? No one calls the police?"

"The missing *missing*," Marty said. "They're —"

I interrupted. "They're people who disappear but no one notices." I nodded. Roderick gave me an odd look for a second, as though something had just occurred to him but he hadn't been brave enough or nosy enough to ask. I shrugged. "They're an obsession of mine," I said. "I don't know why. I've just always found them fascinating. I mean, look around: we've got hobbyist drones. You probably ordered that thing online." I pointed in the general direction of where "Xi" had flown. "It's harder and harder not to be noticed, tracked, perceived." I thought of the talk Roderick had with me about not hunting on college campuses because of the cameras everywhere. I thought of the stories I'd read about the NSA monitoring phone calls and emails and everything else they could get their hands on, hoarding it away in quantities well beyond even their prodigious ability to sift it for anything interesting. "But the number of missing *missing* goes up every year. Where do they go? And why? That has always tugged at the back of my mind." I had kind of drifted into my own thoughts for a second as I spoke and I tried to climb back out. I shook my head. "Anyway. Yeah. So mostly, at their worst, they're just killing their prey and disposing of the bodies and there's nothing to report about it so it doesn't show up."

Marty nodded. Jennifer shook her head in disgust.

"Well," I said, "We're not going to go out and randomly maim people to show up in their data. So we have to use other methods."

To be absolutely clear, there was a part of me just fine with that idea. It wasn't the part of me that pays my credit card bill and drives in the right lane and makes decisions. It was the part of me that's an animal, the part that lives deep down inside all of us. I don't just mean vampires, I mean all of us, including you. The difference between you and me is that the blood makes me learn to let it out once in a while to survive. You probably like to tell yourself it doesn't exist because that's how *you* survive.

It does. Sometimes you even hear its stomach rumble.

"We showed ourselves in a major way yesterday," I said. "Tonight I want to observe what they do in response. Let's not go looking for trouble. Instead, let's just go *looking*. Let's see what they do to regroup or if they try to conduct their own investigation or if they lash out in some way."

Jennifer nodded. "We can put eyes on all the places we hit today—eyes in the sky, even, that they won't see unless they think to look up—and see if they're picking through the rubble or laying low."

I gave her a thumbs-up. "Exactly. And there are some places elsewhere on the island I want to look into with Roderick."

He arched one eyebrow just enough for me to notice—he was curious what I had in mind—but he nodded. "Of course, Cousin."

Beth's eyes finally spun down from the stars above us and she looked at me. "You have provoked them. They will respond."

"But they're essentially paranoid ultraconservatives," I said to her. "They're going to want to know more before they stick their heads up out of the trenches."

"Paranoid ultraconservatives," Beth said. She smiled slowly. "If we have agitated their paranoia they'll lash out in fear. They have one really big gun, right? So, when they unleash the Rhinemaiden out of paranoia, then what?"

Explaining all this stuff to them before they came here—about the war the rebels fought over a century ago; about how the elders didn't want to live amongst humanity but instead to rule over them; about how hiding among them had been chosen as the humane option by people like my maker, Agatha, and the vampires in her cohort; about the Rhinemaiden: neither Old Shoe nor Beth had even once questioned the *reality* of what I was saying. It was like the whole story explained a lot to them, and to be honest it had explained something to me, too: where were all the old vampires, anyway? If we're supposed to live forever, how come I'd never met anyone who *did?*

It was something I'd wondered many times and when neither Beth nor Old Shoe questioned any of this I knew I wasn't alone. Why were no really ancient vampires hanging around? The story our makers had told us was that vampires didn't often survive past a century or two. The world was changing too fast, they said. People aged out of the world they'd understood. Eventually vampires withdrew from life until they gave up on living altogether. It was part of the argument they used to sell us on living among humans, ourselves: stay a part of the world of the living and you'll want to stay alive yourself. I rejected a lot of that when I moved out into the middle of nowhere north of Raleigh, but the suburbs caught up to me and I found myself among humans whether I liked it or not. I didn't know at the time that Agatha was passing along a philosophy for which she fought her own makers; or that it was intended as an antidote to the way the elders, in turn, raised her. I just assumed it was how it always was. Still, a part of the story nagged at the back of my mind: wasn't there some set of circumstances in which just *one* elder might survive? Wasn't that the idea in almost every single vampire movie and story: somewhere along the way there's an ancient to encounter? Where were our Draculas? Who was our Armand?

Agatha always told me there were probably a few, maybe in the larger cities if they possessed some exceptional capacity to keep up with changing society, but more likely in the middle of some absolutely barren landscape. *I've always fancied there being an ancient in the Australian Outback,* she said to me one time when I was young and she was still my mentor. *I rather like that idea: such a desolate place, and in the middle of it, caged behind sand and rock and a few craggy plants in the pale moonlight, an ancient hatred wondering if it will ever again, in what's left of its life, encounter a world it can apprehend.*

At the time, I thought she meant it as a sort of optimistic thing: an admirable example of the will to survive overcoming circumstances that had taken down all this hypothetical elder's peers. Now I knew better. When she said "caged," she meant it. Agatha didn't relish the thought of an ancient still being alive. She relished the idea of it being alive in circumstances it couldn't *stand.* She loved the notion of an elder vampire being tormented forever by an inhospitable setting it would never escape.

"We hope they don't do that," I finally said to Beth. I realized everyone had been staring at me in the silence, waiting to be led. *Shit,* I thought to myself. *I wanted to be the boss, not a leader.* "We try to stop them before they can. And if they do, we make them regret it."

"She has a point, though," Sheila said from amongst the technopagans. "And we have to keep that in mind. We don't want to make them choose the nuclear option. We can't pretend to be surprised if we poke them with a stick and they bite back. We shouldn't be surprised if, when we lunge, they riposte."

I nodded at her. "Point taken, but I have a sneaking suspicion the elders have something else on their minds."

"Something bigger than getting three of their dens blown sky high in the middle of the day?" Jennifer scoffed at the idea.

"No," I said, "But they had a reason for being here before we did that, and it doesn't add up that it would *only* be the Rhinemaiden."

"You think you have figured it out, Cousin." Roderick smiled just a little. I'm not even sure a human would have detected it.

"I think. Sort of. Not completely. But I want to see for myself, and I want to do so as quietly as possible." I nodded at Beth and Marty Macintosh. "You two, hang out with our breathing friends. Get to know each other." I looked at Jennifer. "Holler if Xi finds anything too interesting."

Jennifer looked at me with appraising eyes. She didn't like that I wasn't sharing my theory, but there wasn't one to share. I just had a gut feeling.

"Sure," she said.

I gestured at Old Shoe and Roderick. "You two, come with me."

Chapter 7

London is drowning, and I live by the river.
--The Clash, "London Calling"

Across the Intercoastal Waterway from Sunset Beach was the sort of golf course it takes more fresh water to maintain for a season than the town could drink in a year. In a world where clean drinking water isn't available to every child, your blood has to curdle just a little at the sight of so much of it getting pissed away twice a night so some retired hedge fund manager can pass the ennui of his twilight years double-bogeying his way to hell.

I'm sure it's good for property values, though.

The golf course had no sandy shore on the Waterway *per se*, just a rocky shoreline unsuited to tourists. In the middle of the night, it was abandoned. In the distance, maybe a mile away, we could see the lights of the houses Sunset Beach and, in one corner, the massive, blindingly bright lights the cops had put on the scene of the house Jennifer destroyed as her grand finale the day before.

Closer to us, standing across the Waterway from it, was the dark horizon of dunes and scrabbling grasses making up the Bird Island Reserve, the name of the undeveloped natural area on the southwestern end of Sunset Beach's island property. The water between it and us looked and smelled like marshy ocean because that's what it really was: not so much a river and not so much the ocean as it was a delta in slow motion. High reeds and low trees clung to the edges in hopes it would turn into land sooner or later. There was a sign—WARNING SHARKS—and I wondered at how exactly to read that one.

"You know, boss," Old Shoe said as we stood there watching Roderick strip to the skin and tuck his clothes into a big plastic bag he tied to Dog's collar, "I don't know how to swim." Old Shoe shrugged at me. "Never learned."

"You grew up in a beach town," I said. "You're wearing those damned surfer coral bracelet bead things. You're wearing *board shorts*. What do you mean you never learned?"

He fluttered his lips as he let out a long breath. "Never got around to it."

"Well, lucky us, we're already dead," I replied. "You don't need to breathe so you don't need to swim. You just need to know how to walk." With that I stepped forward and down a few inches. Cold, brackish water flooded my boots and made a horrible sucking sound. "Last one across is a rotten egg."

Roderick stretched from toes to fingertips, head back, naked as fart, and laughed. "Oh, Cousin," he said, "Do not issue such challenges. You know I love to win." He winked, stepped backward twice, then ran forward and dove directly into the water with an impossibly far leap, the strength of a vampire letting him get well out over the water before he dropped lithely beneath the surface and vanished. Dog, without a care in the rest of the world, nor a second thought, stepped into the frigid water and began his slow, purposeful paddle across the Waterway with the strength of a hellhound. The plastic bag of clothes bobbed along beside him.

That gave me a thought, and I laughed to myself. Old Shoe—it felt so weird calling this cute but ultimately eminently forgettable college kid by that name, but I had no idea what his real name might be—looked at me oddly.

"What's so funny?"

"Nothing," I said. "And everything. Watch this." Smiles was sitting next to me and I squatted beside him. With a click of my cheeks, he dutifully climbed into my back and let me grab him by his legs. Hellhounds are sturdy animals. You don't have to be as easy with them as you might a real dog. I turned away from the water, sprinted a few yards onto the golf green with Smiles on my back, and began to run in circles. Just like the time I'd taken Mary-Lou Reinholdt's stupid-ass handgun away from her before she knew it, and the time I'd fought the Transylvanian in high speed, and the time I'd fought Dmitri to the finish before his revenant minions could leap into the room, I spun up the super-speed and *really* put some pepper on it. Faster and faster, my boots tore through the turf in a widening circle. The hedge fund managers were going to wonder who did donuts on their precious putting green.

"Jesus," I heard Old Shoe say in ultra slow motion as I rocketed past him. My feet just kissed the top of the water.

I laughed as I ran. *That's kind of exactly the idea*, I thought to myself. In what might have been two blinks of a mortal's eye, I crossed the river moving too fast to sink, running on the surface of the water itself. I glanced behind me as I went: I moved so fast I left boot prints.

I could see ripples in the depths from Roderick swimming along just below the surface. He had turned on the super-speed, too, so he flashed like a fish and the water frothed around him as though churned up in a motorboat's wake. The idea suddenly occurred to me these were shark-infested waters—just like the sign warned us—the moment *we* stepped in. That made me laugh again. Some nights I really love being what I am.

I hit the opposite shore going hell for leather. Smiles leapt from my shoulders as soon as I let go of him and nimbly touched down on all fours. My own momentum drove me straight up the beach, plowing aside wet sand like a ship run aground. I smashed into a dune and it exploded apart, sand and shells and clumps of wispy little grasses flying in all directions like a grenade had gone off. I slid face-first a good twenty yards into the nature preserve, rolling head over heels and grunting and groaning with each bump and fumble. When I finally came to a rest I staggered to my feet, dizzy and spitting grit all around me. Smiles calmly sniffed the air from thirty feet away.

The world slammed back into regular time with something like a thunderclap and I trudged back down my own trail of destruction to the shore of the waterway. Roderick was standing there, having finished his high-speed swim with grace rather than my tomfoolery. He laughed when he saw me, his eyes twinkling. Dog appeared a couple of minutes later, plastic bag in his teeth, and Roderick began to dress.

"You skinny son of a bitch," I said to him. "You ought to try out for the Olympics, swimming like that."

"I have to say," he replied with a smirk, "It was very enjoyable watching you impact the shore. It was like a meteorite strike—no, like a cannonball exploding in a pirate film."

"I guess I didn't think that entirely through," I said. "I was just so intent on getting across, I didn't think about the landing."

Roderick's hair was slick-wet and so was he, but with a rapid-motion blur he shook himself. He shimmied just like one of the hellhounds, but with the super-speed of a vampire, and in a blink he was dry.

"Now that…" I said. "That's clever." I held out my arms and did the same. Sand flew off in all directions.

Roderick wiped some from his face. "Well," he said. "Thank you for the warning."

I chuckled and chucked a thumb towards the water. "I wonder how Old Shoe is doing?"

We both turned to look for his progress, but he was underwater, doing it the hard way, and we couldn't see him. To be honest, that was also the smart way from the perspective of not being seen by anyone *else*, but my desire to show off simply got the better of me.

I could see a silhouette out on the water, too: one that was not the giant, arcing bridge over the waterway between Sunset Beach and the mainland, nor was it the dunes and grasses of the nature reserve where we were coming ashore. It was a fishing boat, just some old guy in a little dinghy with a thermos of coffee, maybe a pint of bourbon, and a rod and reel. He probably wasn't even trying to catch anything. I saw him leaned back with a longneck bottle held to his mouth and could hear what sounded like a transistor radio playing some old tunes.

This wasn't the hedge fund manager with his golf foursome and a cocktail; this was some gone-native neo-local living the old-fashioned old man dream. A retiree in a retirement town listening to golden oldies on the waterway was about as classic Bullshit Americana as it got. I was a little worried he saw me run across the river or noticed Roderick's meteoric swim, but then I heard him belch with satisfaction at the end of that beer, and he turned up the music: mission accomplished. He was probably a little toasted and didn't notice a thing. Vampires make our bread and butter on mortals being lousy at seeing what's right in front of them.

The oldster got a bite right about then and all of a sudden his attention was on trying to reel in whatever was on the hook. Whatever it was, it was big and strong and had plenty of fight.

For a moment it looked like he was winning as the reel suddenly started turning and he leaned backwards as he brought up his catch. At the last second, just as the fisherman was making some cackle of victory, I caught a flash of white emerge from the water. It wasn't a fish: it was a hand with a coral bracelet around the wrist. It grabbed the guy by the wrist, yanked with the unnatural strength of a vampire, and pulled the guy into the water so fast he only got out the very first spear tip syllable of what he meant to be an ear-splitting scream.

The water foamed and thrashed for a few seconds while Old Shoe got his teeth in the guy, both of them under the surface, but then it went still.

Old Shoe beat the fisherman at his own game, I guessed.

Eventually I heard a sloshing noise and the guy's corpse floated on the surface. Old Shoe knew to lick the wound clean so it wouldn't show. Now there wouldn't be an inconvenient mystery: there would just be a guy who got drunk, fell overboard and drowned. Hell, if there really were sharks around, the blood would probably lead them right to the body and disguise *any* sign of the unusual. It was a tidy, open and shut case, just the way we like to leave them.

It was also one of Marty's various tangential categories of data: shark attacks in places or at times other than expected. I wondered if anyone would notice it.

Looking up at the massive arch of the bridge spanning the Intercoastal Waterway, only the blinking red lights along its edge winked back. If anyone noticed, they weren't standing out here right now.

Jennifer and her gang—that's what I think of the technopagans as being, a kind of gang with a very special set of circumstances surrounding them, because they do it partly for prestige and partly for profit and some of it sounds pretty illegal, and sometimes they have scuffles over turf—were sitting in the van in the parking lot of that coffee shop that was closed down for the off-season.

Ramon was in the passenger seat. In his lap was a tablet he used to track the movements of Xi 2.0. The drone was navigating over the island from north to south and east to west in a complex grid pattern. On the tablet, Ramon could view the camera feed, monitoring the ground and the many rooftop decks and backyard boat docks of the houses on the tiny island.

On Sheila's computer, the drone's movements were drawing a pattern on a map overlay of the island. She could see the drone's path unfold superimposed over the island, not the drone or its feed itself. Like a long stroke being drawn in the absence of a pen, Sheila's map began to reveal a complex geometric pattern I would later hear described as "a kind of cross between a fractal and a sigil."

"You guys are doing magic," Marty asked it of Sheila after a very long time of considering whether or not to speak. He and Beth were seated in the back, watching the others work in silence. "Right? What's the point of that design?"

Jennifer was the one who answered. "She can't answer because she's meditating to maintain the focus of the spell." Her eyes met Marty's in the rear view mirror. He shrank a little but she kept talking. "The spell expands our ability to surveil small pieces of the island into a persistent magical presence over its entirety. When we look at the pattern as a whole, we know also—due to the nature of a fractal—that we can then look on any part of it and find it as valid as the whole. That's how fractals work: any suitably chosen part is similar to a larger or smaller component of the overall shape when enlarged or reduced in size."

"It's a magical microscope," Marty said. "You can zoom in or out wherever you want."

"Exactly," Jennifer said. "In this case we're specifically tracking supernatural presences on the island." After a pause, she went on. "So you're good with numbers?"

"'Surveil' is a mutant word," Beth said, staring out the window at the darkness and the water. "It was created in reverse by dropping the end from the pre-existing word 'surveillance.' It's debatable whether or not it's a real word in English." Her tone was flat and steady.

Marty nodded, still looking Jennifer in the eye in the rear view mirror. "It's like a fractal word-origin. 'Surveillance' was a valid word, so a smaller portion of that word is also valid."

Jennifer was quiet for a moment. "Okay. I see where you're going there." She ignored when Ramon mouthed the words *so crazy* to himself. "So, what sort of data do you work with?"

"I like to think of myself as more of a computer geek than a numbers geek. It just turns out computers are really good at math. What's the third computer doing?" He pointed at Dan. "What is his part of the ritual?"

"I'm mapping the course of the car and the hydraulic lift and anything else we've done to drive around the island for the last, say, 72 hours," Dan said. Marty leaned forward and peeked over his shoulder while Dan spoke. "If we lace together the patterns derived from Xi and from our own movement on the grounds, we create a magical synergy: two images generated with the same *intent* but using different means. Our ground-level view and the flying perspective of Xi complement one another. They reinforce our ability to study the island from either perspective by intertwining the output of each."

"As above, so below," Marty said. He blinked at Jennifer's reflection.

"Yes," Jennifer said. She smiled a little. "At least, that's what they tell me."

"Aren't you a ritual magician?" Marty sounded confused for a moment.

"Only sort of," Jennifer said with a little shrug. "Originally I was just a computer geek like you. It turns out computers are really good at magic, too, because maybe magic is just fancy math, and I needed magic to keep up with everything going on. It's not that simple, though. Magic seems to work when you really *need it*, and it's like it knows. It's like there's something behind it: a force, maybe an intelligence, and it's listening to see whether it thinks you really *believe*. It turns out I'm also pretty good at that part. I'm good at spontaneous stuff. I just don't have a ton of training." She looked as though she might keep going, but she and the other technopagans all drew in their breath.

"Did you feel that?" Ramon asked.

"Yeah," Dan said.

"Jennifer," Beth asked. "Do you believe in devils?"

"We're not Satanists," Jennifer said with something of a sigh.

"How are you in charge if you aren't trained as a witch?" Marty looked slightly worried about that, as though it weren't natural.

"I didn't ask if you are Satanists," Beth said.

"I've been initiated, but I'm more *techno* than *pagan*," Jennifer replied, stepping on Beth's statement.

"They know we're here," Sheila announced. She didn't open her eyes, but her voice carried the urgency of someone who's just heard the boss' footsteps in the hall. "They know Xi is there."

"They have magic, too," Beth murmured. "They have magic from a devil they created. That's what Seth told me. Seth told me all about them. All about the thing they created so they could worship it." Her eyes slid off the endless burble and flow of the Waterway, just barely visible from the coffee shop's lot. Her gaze fell on the back of the seat behind her, or a speck of dust in front of it. "They have magic they sacrificed their own kind to get. The thing they worship is like a demon but it isn't from Hell. Seth told me they made it themselves so they would have someone on whom to blame their failures. He said they always knew they would lose. Seth thinks most of them are just hoping to stick around long enough to watch the others die first. They're like castaways on a desert island who find the last coconut and look at one another with hunger in their eyes. At best, the victor will live longer than the loser by a meal or two."

Everyone was quiet for a very long time. "Tell me about this magic they've got," Jennifer said.

"I don't believe in magic," Beth said. "I think Seth was just being funny." She smiled and leaned forward in her seat to speak to the back of the others' heads. "I think he just said it to make me laugh."

Jennifer chewed her lip but didn't say anything to her. Instead, to Ramon: "What's their status? Is Xi seeing movement?"

Ramon leaned close to the tablet, hunched over it like a jeweler at his task. "There are... yeah, there are targets in the street. They're looking up at Xi. So, like Sheila said, they've seen him. And..." He made a noise in the back of his throat. "There are a *lot* of them, and they're *waving at us.*"

A couple of minutes later, Old Shoe trudged up onto the sand. Brackish water streamed from every corner and hem he had. His phone and wallet were in a sandwich bag but the kid's clothes were drenched. He looked at us and said, "Where did you learn to do that?" He sounded offended, almost, like it was yet another unfairness heaped upon him. To be fair, if I woke up looking like he did every night, I'd probably resent some shit, too.

Roderick smirked at him.

I just shrugged. "What, haven't you learned to move fast? That was one of the first things I realized about myself," I said. I chucked a thumb behind me, in the direction of the ocean, across the width of the island. "I see lights in the distance. We need to get moving."

"What are we here to see, anyway?" Old Shoe still sounded sulky.

"I think the vampires in this place and a few humans from a local *historical society* are all looking for the same thing. Or maybe the vampires are trying to protect it and the humans are trying to find it. I want to see what they're looking for, because I think it's the Rhinemaiden."

Old Shoe opened both eyes wide. "Wait, you think some folks from the local tourism board are out here going toe to toe with the ancient vampires you think are trying to wipe us all out? That doesn't make any sense. Why wouldn't the old guys just bump 'em all off in a night?" There was a panicky edge to Old Shoe's voice that surprised me. Maybe the kid hadn't seen much action, sure, but we're all vampires. Not a one of us is a stranger to violence.

I shrugged. "Because people would notice. Because one of the people in the historical society—at least one, maybe more—used to be a thrall and now he hunts our kind. I think he escaped from one of the ancients and wants to find the Rhinemaiden so he can use her instead: to put a hurt on his old masters."

Roderick was just finishing tugging on his shoes. "Cousin," he said, in a much more measured tone than Old Shoe, "This would explain some things about our interactions with the deputy. I do not understand how *you* have arrived at some of these conclusions, however." He smiled a little, looking back at me.

I grinned a little. I couldn't help savoring knowing something Roderick didn't. "I have my methods," I replied, hands spread. "But also because I went and knocked on Deputy Crew Cut's hotel room door. The guy is larded up in magic like you wouldn't fucking believe. It reminded me of the shit we saw in that garage, except this time all the blood was still running around in the veins of a bunch of living animals. He's got one of the same maps of the island, too. I think they've both..." I struggled with the terminology. I'm a supernatural creature, sure, but I'm no mystic. "I think they *divined* the location of something, and we all only know one thing they'd be out here trying to hide or find. So, two plus two..."

Old Shoe didn't like it one bit. "And we're just going to walk up to them and ask what they're doing? How do we even know the people out there where those lights are…" He looked over my shoulder suddenly and shivered. Funny, since vampires don't really get cold. "How do we know they're these blood bags? How do we know they aren't, like, a few elders standing guard?"

"What, you worried they'll catch you?" Sometimes I have little patience for a vampire who won't get his hands dirty. "Oh, that's right, *you* can't *run*."

"Be fair to the boy, Withrow," said a voice I hadn't heard in a very long time. "You've had decades to learn about yourself, and a maker who was willing to teach."

Dog and Smiles both began to growl with the deep, bone-rattling intensity of Hellhounds who know an enemy when they smell one.

We all three turned at the fourth presence standing there, one that hadn't been there before: Ross, the "demon" who played a flirtatious game of cat and mouse with me once before, and the source of all the elders' magic thus far.

Ross was tall, athletic, and shapely in a defined but not beefy sort of way. His body was covered in silver-tinged blue scales that reflected the light of the moon and the stars, and his eyes were a cloudy shade of amber-yellow suggesting fool's gold in a cup of curdled milk. He had no hair and he was wearing a t-shirt for a band I never heard of and a pair of swim trunks that showed everything in them—everything—in obscenely perfect detail. The last time I saw him it caused something deep inside me to well up by surprise: a kind of physical yearning I hadn't felt in decades. It was the sort of lust I left behind when I let Agatha turn me into a vampire. Back then I wanted to escape a world in which I was not considered a sexual object and until Ross came along I succeeded.

I was a little surprised to realize it was not happening this time.

"Hello, Withrow." Ross's voice was deep and smooth and sounded like a peanut butter cup selling a used car. He looked at Roderick—who froze mid-button of his shirt so he looked like a statue—and nodded. "And Roderick. I should have known you wouldn't be far behind."

Roderick normally has a saucy retort ready to ship at a moment's notice but he didn't say a word. Instead he went back to buttoning, his eyes never leaving Ross' handsome features. Something like a smile was on Roderick's face, but note how I said *like*. I knew my cousin well enough to recognize murder in his eyes.

Ross looked over at Old Shoe. "Hello, Brodie."

I blinked and finally found my voice. "Brodie?"

Old Shoe didn't say anything. He just stared at Ross. A vampire like Old Shoe, who didn't even know how to run fast, must've never seen anything like Ross before. I told him and Beth that the elders had supernatural powers at their disposal beyond what we would normally expect but I maybe didn't go into a *ton* of detail with them about things like blue-scaled demons who made you horny. It just sounded so fucking crazy whenever I said it. Roderick had this crazy idea the demon was a tulpa, a thing people make real out of nowhere by believing in it real hard, and that didn't help summarize things at fucking all. Besides, I was a little embarrassed by the way Ross made me feel. I didn't want to have to go into explaining they should stay away from the thing I made out with so hard I wrecked the stockroom of an ÜberBargains.

Ross turned to me with a smile. "That's your friend's name." He arched an eyebrow. "Isn't it? We have a knack for knowing these things."

I harrumphed at him and shifted my weight, folding my arms across my chest. "Don't waste our time standing around looking pretty, Ross. What the hell do you want?"

He smiled more broadly this time. "Tsk tsk, Withrow. Life would go so much better for you if you became a little more sociable."

I heard a sound come from Roderick, way down, and I realized abruptly he'd started to growl just like the dogs. Dog started shaking his hips, but my cousin put out one hand and his Hellhound fell silent. This was Roderick's squirrel to chase, not his pet's. Roderick had a real hate-on for Ross and I've never totally understood why. He claimed he destroyed one before but he wouldn't tell anyone *how*. I just figured it was a story he told to sound like a badass, a vampire's version of having a girlfriend in Canada.

Ross laughed lightly at the growl Roderick was working up, and looked back at me. "My… clients know you are here. They also know your mortal friends are here. It's odd, don't you think? A vampire who would work with humans to destroy other vampires? You so recently fancied yourself a loner with no need for human interaction at all and here you are working with them to betray your own kind?" Ross shook his head. "Anyway, your little friends aren't the only ones with something like *magic* on their side. I mean, if you want to sully the word magic using it to indicate what pathetic little mortals can do. Terribly weak compared to what my clients have at their disposal."

"Get to the fucking point," I snapped.

Ross smiled and he had dimples in his cheeks. "They've asked me to inform you it's not too late to join them." He initially stood with his hands folded together before him and now he brought them up and apart in a slow-motion gesture of pleading, like a lawyer addressing the jury in his closing statements on a bad courtroom drama. "Give up this quixotic quest to preserve your maker's rebellion. Give up this uninformed notion the eldest of your kind are your enemy. Withrow, the two examples of the elders you've actually met were, frankly, poor representatives: a redneck on a power trip and a fetishist bogeyman courting mad science in faded suburbia are not exactly the center of the bell curve. The eldest of your race are not monsters. They are *survivors*. You have a lot in common with them. The elders just want you to hear what they have in mind. Give them a chance to persuade you. Don't assume your maker wants what's best for you. Don't make the mistake of thinking the elders want to harm you just to harm you. They only want to retake their rightful place at the top of the food chain. They have no intention of interfering in your life once you've shown them proper respect."

That word, *respect*, landed like a kick in the stomach. It felt like being bitten in the neck. I balled up my fists and had to work hard to keep a handle on the monster that lives inside. It lunged at Ross, deep in the cage of my soul, and it was an act of willpower to keep it in check. "Let me tell you what your clients can do with their proper respect," I rumbled, but Ross put up his hand and there was something in his eyes—some evil sparkle, some hint of iron and stone—that touched an ancient human part of me, deep down, and made me shut my trap. Whereas the last time we met, Ross made me feel a desire I'd thought long gone, this time he made me feel *fear* in a way I hadn't in decades. Even the monster inside whimpered in fear.

"I think now might be a good time to let you know the fate of your friends relies on your answer." Ross grinned with perfect teeth and it could have curdled fresh milk.

"Ah," Roderick said in a very quiet voice. "Of course."

Old Shoe had been standing there adjusting his coral bracelet with the opposite hand nonstop, a nervous gesture, and he said, "Boss… what's he talking about?"

Jennifer cranked the mini-van's engine and threw it in reverse. "They know we're here," she said to the car in general.

"Where are we going?" Dan's voice shook.

"One of them just pulled out a pistol and pointed it at Xi," Ramon said, "But another made him put it away and picked up a rock… and threw it? Xi's been hit." Ramon was still hunched over the tablet.

"Xi is returning to his point of origin." Sheila's voice was flat, no more emotional than text on a terminal screen. She didn't sound worried because she didn't sound *anything*. She was still locked into the meditation.

"Without his complete pattern, our surveillance rune is shot," Dan said.

"We're aborting," Jennifer said. It was an order, not an opinion. She stepped on the gas and the engine roared. The back wheels of the mini-van shrieked and kept shrieking. The van didn't move. Marty and Beth, seated in the last row, looked backwards.

"There is a woman," Beth said. "She is holding the van in place."

Marty noticed, just at the edge of his vision, Beth's eyes widen slightly in fear.

Jennifer looked in the rear view mirror. A lone woman, looking to be in her 60's, stood there with one hand on the back gate. The van's engine was at maximum revs, roaring like it was about to throw a rod, but it couldn't move an inch.

Marty licked his lips. "The force exerted by the engine of this van at maximum output, expressed in pounds per square inch across the surface area of an average human hand is –"

Jennifer shifted to drive and gunned it again, but the rear axle of the van merely lifted off the ground as the woman behind them picked up the whole thing using the back bumper.

Another pair of figures, a man and iwoman, melted out of the darkness at the edges of the parking lot and moved in. One approached the driver's door and the other walked slowly toward the passenger door.

Jennifer reached down and hit the automatic lock.

Dan laughed at the mechanical clunk noise and he sounded a little hysterical.

"Jennifer," Ramon said, his voice very quiet. "Are we about to die?"

"No," Jennifer replied. "*We* are not."

"Boss," Old Shoe said to Withrow, a mile and a half away and infinitely further in terms of his ability to affect anything about the situation. "Boss, maybe we should listen to this ugly asshole."

Ross' eyes flashed at Old Shoe—a searing burst of hate—and the kid just shrugged.

"Sorry, but it is what it is," Old Shoe said. Looking back at Withrow he begged for consideration. "Seriously, boss, if they've got Jennifer and Beth and Marty and everybody else, and if all they want is for you to give the salute or whatever, I mean, why not?"

Ross' features settled back into something like placid handsomeness and he turned half-lidded eyes and a very subtle smile at Withrow and then Roderick as he spoke. "Your junior colleague seems to understand the situation. You should take his advice."

I turned my whole body, very slowly, away from Ross and towards Old Shoe. I wanted him to understand what I was about to say was more important to me than a literal (*maybe*) demon standing in front of me talking threats. I wanted Old Shoe to understand Old Shoe, himself, was more real to me, more important, and I was more likely to hurt him—to reach out with my hands and break him—if that was what it took to get my point across.

"No," I said. My voice was very soft. "I will not ever take this thing's advice." I hooked a thumb at Ross. "I don't know what he is or where he comes from. I don't know whose side he's really on, or that it matters, or that there are even really 'sides' in this. But I know he lies, and betrays, and takes pleasure in the suffering and torment of others. I think he takes his greatest pleasure from getting people to torment *themselves*. He makes people think there's an easy solution." I looked right into Old Shoe's eyes, blandly brown in a forgettable face. "There are no easy solutions." I drew a breath. "Do you understand me? There never is. It is always a trap."

Old Shoe's youthful and perfectly neutral face was as uncertain as any expression can ever be. He looked like he wanted to object but didn't know how, didn't know what to say, what appeal would find purchase with me. After a moment he swallowed some air and started to say something and I shook my head.

"I won't say it again after this: no. And no one will be permitted to suggest otherwise. Old Shoe, I will let another vampire live her life how she wants any night of the week, no matter how dumb I think they may be, right up until their choices threaten me. Giving this thing a moment's consideration is that kind of choice."

Ross sounded slightly exasperated when he spoke. "Do you see, Brodie? This is the sort of rhetoric I hear all the time from fanatics like Withrow. He claims to know the elders' intentions and that those intentions are sinister. He says his own intentions are…" Ross trailed off. "Actually, have you ever said what are your intentions, Withrow? Have you ever said what it is *you* want?"

I turned my head to look at him. Roderick was still growling, standing stock still as he did so. Not a muscle in his whole body had moved the entire time. His eyes had not left Ross. He would leap upon the pseudo-demon and rip him into blue confetti if I said the word. Maybe if I didn't, too. I spoke to Ross with all the calm I could muster. "I want freedom. I want to live my own life without someone else thinking they can tell me what to do just because they're older than I am. That's why I quit working for my maker and came here. That's why I knocked off my predecessor and took power. That's why I do everything, more or less." I smiled a little. "It probably sounds too simple, too easy, but it's true. All I've done has basically been to guarantee my own right to live my own life."

Ross smiled, but at Old Shoe, not at me. "See? He says it himself; or rather, he does *not* say something important: what he thinks of *your* freedom. Withrow is full of the importance of his own happiness, his own liberation, his own prerogatives, but never anyone else's. The gift his maker gave him by turning him into one of your kind? Thrown back at her so he could go have adventures of his own. The previous administration of your state was murdered down to a man because Withrow didn't want to be bothered with learning to live in the world as we find it the way the rest of us do. When was the last time Withrow asked you if you needed anything, Brodie? When was the last time he offered to *help* you rather than merely to tolerate you?"

"When," Roderick said, a dry rasp between lips still practically sealed together, "Was the last time one of your followers didn't *die* for having worshipped you?"

Ross chortled aloud, a laugh fighting its way out of his too-handsome face, a smirk wrinkling his so-perfect snakeskin cheeks. "Oh, Roderick," he said around a chuckle, "Who are you to criticize someone on the grounds of death? Does the world even know how many people you've murdered? Do you even remember, yourself? At least I'm honest with those who choose to become my clients. My relationships are purely transactional and above-board. The elders know what they're getting into when they work with me and they do what is required of them by their own choice. I've never compelled a single soul against his own will."

Roderick stepped forward and reached out. I thought he was going to grab Ross by the front of his shirt or the scruff of his collar or something, but he reached out and simply held his finger an inch from the center of Ross' chest. He had stopped growling, had stopped smiling or smirking or anything of the sort. Roderick's face fell blank like that of someone in deep sleep. The dead usually wear an expression—trust me—but a sleeper's face wears the emptiness of being a body whose mind has gone somewhere else. Roderick's face had that kind of emptiness now. His eyes were not totally focused and I thought to myself this was the closest I had ever seen Roderick to going full-on red-mist murderous psycho. I had hunted with him in the past, in Seattle and in Durham. We had killed together: mortals aplenty and occasionally a vampire. All those times, Roderick seemed to *gain* clarity when he resorted to violence. The moment he moved to take a life was when Roderick seemed to awaken, not to fall away. It was one of the things I found most worrying: the possibility he could only see the world clearly through a fine sheen of someone else's blood. Now I felt a fear more terrible than that: the possibility even Roderick could become so furious, so livid, he would lose himself to the monster inside. I had always thought Roderick ran neck-and-neck with the animal that lives under the skin of every vampire, but no, now I realized it was possible even my cousin could stumble and be outpaced.

Roderick didn't look at Ross when he spoke, he looked at his finger, or at Ross's chest so close to it, as though a part of him were wondering how hard he would have to press to leave a mark. Roderick licked his lips absently, halfheartedly, his tongue having to feel around as though it had never been used before. "I," he said, and paused, as though he wasn't sure how to finish the sentence. He tried again. "I am going to destroy you. And it will not be by violence. It will not be the ways you might think it will be. I will not use my teeth or my hands or a knife or a gun. I will kill you with my mind."

Ross did the worst possible thing I can imagine someone doing, in terms of infuriating me. He looked at Roderick with something like pity before he turned to me to say something. "Withrow, I think your cousin is—"

With a flourish, Roderick produced a shining silver coin. Starlight glinted off its edge and my vampire eyes had no trouble seeing it clearly: it was a Peace silver dollar, the kind we used to have floating around when I was a kid. They were a post-Great-War thing, with Liberty on the face and an eagle on the reverse. It was one of the last coins minted by the United States composed of at least 90% actual silver. Roderick seemed to be looking at the coin, but also through it, past it, maybe *into* it. He sounded sleepy when he spoke: distant and thick. "I know this will not kill you," he said. "But it will cause you *tremendous* pain." With the speed of a vampire, Roderick pressed the coin to the flesh of Ross' face, right across those beautiful, lying lips, and the demon's flesh sizzled like bacon in the pan.

Ross tried to roar but couldn't, stumbled backwards, and screamed at the top of his lungs.

A mile and a half away, at that moment, Jennifer looked in the rear view mirror at Beth and Marty. The vampires approaching the car stood by the doors at the front and were reaching for the handles. "Vampires down," Jennifer said. Marty and Beth blinked at her, not understanding, and she shouted at them as she pulled out one of those giant water guns built like a gallon drum made of neon-colored plastic. "No, seriously," she yelled. "*All nice vampires need to hit the fucking deck.*"

CHAPTER 8

Holy water—the real deal, the stuff that actually works—is a hell of a thing to come by. I have never known where to get it, never was totally sure it would work, but the technopagans had a source for the real stuff.

The stuff you find in a church? That doesn't cut it. That stuff is just water some guy in a collar talked at. The real thing can come from any religion but the person who makes it has to do more than believe. They've got to *know*. Lots of religions believe in sanctifying water in one way or another for one reason or another. Buddhists have about a hundred different definitions of "holy water." Shia Islam has a version they drink as a kind of magical cure-all. Christianity's just lousy with the stuff, of course. Neopagans love it, Hindus literally bathe in it, some religions have rivers or lakes they consider inherently holy, and a million other examples exist beyond those few. Go looking around for holy water and it's a wonder there's any left that *isn't*.

In practice, none of that means a lick to a vampire. I could go skinny dip in the baptismal pool at the back of the craziest, most fundamentalist, fire-and-brimstone-preaching-est, full-immersion Southern Baptist church in the scariest little inbred corner of Creation you can conjure up. All I'll get is a stern look from whoever sees me.

Unless the person who blessed it happens to be a little magical in her own right.

Jennifer told me one time they're called *extempore* witches. Nobody knows why they happen but they're basically witches who've never been trained and may not even know they're working magic. I'm not convinced it's *magic*, actually. I suspect these people are just lucky or something. Maybe they're psychic or some shit and they use it to shape reality to their expectations. Of course, Jennifer told me that *is* a witch: someone who reshapes reality to align with their vision of it. Hell if I know. Apparently, if you can find an extempore who is also a recognized religious leader—a priest, a cleric, an imam, a monk, a rabbi, whatever—and get them to bless some water, voila, you've got something that will turn a vampire into slag with a splash.

Jennifer and Dan each had a liter of the stuff in giant water guns and, next to them, power windows. They opened fire the second their windows were down. The vampires about to yank open their doors didn't stand a chance. Water splashed them in the face and their heads simply weren't there anymore. Their bodies didn't thump against the pavement because they exploded into wet dust before gravity could catch up to them.

Beth grabbed Marty by the shoulders, dragging him into the floor of the mini-van next to her, between the bench seats, as Jennifer and Dan each shouted a war cry and rolled out of the van in opposite directions. Sheila snapped out of her trance and slid into the driver's seat. Ramon grabbed a third water gun from the floor by his feet, leaned over the back two rows and jabbed his finger into the hatch release so it popped open on hydraulic arms. Flying open, the hatch clocked the vampire holding up the back end of the van.

Stunned, she dropped the back bumper, the wheels hit the ground spinning, the tires shrieked and Sheila, foot on the gas, yelled, "*Eat Detroit polypropylene, broccolis!*"

Roderick sprang forward, his eyes suddenly sharpening and his focus seeming absolute. I spun up to super-speed and ran around behind Ross to grab his shoulders and hold him still so Roderick could do whatever it was he could do with a silver coin. I had no idea what Roderick was thinking, but I was one hundred percent on board.

There was a time when I felt a powerful attraction to Ross. That was before I knew the things elders did at his behest: the rituals knee-deep in blood, the deception, the betrayals, the way he took what people wanted and used it against them. There are plenty of ways that parallels what a vampire does to mortals and I'll be the first one to cop to that, but the truth of the matter is that there is something, to me, *honest* in a vampire's dealings with a human. We need food and we need it in a specific way and—importantly—we can get it without killing them and without leaving them traumatized if we choose to operate with something just a little bit like mercy when we hunt. That isn't just different from what a demon does. That's different from what McDonald's does. Not a lot of hamburgers get made where the cow sleeps it off later.

Not all vampires try to operate with mercy, either, but one of the reasons we keep each other in arm's reach—and one of the tasks I set myself as the boss of North Carolina—is to step in and act when a vampire has done evil too much or too often just for the sake of having fun.

Something about this demon, about the way demons act in general, about Roderick's pet notion Ross might not even be a real thing but instead was something the elders dreamt up out of whole cloth: it all added up now to make me feel an overwhelming revulsion and hatred where I once felt a long-dead sense of longing. Maybe that was a part of why I hated him so much, if I'm really honest with myself. Maybe I was just furious at the way his original flirtatious attempts to distract me reminded me of how alone I was for decade after endless-and-unnoticed decade.

Maybe all I really wanted was to help murder the one and only guy who said he was into me since the night I gave up on ever having anyone be interested again.

I grabbed Ross' upper arms with all the strength the blood would give me and Roderick brought his hand around in an open-faced slap at hyper-speed. The silver coin was in his palm and burned an ugly purple scrape across Ross' silver-blue scaly skin. Roderick's other hand came up and around to mirror it and moving as fast as I was—even faster than Roderick—I had time to read the date on the silver dollar: 1934. The second slap burned Ross' skin just as badly as the first, the other way across his face. Roderick spun with the momentum, brought up both hands in front of him like some kind of kung fu master, and slapped his hands forward. The shirt Ross was wearing must have been a part of *him*, because the coins touched what looked like fabric in the middle of Ross' chest and gouts of black smoke bubbled out from between Roderick's hands.

Roderick's eyes were open, his pupils tiny, his gaze as sharp as a scalpel. His fangs were bared and he was growling like a wild animal.

We were moving so fast Old Shoe didn't even have time to turn around. He was able to see what was happening, but his eyes were wide with horror and he looked to be taking a breath to say something. I wished him luck: I wouldn't understand a thing at these speeds.

Dog was still obeying Roderick's order to remain still, but Smiles was—very slowly—leaping forward with his mouth open.

Roderick pulled his hands back and flipped the old coins between his fingers like an illusionist doing a close-up magic show: now you see them, now you don't. They reappeared between Roderick's fingers, jutting out edgewise between his digits like a couple of claws. He reared back to strike, ready to plunge them into Ross' flesh, when the demon bellowed deep and long and low, a roar distended by our own time distortion and by the rage and pain he must have been experiencing. It sounded delicious to me, one of the best things I ever heard, as satisfying as the hot wet smack of blood against the back of my throat. A kind of satisfaction washed over me in guiltless, unrestricted, unmitigated waves. Trying to kill a demon—and especially with my cousin helping me—just felt *right* to me in a way I did not expect and also did not question.

The moment before Roderick could drive the coins into him, Ross disappeared in a puff of angry yellow smoke and a bright flash of cobalt blue light. I could *feel* the magic he used—or whatever—tear him apart and whisk him away, right out of my hands, like sand through a sieve.

Roderick and I, unable to stop our momentum, slammed into each other and tumbled to the ground like two of stooges. Under us, where Ross had stood, the sand was covered in sticky black tar—or something like it. It seemed to be the residue of whatever he did to get away.

I dropped back into normal speed as I landed sprawled in the sand and Old Shoe—with his generic, forgettable face and his youthful expression of something like naiveté despite being my town's resident blackmailer—was shouting out. "What the hell are you doing," he cried. "What the fuck is going on?"

Jennifer and Dan each tumbled in a barrel roll to come up standing. Dan was screaming something non-verbal, just a plain screech, but Jennifer gritted her teeth and came to her feet in silent and utterly grim determination. She and Dan were both pumping water out of their UltraSoak 5001 With Bonus Tank & Lighted Barrel water guns. Elder vampires—or their minions, or their spawn, or whoever—were *pouring* out of the darkness now. They looked some combination of amused and confused until a stream of water thirty feet long shot from Jennifer's gun to one of the vampires. He looked like he was about 25 but he stood with a straight-backed, haughty regality modern sensibilities classify as being a one-percenter. Older eyes recognize it as nobility. He probably once had a title and land somewhere, and then he came to America to feast on its all-you-can-drink buffet of native and enslaved blood, and then history happened. Now he was just some asshole in a little beach town, polishing the knob on his plan to rule the world.

The next second, he was dust on the wind.

The vampires all blurred at once and instantly two of them were on Jennifer: one in front and one at the side.

She felt vampires' bodies press to her and she let herself cry out once as something sharp grazed her skin. She always wondered if this—all this, the business of chasing vampires, of trying to understand how they worked, how the world worked, the secret mechanisms behind the world most people saw—was what would be the end of her. Now she was going to find out.

The first set of teeth sank into her flesh like burning, jagged knives. A vampire's bite does not have to hurt but many of us take pleasure in causing pain and the elders who survived the rebellion of the 19th century were ones who especially savored the suffering of others. This one was not being kind. He was being especially cruel.

Blood shot out of Jennifer like it was under extreme pressure. Her heart was pounding, adrenaline flooding her system, and she saw red spurt once, twice, three times as the vampire tried to tear with her bite rather than necessarily *drink*. She was a middle-aged woman, or looked like one, and she was using her fangs as a weapon.

The one at her other side tried to bite into the skin at the base of Jennifer's neck, through the high-collared workout fleece she was wearing, but under that fabric Jennifer had secreted what's called a "twisting" balloon: the long, skinny kind used to make animals at the county fair. Jennifer filled this one with more of their special holy water, but not so full it kept its shape, and draped it around her neck under the fleece. The vampire's teeth burst the balloon and that vampire—she never even saw what he looked like—exploded in a cloud of greasy ash.

Dan was being mobbed, too, but he was packing water balloons under his armpits. When they tried to hold him down to bite, those balloons burst, obliterating both of his attackers.

The one who'd managed to get her teeth into Jennifer finally clamped down, sucking at the wound like a giant, sloppy leech, confident she was in control of her prey and ready to savor the kill, but Jennifer got her water gun up against that vampire's neck and squeezed the trigger.

An instant later, Jennifer was staggering, free, bleeding profusely but alive and unrestrained.

The van was screeching forward and one of the enemy vampires cried out as the front end plowed into him, knocking him airborne and, even as the vampire—apparently a kid of no greater than thirteen or fourteen, but Jennifer knew that meant nothing—flipped backwards through the air to land on his feet, the van surged as Sheila put the pedal down. The vampire-child landed in a crouch just in time for the van to hit him again, knocking him backwards and down, dragging him forward, pinned under the front axle. Sheila plowed it into a low wooden fence at one edge of the parking lot.

Wooden pickets drove through the vampire's back and erupted from his chest, thick black blood welling out of gaping wounds. Ramon shot out the side door of the van to pump water into the vampire's face.

More vampires were coming out of the woods, blurs of shadow leaping from the darkness. Jennifer wondered at first if this was a kidnapping but no, she realized, this was a hit squad. Running for the van, she yelled into her smart watch, "*Fast forward!*"

Reality rippled around her as the keyword set off a spell she kept in reserve. Time slowed for her as she spun up to super-speed.

The vampires were still faster.

"Politics," Roderick said to Old Shoe. His eyes had unfocused a little again and I could feel him slipping free of the grasp of the here and now in the way one does when they sit by a patient in a hospice or a psych ward. Roderick's presence in the moment wavered but he seemed more or less to home back in on our current coordinates in space and time. "Politics are what is happening."

"How did you know silver would hurt him?" I was knocking sand out of my hair, my coat, off the knees of my pants.

"Because it hurts them in the most popular and widely read demon fiction in America," Roderick said.

I made a little 'o' with my mouth. "Which… is…?"

"Dungeons and Dragons," Roderick replied. He shrugged. "Ross is a product of the belief in him, and the rules by which he operates are the rules those beliefs set around him."

I rolled my eyes and looked at Old Shoe. "Anyway: no, this is not politics." I said. I shook my head at the ground where Ross had been before he disappeared, the place where we'd finally, for just a moment, held him down and made him suffer for the things he did to us: not for the things he did in general, not for being the thing he was, not for being *bad* as though we were some definition of *good*, but for the things he did to us in specific. "Revenge is what's going on." I looked at Old Shoe and nodded in Roderick's direction. "There's some politics, too, but I'm going to tell it to you straight, Old Shoe, and I always will: this is mostly about revenge. That thing lies. Always. Do not forget that. It tells people what they want to hear. It's a demon with all the crazy shit that suggests. But to be honest, I just want to get revenge, plain and simple, for what it did to *me*, and for the lies it told some people who didn't deserve to die."

"A tulpa," Roderick corrected, voice quiet and still a little dreamy. "I am still fairly sure demons do not exist as an independent type of entity."

I waved that off. "Whatever it is, wherever you want to put its picture in the encyclopedia of the strange, some good people got hurt or got killed because of that son of a bitch. Ancient vampires have been using it for over a century to try to survive a rebellion against them."

"Withrow…" Old Shoe sounded a mixture of uncertain, amused and frightened. "We're vampires." He bobbled his head as if to say *duh*. "*We* deceive. We use humans. Sometimes we kill them. We don't care about *people*. We feed on them."

"The hell we don't care!" My voice rose all of a sudden and my teeth dropped down and I pointed a finger right in Old Shoe's face. I caught myself suddenly. I saw in Old Shoe's eyes just how sudden my rebuke had been, how out of character. I was the boss of all the vampires of North Carolina, with some fine print at the bottom of that assertion, sure, but I styled myself as the easy going kind. "Okay, so I'm the most hands-off boss this state has ever had. But I'm also the first one to give an actual fuck about the rest of us. Oh, sure, at first I was just the nice fat guy with a joke for every occasion, who didn't really care what you did, but these last few years—since I got dragged into saving people who never knew the irony of having a vampire save the day—well, I don't know, it's all fiddled with the gears in my head in some way. Old Shoe—no, *Brodie*—don't let yourself forget the importance of there being other people in the world. Don't fall down the well of thinking you're the only thing that matters in your whole damn world. That's what makes *them*—the elders—go fucking crazy. That's what makes them monsters. Working with other people reminded me it was possible to respect some of them. Eventually I realized I even *liked* them."

Shit, I thought, *I'm getting too soft*.

I dove ahead while Old Shoe stared at me. "Once I liked them, some of them were taken away. That hurts. I didn't know I could hurt like that, but it hurt me in my heart." My eyes softened a little, just for a moment. "It hurt me in the place where I used to have a soul. Now I am just *so* ready to punish the people who did that. I want revenge for the twins who got turned into an all-you-can-drink buffet. I want revenge for children who got turned into a squad of murderbots. I want revenge for Ross manipulating my feelings in ways I didn't even know could be done anymore." My voice fell, and I said aloud what I'd been ashamed even to think before. "The way he made me feel excitement and lust, the simple flattery of feeling desired… that hurt, too. Part of why I said *yes* to Agatha was to escape a world that wouldn't let me live as who I am, a gay guy in an era that only used "gay" to mean "merry." I thought all those parts of me were dead, but Ross brought it all right back like he flipped a switch in my brain—and then he used them against me."

Old Shoe's shoulders sagged and he blinked. "Dude."

"More than anything," I said, ignoring whatever he was about to say, "I want revenge for The Bull's Eye. She was a hero—an honest to God super hero—and she went toe to toe with a real mad-cackles-and-stolen-costume super villain. She was willing to die for the people of her city. Sometimes, when you're around genuinely good people, you can't help but let a little bit of goodness rub off on you. I never told this to a single soul, Old Shoe, but being around the Bull's Eye made me want, just a little bit, to be a hero." I drew a long breath and it shook a little. "Killing zombies to save my neighbors just made me want to be forgotten. Avenging an old friend back home made me want to be powerful. Fighting beside the Bull's Eye made me want to be *admired*. I want something new, now. The enemy knows I'm here and thinks it's OK to use my heart against me, so now I want to end them, once and for all."

Old Shoe stared at me with wide eyes and an almost blank expression. The only thing I could pick up from it was that he was horrified. I didn't know by what: by me, by Ross, by this whole situation in which he found himself. He was mostly still just a kid like any other trying to find a way to fit in. Everything about him said he wanted to blend in or otherwise go unnoticed: when he healed his eternal injuries he looked indistinguishable from any other kid in an ad for a cheap beer and when he wore those injuries he had to live in the shadows.

And here we were, dragging him headlong into a fight where the whole point was to be seen, to make an impression, to be remembered.

Roderick turned to me and said, his eyes still a little unfocused, "What is that thing you want right now? What do you want in *this* moment? Not in terms of goals, cousin, but in terms of *feeling*?"

Without hesitating I said, "I want to be feared." I blinked at him, pausing a moment. "I want to destroy their secret weapon and destroy Ross and put them right back where they were a century ago: hunted, outnumbered, with nothing to do but turn on one another. I want them to know I took away their pretense of having a fighting chance. I want to be the shadow on their doorstep. I want to take away their *hope*."

"Then we must find the Rhinemaiden," Roderick said, "And destroy her before she is used against us." The wind kicked up then, and whistled across the dunes like the sound of a knife across flesh.

"So let's go look and see if she's over there," I said. I chucked a thumb in the direction we originally were to go. "The sooner we look, the sooner we know."

Roderick straightened his shirt. "And Jennifer and the others?"

I shook my head. "I don't think they're actually in danger," I said. "I think anything Ross says, we should assume the *opposite*."

The van backed away from the spot where Sheila drove the ex-vampire into the fence. Its tires spun on wet, sandy gravel, and as the wheels turned sharply to the right, Sheila let off the gas, whipping it around. Jennifer heard the car's transmission howl as it popped from R to N. The engine roared as Sheila put the pedal down with the car still in neutral, then yanked the shifter into D. Gravel pelted everything in a thirty foot arc, Jennifer included, as Sheila hit the high beams at the end of her perfectly-executed J-turn.

The high beams were sun lamps.

Where the holy water made vampires explode in wet dust, sunlight merely made them explode. Three were running for the front of the car when light siphoned directly from the literal other side of the world struck them full on. No one even saw what happened to them: they simply went off like bombs.

The front of the minivan flew off the ground from the force of the explosions, like Jennifer imagined happens to Humvees driving over IEDs in the various horrible places the United States likes to invade. There were screams from inside the van and screams from the shadows. Apparently vampires didn't like watching sunlight happen to other vampires.

Jennifer was up and moving before the van came back down. Moving faster than any vampire would expect of any mortal, she plunged ahead into the shadows sharply contrasted by the beams of sunlight. "*Cat's eye*," she said aloud, and with a blink she could see in the dark. It hurt, though: magic always has a cost, and the on-the-fly stuff like this usually took its fee in pain. Best-case scenario, Jennifer would have a hell of a hangover the next day. Worst-case, she would be blind for a week.

There were five more vampires standing there, dropping out of super-speed to gape at what just happened. Jennifer hit one with the water gun, then a second.

Dan, slow as molasses, came running, screaming, around the front of the van, right into the chaos. With a ridiculously slow barrel roll Dan cut across the lines of attack between the remaining vampires and the van and came up standing *in* the light. *Yes*, Jennifer thought, *Always thinking!* With a shrill war cry, slowed hilariously by their different paces, Dan reached under his shirt and pulled out a giant silver medallion. It was the reward he'd gotten for running a race somewhere, and the light from the sunlamps played across it and out over the parking lot in wide, shimmering, disco-ball rays. They shot through the dust and smoke of the impromptu battle. Jennifer tried to shout—the explosions would surely kill him—but Dan would never understand her.

The three vampires screamed, but none of them exploded where the light touched them.

Jennifer seized the moment and shot one with holy water. The other two snarled and roared, but they were on the other side of the high beams and couldn't step through. With a blur, they were gone. Jennifer realized she was moving just fast enough to see them: they were simply running around the back of the van. One came at her and took a hit of holy water in the face. The other stopped at the back of the minivan and ripped the hatch right off of it, then came running at her holding it up like a shield—or a weapon.

Jennifer squeezed the trigger on her water gun, but it was empty. There wasn't much to begin with and she used it all up. Jennifer could feel her super-speed starting to slip, too, and the minivan was pointed the wrong way—possibly entirely out of commission—for the high beams to hit the vampire.

Dan was just now starting to realize the vampires did not explode. Looking around, he saw the remaining one running towards Jennifer with the giant sheet of metal from the back of the car. Dan lunged forward, and Jennifer realized if they were going to make it through this they were just going to have to fight the vampire the old fashioned way.

Roderick's eyes went unfocused and he turned away from me to look back, towards the mainland, and he shook his head. "I believe Jennifer is in danger," he said quietly.

"Why?"

"Dan and I…" he said. He blinked again, slowly, still looking that direction. "We are linked."

I rolled my eyes. "I thought you said you wouldn't describe what you did as 'dating.'"

"I asked him to alert me were he ever in serious danger," Roderick said. His voice had gone dreamy again. "It… seemed the romantic thing to do at the time."

"Great," I grumbled. "Just fucking great." I pointed at the lights on the horizon, on the other shore of the island. "Listen, Ross is making shit up. It's what he *does*."

Roderick waved a hand. "Cousin, it is important. Go. See if the Rhinemaiden is there." He still looked the other direction, though. "But I…" He hesitated. Roderick, my cousin who isn't always exactly *here*, I admit, but who is at least always sure of what he's going to do, and of himself, seemed uncertain. He took one step back towards the Waterway, and towards the mainland beyond, where we knew the technopagans were conducting whatever reconnaissance mission they cooked up. With agonizing slowness he took another. Then another, but his steps were slow and trudging. I wasn't sure whether Roderick was fighting the urge to go or the urge to stay.

"And you go…" I sighed long and loud. "*Check on your boyfriend.*" I put a little hoodoo behind it. It was freaking me out to see Roderick not sure what to do. Roderick moved more freely and, fresh clothes and all, dived into the water to swim away. Dog dove in right behind him.

"Shit like this," I said to Old Shoe, "Is why I don't date."

The vampire was slowing down, too. In fact, he stopped running and slowed to a stroll, minivan hatch held aloft in one hand. "Mortals," he said, the way you might say "maggots," or "Uncle Bob." The loathing in his voice was a living thing, with a history and a heft to it. It was its own undertone, a distinct harmonic. He wanted to make sure Jennifer and Dan could understand him.

Jennifer noted the driver's door of the van popping open as Sheila got out. Ramon, slow the whole time, came jogging around the end of the minivan.

"*Magic users!*" The vampire was dressed like a suburban dad: khakis, a golf shirt, but both were dated. He looked like the men's casual wear section of a JC Penney catalog from 1964. "Do you think your petty mumblings can really stand up to the full might of the vampires of old?"

"You're dressed pretty 'now' for somebody talking a lot of shit," Jennifer said. She ducked into the other of the high beams, putting Dan and her out of the vampire's reach. He had that door, though, and he could use it from a distance. All he needed was decent aim.

"Why didn't the reflected high beams work?" Dan sounded a little panicked.

The vampire snickered at him. "So clever, and so stupid. Typical." He pointed up: the moon was overhead. "Reflected sunlight means nothing, *boy*, or the moon would be as deadly as the sun." With a flick of the wrist he threw the door, but Dan dodged it—and fell out of the beam of light.

The vampire's fangs shot out and he started to crouch to make a leap *over* the beam to get to Dan.

"*ROUNDABOUT*," Sheila shouted, and Ramon and Dan both shouted guttural screams. Jennifer joined in, and so did Sheila. Jennifer could feel the magic pulling at her, pulling something out of her. Sheila wasn't just focusing her will to execute a spell. She was pulling power from all of them there, pulling energy, and it *hurt*. As they screamed the light from the headlights bent. Impossibly, defying all the laws of nature—but then, that's what a witch *does*—the beam of light arced around in a circle like a bendy-straw in a milkshake. The light struck the vampire and he, like the others, erupted in light and fire, a bundle of ancient death exploding in the light of the life-giving sun.

Thirty seconds later, Jennifer came back to consciousness. She was lying fifteen feet away, on her back. Her face was wet, and she could smell blood. The van was a wreck. The lights had been turned off, or had burned out—sunlamps didn't last very long. Sheila was staggering to her feet. Marty Macintosh seemed to be helping Dan to stand.

Before Jennifer opened her eyes she realized someone was very close: perhaps right over her. She fluttered her eyes open and found Beth crouched there, sniffing. With a motion like a snake, or like a frog catching a fly, Beth's tongue shot out and ran up the side of Jennifer's face. Glistening with blood, it shot back into the vampire's mouth. Jennifer gasped, then held her breath.

Beth did it again.

Jennifer made a small sound, something between a squeal and a whimper.

"Oh," Beth said, looking her in the eye at last, "Are you awake?" Her mouth opened, but Jennifer scrabbled back across the gravel.

"Don't," Jennifer said. Then she grabbed her forehead and cried out in pain. The magic—there had been *so much* magic. The others warned her against this when they started to teach her, when she became the executive they so desperately needed, but she always chalked that up to the timidity she was constantly trying to work out of them. Her head hurt just thinking about all that energy they used. This wasn't the next-day hangover she figured she would get. This was her body and her mind reacting to all the magic she used like a liver reacts to alcohol poisoning. She was going to be down for the count for a nice long while. Magic *always* has a price.

Beth blinked at her, all innocence. "Was that impolite?"

"Did you call them 'broccolis'?" Dan said aloud to Sheila, though he was still panting and still staring wide-eyed at the places where vampires had been.

"Well," Sheila said, much more matter-of-fact and in the moment, "Ending a statement with 'bitches' for emphasis always struck me as misogynistic." She paused, drew a breath, winced, put a hand to her side. "And I've never liked broccoli."

On the other side of the van, Ramon threw up.

CHAPTER 9

The slumbering apparitions that they've come to wake up.
--Panic! at the Disco, "Nearly Witches"

I turned from Old Shoe and said, "Catch up when you can," over my shoulder. Then I took off across the sand at top speed, with Smiles right beside me. The Bird Island Nature Preserve is a long field of dunes covered in scrub grasses: steep angles and sharp curves, and easy as hell to get lost in. At times I ran so fast I just went right up the side of a dune, but other times I had to go around, double back, or tack right or left. I needed to jump as I ran, bounding high into the air, to get oriented. Smiles seemed to know exactly where he was going, or at least where I was going, and I could tell he loved running like this: wide open, no subtlety, pedal to the metal.

Ahead of me, maybe half a mile or three quarters, were lights in the night. I didn't know exactly what was there, but I knew it was important. I knew if it wasn't the Rhinemaiden then it was something that would lead us to her. I *knew* this. I don't know how to explain that other than to say this was not information that came to me: this was information I felt like I already possessed. It was certainty, not supposition.

A hundred yards out, I slowed again and started creeping along, hunched down, like a bad movie ninja. The lights ahead were bright, but they were also shielded so the light was directed rather than producing the maximum possible ambient glow. That was interesting to me: whoever was doing this needed light but they didn't want to be seen from a mile away. I could see them, but I'm a vampire. Humans probably could not see them at all. It suggested these were mortals, and it suggested they were breaking the law.

At fifty yards, I could hear their voices over the otherwise deafening background roar of the ocean. It was low tide, and in Sunset Beach low tide is *low*. The water was easily thirty or forty yards farther out than what I imagine it would be during the day, with people on the beach. Still, that surf is a hell of a white noise generator. I continued creeping along, confident in my ability to hide in the dark, and listened. Smiles was as silent as the sky as he slunk from one shadow to another.

I could only catch snatches of what the people were saying to each other, but it was plenty intriguing:

"…But this is where the map…"

"…Divination is unreliable!"

"…Sources tell me it's got to be here."

"Bastards from South Carolina probably got here first."

"We would know. Trust me."

That last one was the voice of the old guy who'd been such a dick to me when Roderick and I barged into their little historical society sales pitch chasing Crew Cut. I clambered to the top of a big dune overlooking the beach itself. Beside me—at least a mile from the nearest house—was a wooden post and, atop that, a mailbox: a plain black residential mailbox with APPROVED BY THE USPS stamped on the back. It was one of the big ones, the kind you can put a couple of packages in, like maybe you'd see out in front of a business instead of a house. The mailbox gaped open, and inside I could see a bunch of spiral bound notebooks with pens and pencils tied to the wire binding them together.

You can read about this mailbox on the Internet. Tourists come and write notes and poems and letters to no one in the notebooks inside. They're like a guestbook but they're for the whole town and you have to walk a mile to try to find them.

I hunkered down beside the mailbox, gritted my teeth, and peeked over the edge.

On the beach, well into the area that would be underwater at a higher tide, were all the people who were in that metal detector sales meeting a few nights before. They were still dressed in the dumpy, frumpy clothes of a weekend gardener who knows she's going to get dirty, just like before, but they were also wearing long black opera capes a la Count Dracula himself. Standing in a circle around a hole—maybe ten feet across and deep enough I couldn't immediately see the bottom—they looked to be taking a break from digging: work gloves off, arms folded, breathing hard. It sounded like an argument was going on and maybe they were ready to start laying out the blame for something. The same interpersonal politics bullshit can take down any team, whether they're playing football or doing the devil's work.

The clown who sassed me wore a comically high collar on his cape. It marked him as being in charge. So did the ten pounds of costume jewels all over it. He bedazzled his ritual cloak. Take a second to picture that. I shook my head and stifled a laugh.

"It. Is. *Here.*" He spoke with the firm, pausing words of someone trying like hell to ride the bucking bronco of his flock's sudden disbelief. "All the signs point to it being in this place."

"We should have bought the *big* metal detector." One of the women in the group shook her head as she said it. "It would be a good investment."

"No," another said, "We would have every cop in Sunset Beach all over us in an hour if we tried to drive that thing out here."

"This is the best plan. We've all agreed to that. Now *pick up your shovels and dig again.*"

The thing is, when he said that, even I almost looked around for a shovel. He was using the hoodoo, and it worked.

On the wind, just faintly detectable under all that sand and sea, I could smell the same scent of a vampire I'd picked up when I talked to them before. I thought it was Crew Cut sweating out the blood of whoever had made him a thrall, but doubt crept on cold toes across the back of my neck. Now I was forced to wonder, what if that asshole in the fancy robe was a vampire and I somehow didn't recognize him as one?

The others grabbed their shovels and started digging with enforced enthusiasm. I slipped back behind the dune and pulled out my phone.

Are there vampires who can turn into people again as their Last Gasp?, I texted Roderick. There were undoubtedly better ways of phrasing what was running around in my head.

The phone thought about it for a second then sent the message. I put it back inside my coat, put my back to the dune, and listened.

Roderick pounded down the pavement of the empty streets of Sunset Beach in winter. Dog—old as dirt—padded behind him on giant paws. Roderick didn't try to hide his approach in any way. His boots slapped asphalt like clapping hands and, at the speed he was running, anyone perceiving events in "normal" time would probably have heard them like a playing card in the spokes of a bicycle wheel rather than footsteps.

Rounding a corner he saw the minivan sitting in a heap in the parking lot. Finding them was easy: there was smoke billowing from the wreck. Jennifer was bleeding but standing upright. The others all seemed to be alive, too. They were gathered at the edge of the parking lot for a quick conference but turned, guns pointed up, as Roderick blurred into view.

"It is I," Roderick said with a smile. He held up his hands, but then brought them together in a single excited clap. "They engaged you! Tell me you used the holy water!" In the empty lot, even with the gentler breeze of the waterway instead of the powerful wind of the Atlantic itself, he could be heard as clear as anything.

"You scared us," Jennifer said with a sigh, her hand against her head. "Call out or something before you come tearing up the street like that."

"You would not be able to understand me if I did," Roderick said. "It would sound like a shrill scream. I do not think you would react better to that." He smiled.

Jennifer glanced around. "No, I guess we wouldn't."

Roderick then nodded towards the island. "I observed Xi's return over the water. He appeared damaged. Did he have to abort his mission?" He looked around at the crushed fence and the greasy, ashy clothes scattered across the ground. "There were many of them. An ambush."

Jennifer sighed and nodded. "Xi had to abort. He went back to base on an auto-return sequence after being too damaged to continue. They spotted him and threw a rock." She sounded disgusted with herself. "A fucking *rock*."

"Ranged weapons are for cowards," Roderick murmured. "I have much greater respect for someone willing to kill with her hands and teeth. Murder is the sort of thing one ought to do by one's own power."

The others—with their super soakers and their sunlamp headlights—looked at him for a long moment.

"Present company exempted, of course. You need tools to do your work. Using a hammer to drive a nail makes perfect sense."

The historical society cult—*Jesus Henderson Christ*, I thought to myself, *the world is a fucking weird place*—kept digging in silence for a while. I could hear someone stomping around in the sand, and I guessed it was the Big Cheese since everyone else was digging at his command. He sounded pissed off. The more I listened, though, the less he sounded pissed off and maybe instead a little bit infirm. His heavy steps were just *slightly* uneven. He was landing harder on one foot than the other.

Vampires are exceptionally good at picking out the weak member of the herd.

I decided I needed to risk it, so I peeked back over the dune between tall stalks of the hardy grasses growing in the preserve.

Big Cheese was indeed favoring his left foot. It was very faint, but I could see it in his walk. The humans around him probably didn't even notice. I don't know why that struck me as odd, but it stuck. Details are funny like that.

Sand was piling up around them. They weren't literally tossing it over their shoulders, but they were filling a central bucket and lifting it out, over and over. As it filled, they got deeper in the hole. The hoodoo made them really go at it, so they started getting lower a lot faster than I think they would have done on their own.

Crew Cut was in there digging, too, the hoodoo working on him even better than it would another. Being turned into a thrall makes someone especially susceptible to suggestion. That raised its own question, though: what was he doing here trying to hunt the elders *and* taking part in a little cult being led by one? I mean, if the boss actually was an elder who could, I don't know, disguise himself as a human somehow? Thoughts of the Last Gasp ran around in my head. No one knows the full range of possibilities for the power a vampire will manifest at their second death—the moment there isn't a living soul left who knew them when they were alive, so they pass entirely from living memory. There's a taboo against vampires discussing the Last Gasp, too. It's seen as intensely personal. I've always assumed that's just a polite cover for no one wanting to give away what card we've each got tucked up our supernatural sleeve. The end result is none of us knows a ton about what it might be or do for anyone but ourselves—and we have to kill experimentally just to figure out our own.

Crew Cut seemed to be surrounding himself with the magic of life, back in his motel room, and I guessed it was to shield himself from the death magic the elders practiced. Was it possible he was trying to shield himself from the vampire right in front of him?

Was it possible that vampire's powers of disguise were sufficient for Crew Cut not to have realized the guy was a vampire?

"Herman," someone in the hole called out, putting her shovel to one side. "*Herman*! We've got company!" I froze, stock still, cursing myself for being so foolish as to peek over the top of the dune, but she wasn't looking at me. She nodded her chin to point down the beach away from town, towards the southwestern tip of the island, past the South Carolina state line. She was looking at the end of the island where ships came and went from the waterway. Beyond that, the lights of Myrtle Beach—the South's trashy cousin of Las Vegas—glowed just beyond the horizon.

All their eyes turned, and I saw the Big Cheese—Herman—put a hand up to shield his eyes as he blinked them rapidly. He looked uncomfortable, like maybe his eyes didn't work too well, but he didn't have any problems with them the other night. I noticed at the time how sharp his eyes were. He shifted back and forth from tiny print on one end of the room to me, right next to him, without batting a lash.

Huhn.

After a second, I looked where they were pointing, because they all stopped what they were doing. Off in the distance, maybe two hundred yards away, there was a figure in the darkness. My vampire eyes zoomed right in on the vague shape and if I froze any harder I'd've turned into a block of ice.

Hand to the gods, there was a ghost walking up the beach towards them, looking right at them.

She was regal. I think—no, wait, let me expand on that. I don't know why, but every time I think of her, "regal" is the word that comes to mind. I don't mean she looked like a cover model or a movie star. I mean she had that same air of command about her old queens like me see in our favorite stars of yesteryear. From two football fields away I was struck by the same quiet command possessed by someone like Bette Davis or Lauren Bacall, or these nights maybe by Cher or Beyoncé: eyes that say *do not fuck with me* set in a face wearing a measured passivity. She had the look of someone who was a victim at some point and will never, ever be a victim again.

I liked her right away. I just immediately felt like she was someone whose hand I'd want to shake if she weren't also about half-transparent and obviously insubstantial. Behind her—through her—I could see the sand and the water and those Myrtle Beach lights just as plain as my own hand. The woman walking toward us was also gray. I don't mean just her skin tone, or her hair, or her clothes. I mean she had the features of a young woman but she was monochromatic from head to toe: one largely undifferentiated shade of gray, her features distinguished only by the lines of her face and the deep black wells of her pupils.

I knew instantly I had seen her before: she ran in front of my car the other night when Roderick and I were driving around chasing Crew Cut. So much for my plan of just pretending I never saw a ghost.

Herman—the Big Cheese—barked at his crew. "Dig, goddamn it. *Dig.*" The hoodoo worked, and they went at it double-time, glancing up at the figure as it strode towards them slowly, but digging nonetheless. Something had been odd in his voice, though: the words were accented this time. Something thick and guttural was there that wasn't before.

Herman began walking toward her, slowly at first, then stumbling into a trot. He looked like he wanted to run, but his aging body wouldn't let him. More possibilities about what was going on with him—possession, shape-shifting, body-jumping—all sprang to mind but I pushed them aside. Herman was about to have a moment with this ghost, and I wanted to see it.

The ghost was maybe 180 yards away now, walking slowly but certainly. In a blink between seconds, it moved closer by a third of that. Another blink and it jumped forward just as far. Now Herman really did try to run but stumbled and almost fell.

"*MISTRESS!*" His voice rang out across the dunes, subtlety be damned, and he threw his hands out towards her as he screamed. His voice didn't sound at all like the old redneck he'd been at that metal detector sales pitch. He sounded younger, and he sounded… European? "My mistress," he shouted. "Please come back to us! Mistress, we will make you whole again!" He stepped wrong, on that leg he was favoring, and finally went down on his knees, his face in the sand, his arms out in front of him. Whether he meant it or it was an accident, he landed posed for supplication and he didn't stop shouting for her favor even as he buried his face in the surf.

The ghost—goddamn nothing ever being fucking *easy*—blinked forward again and this time went right past him. I looked around for her: she stood by the edge of the hole where the historical society was digging. The hoodoo Herman used on them was still working—they were digging hell for leather down there—but they were staring at this apparition in front of them and gaping in terror at the same time. Sand was flying around, shovels were banging into each other, but none of them could turn away. None of them could stop what their bodies were doing and none of them could stop staring at what their minds refused to comprehend.

The ghost woman opened her mouth in a big, toothy grin, complete with vampire fangs. I shuddered involuntarily, because her jaws opened like those of a great snake and kept opening. Her whole face folded backwards with horrifying slowness, like a convertible car opening its roof to expose a Sarlacc pit inside, and in a moment she was just a giant ring of ghostly teeth sucking air, her face dangling backwards from the stump of her own neck.

The people in the hole started screaming—all but Crew Cut, whose jaw was open but who did not shout—as the ghost lifted her arms out to the sides. She looked like a diver about to jump from *way* up there, one of those tall diving stands they use in the Olympics. For a moment all was still except the screams of the humans and the crash of the waves. The water itself ran back, perhaps building for a real chest-slapper of a wave, perhaps running away from this horrible tooth-woman-monster-ghost standing half-visible in the bright artificial lights. Smiles couldn't even see what was happening but the screams agitated him. He started to growl, deep down, until I pointed at him with one finger: universal owner-speak for *no*.

Herman got to his feet, his gray hair matted, his beer gut soaked, his dime store ritual cloak drenched and clinging, the bedazzled collar crumpled. He staggered back toward the hole, screaming again, and I could just make out the words over the surf and the humans shrieking: *We can make it right, mistress, we just need another chance.*

The ghost looked for a moment like it might dissipate, going briefly fuzzy, an image out of focus, but instead it turned to something like smoke—no, like a swarm of bees—and shot forward at the woman seated next to Herman at the sales pitch: the frumpy woman with the white hair and the very sincere sweater vest. The woman's hands dropped the shovel she was waving around. The swarm of smoke-bees surrounded her and *invaded* her. The scream in her throat turned to gravel and then to choking gasps, then stopped altogether. Her hands scrabbled at her own neck. Her eyes rolled back. The hoodoo finally broke and the others started dropping their shovels and diving in different directions—none to *help* her, all to get away—as the woman clawed at her own flesh.

I saw blood fly out from between her fingers.

Glistening red fired out of her neck and ran down her sweater-vest. She stopped screaming and stood stock still, mouth open, then slowly began to cave in on herself.

Like an old stop-motion effect, the woman shriveled and shrank, light spilling from within herself as she turned to something like thin paper around a skeletal frame, then crumbled entirely to dust, her cape and that sweater vest falling down and fluttering away on the whipping wind of the Atlantic Ocean.

There was a sound like a thunderclap and a gust of wind going the wrong direction threw sand everywhere. I raised my hand to shield my face, turned the other way. Smiles squeezed his eyes shut and showed his teeth but didn't *quite* growl.

A half mile or so back, from about where I stood with Roderick and Old Shoe to slap Ross around a little before he disappeared, I saw a flash of cobalt blue light. It occurred to me to wonder why Old Shoe hadn't caught up by now.

Shit.

Digging into the sand, I started to run back that way at top speed. With everything they just saw, there was no way Herman or Crew Cut or the rest of these shoveling mortals would notice one more idiot running away into the night. I pounded across the sand, stumbling and staggering on the loose dunes, the wind buffeting me every time I reached a peak and screaming past me overhead as I dipped into the valleys. I was as loud and as fast as I could be. Subtlety was the last thing on my mind. *Fuck this shit*, I thought to myself. *Fuck everything about this shit.*

Around me, every bird of every type rose into the air and took to the sky en masse, like they were giving up on the island if it could hold monsters like that ghost thing back there. They shrieked and circled, nearly banging into each other as they flew, and with a few whirling turns they all eventually pointed themselves in the same direction: towards the mainland. They took off together on the thunderous applause of what must have been a thousand wings.

"So you were doing a surveillance ritual?" Roderick looked more than interested. He looked *intrigued*.

"We were," Ramon said, "But without Xi we can't finish."

Sheila nodded. "We have to inscribe two opposed designs onto the area. Xi was carrying a GPS transmitter for them. He was going to fly one pattern, then turn around and fly the other. Our position would provide the third point of reference to obtain a magical triangula…" She trailed off. "Well, anyway, we need him to finish it. Unless you can fly."

Marty perked up a little and seemed to snap out of his shock at the mention of maps. "Can you…" His voice faltered for a second. "Can you show me the route he was going to fly?"

Marty, Sheila and Ramon conferred for a moment. "If we had someone who could move very fast or jump great distances with a lot of…" Marty hesitated again. "With a lot of agility? If we had one of those people, and they carried Xi's GPS transmitter in their hands, I could describe the route they needed to run." He blinked, eyes wide, then narrow again, as his mind leapt hither and yon. "You know, on the rooftops?"

Beth held out her hand to Sheila. "I can map it." She said it with her usual dreamy quality, as though trying to join a conversation while just waking up. "Marty can tell me where it needs to go."

"But…" Marty licked his dry lips. "You would need to be able to jump the gaps between houses and, looking from here, I would guess that averages to be approximately fourteen feet, four inches."

"We're…" Jennifer blinked at him. "We're standing at least half a mile from the nearest house on the island itself. We're at one of the widest points of the Intercoastal Waterway."

Marty nodded. "I could be more precise if we were closer. I'm sorry." He shrugged. "The average person can jump a gap of at most ten feet and only with a running start of at least forty feet across level ground but none of the roofs are level and—"

Roderick's abrupt laughter at Marty's naiveté made Marty stop. "You…" Roderick paused. "I apologize. I should not laugh. You have not spent much time fighting other vampires, or running away from the scenes of your meals?"

Marty shook his head.

Roderick nodded. "Another vampire unaware of his capabilities! Martin, a fourteen foot gap is trivial for a vampire." He clucked his tongue. "I have been too lax in your education. We will work on this when we return to Asheville."

Beth looked at Marty again. "Give me the route," she repeated.

He and Sheila produced a tablet computer with the route Xi was meant to take. Beth stared at it a moment and nodded. "Thank you," she said. "Wait here." She stepped away, just a few yards, and in perfect silence on bare feet walked up to the edge of the parking lot. One of the countless little sea birds that populate the coast—driven away when the fight broke out—had returned and started pecking at the asphalt again in search of food that wasn't there. With the speed of a vampire, her hand shot out and her fingers gripped it around the body. It produced a chattering cry of protest but Beth was gentle with it. She lifted it up to hold it in front of her face, looking into its mad, black eyes.

Beth studied it for a second, held that way, then plunged her fangs into its tiny body and in an instant drained it dry. The humans gasped, even Jennifer, who saw a vampire feed the very first time she met one. Roderick opened his thin lips for a moment and his eyes flashed with something like shock. We can feed from animals, and there are always rumors of vampires who do, but I've never actually met a vampire who truly only ever ate from animals. It isn't like with human vegetarians who are perfectly capable of getting what they need without eating animal proteins. A vampire can in theory subsist on animal blood alone but that blood tastes… incomplete. There's something missing when we drink an animal's blood: some quality to it we can't get otherwise. I don't know what that is, and I don't care. A vampire feeding from an animal is, to another vampire, sort of like seeing someone pick their nose. We've all done it but that doesn't mean it isn't gross. Animals don't deserve the cruelty of being drained, anyway. It's never hard to find a human who has it coming.

Beth dropped the corpse of the bird and leaned her head back with her eyes closed and her hands outstretched, her arms up at an angle. Roderick felt that sixth-sense ripple in the air of another vampire using their Last Gasp. In the distance, even over the constant wind on the water, they could all hear a massive number of birds taking flight.

Appearing as a dark mass in the sky, dozens upon dozens of birds of all sorts rose from between houses, from the water, from the side of the island facing the Inter Coastal Waterway, from the nature preserve, and from anywhere else they might roosted at night. Gathering together overhead, they descended all at once, some landing on Beth, up and down her arms, across her shoulders like a shawl, and arrayed around her on the ground.

Perfectly silent, without a sound other than the thin, slicing whispers of their bodies in the air, they stood and stared at her with the alien eyes of the ancient dinosaurs whence they were descended. Beth did not look back at them: her eyes were closed and she turned her face to rub her own cheek against the body of the bird closest to it on her right shoulder. She looked like she was greeting a favorite pet after a long vacation.

No one spoke as Beth and all those birds—large and small, light and dark—communed in silence for a long span of seconds. Then two of the same type, white with grey wings and black tails and rings around their beaks, flew up and took the GPS tracker between them, right out of her open hand, and flew away. The remaining avian mass shot back into the sky and formed a living debris field around the two doing the carrying.

At a couple of hundred feet—invisible to the humans, but visible to the vampires—they began a slow, looping flight.

Beth lowered her face, opened her eyes and turned to Jennifer. "My birds will run the rest of Xi's assigned route. If the elders fire on them, there will be many birds between the ground and the ones carrying the tracker. They will return to me when finished."

Everyone stared at her. Jennifer opened her mouth but had no idea what to say. Finally, she got out something so normal in its good manners it made Roderick laugh aloud. "Thank you," Jennifer said to Beth. "That's very helpful."

"Well," Roderick said after he recovered. "You have just been attacked and survived. We should prepare to leave as soon as possible lest the elders send a second wave."

"My birds will run interference while we leave," Beth said. To her it seemed completely obvious.

Jennifer shook her head. "They saw us take out their colleagues without a single injury," she said. "They're not going to fight us."

"Without *serious* injury," Roderick corrected. "Why would that stop them?"

Jennifer smiled a little. "Because each individual vampire values his own survival above anything else," she said. "Your cousin told me that at UberBargains when we met."

Roderick opened his mouth to speak, held it that way a long moment, and then produced words as though from far away. "I suppose that is why we became vampires in the first place. We want to live forever, and to hell—perhaps literally—with anyone else who has to die in the course of that pursuit."

I skidded down the last dune to the place I left Old Shoe standing. The dark, sticky pit where Ross teleported away was still there, but fading: turning gray, and sand was sticking to it. Soon enough even this unstable patch of earth would wipe from its mind the memory of a thing like Ross.

A few feet away, right where Old Shoe was standing when I last saw him, there was a second unholy stain.

In the distant sky, I saw all those birds start to return.

This time I didn't silence Smiles when he started barking. A barking dog was probably the most ordinary thing going on for two miles in any direction.

CHAPTER 10

Today we are all demons.
--Combichrist, "Today We Are All Demons"

I didn't know what was up with the birds, but they went to—and came back from—the same direction Roderick went to check up on his boyfriend—ex-boyfriend, "date," whatever. I figured that was a safe bet. I ran back across the water, Smiles on my back, and up onto land and right down the middle of the street.

When I rounded the corner, Sheila was in the driver's seat of their wrecked mini-van and the rest of the coven were trying to push it from behind. I glanced at the back seat of the van, where Beth and Marty were just settling back in rather than, you know, using their vampiric super-strength to help. I wondered why in the hell I let them come here. Did either of them even know how to defend themselves? I assumed every vampire fought as often as I did. I assumed we've all had to kill hundreds of times by the time we've been dead ten years. The look on Marty's face sure as hell told me how wrong I was.

Ramon filled me in on what had happened. I tried to help move the van, but it was dead. Two tires were blown, one of the vampire explosions had done something bad to the front end, the headlights didn't work—hell, the hatch was ripped off and one of the doors wouldn't shut. We were all in for a long walk back to the hotel. Out there, they didn't even have Uber.

The others gathered together their stuff. As they did, Roderick looked expectant. I wasn't ready to tell him Old Shoe seemed to be gone just yet. I wasn't ready to interpret what that text was supposed to mean.

I couldn't believe how selfish I was in bringing these kids here to help me settle my own score. I was the boss. I was supposed to protect them, not ask them to fight in my place. *If you were worth your fangs, you'd go door to door from one end of the island to the other, right now, and murder everything that moves.*

150

That's what the animal deep inside my gut said, anyway. It always pulls at its chain, always tests the fences we put up around it. That animal is not a rational man. It is not the part of us that used to be human. I used to think it was the part of us that came from outside when we get turned into a vampire: the part that gets poured down our throat, the part that kills off everything we used to be with the significant exception of our appetite. We don't talk about it to one another, but it's easy enough when vampires disagree to see that flash of lightning behind our eyes and know the monster in our belly wants to assert itself.

Sometimes, though, I'm not so sure. I think maybe that animal is a part of all of us, human and vampire alike. If it's the part of us that hungers for life in its purest, reddest form, it's also the thing that used to hide in the back of a cave when lightning struck outside. It's the part that came down out of a tree for the first time because it wanted what another monkey had. It's the thing that shivered with cold fear when a predator walked past and then raged at its tracks once they were cold.

Just as it did in Mary-Lou Reinholdt's house—and at the ÜberBargains on Thanksgiving night, and when I stood over the corpse of my last mortal friend, and so many other times in recent years—I felt that animal yank with vicious strength at its chain in the kennel of my heart. Would it be nice to go door to door and kill? Sure. It's a great way to pass an evening. It wouldn't get Old Shoe back, though, and it wouldn't make the humans feel too great about helping us.

Before we left the parking lot, Roderick walked over to a utility poll and, using his own strength, drove a nail into the wood to post a handbill. He then walked to another, did the same, then another, and did the same. I looked at them: hand-drawn caricatures of Ross suffering various awful fates. In one he was being trod upon by a giant foot; in another he was simply lying in pieces with cartoon X's for eyes.

"Alright," Roderick said, "We may go. And no, you may not yet ask."

We walked as a group, right down the middle of the street. To hell with caring who saw us, or asked what we were doing. It was that kind of night. It didn't seem to matter, anyway: the houses were almost entirely dark and the ones with any lights at all only had one or two. Partly I attributed that to it being the dead of winter and partly I attributed it to the elders' time as their neighbors in this tiny place. Like the villages of yesteryear, the people who lived here over the winter probably grew terrified and in that terror they fell silent.

I was right back to thoughts of that animal inside, the ghost of whatever ancestor was forced to hide from the dark and all the things in it—and resented every moment. It occurred to me the elders were destined to lose eventually, either to the humans or to us, because this was no longer a world that would support open enslavement. People have to be bought these days—bought by corporations, by cheap toys and next year's model and this year's nostalgia. They could be quelled for a year or maybe a decade, as the people on this island seemed to have been quelled for a season, but sooner or later people grow weary of cowering.

Without noticing it, I fell behind the others, first by a few paces and then by more. Eventually I looked down from the stars above, where I stared as I walked. Roderick was beside me and the others were at least fifty yards ahead. Dog and Smiles were behind us, looking around, sniffing the ground. Sometimes the creepiest thing about a hellhound is when they suddenly act like a normal dog again.

"Where is Old Shoe?" Roderick asked it without preamble. That's my cousin: no beating around the bush.

"He…" I sighed and looked at Roderick. "I don't know. I'd like to think Ross kidnapped him. He was gone when I went back for him. There was another one of those sticky scorch marks."

Roderick showed no visible reaction. "Where were you?"

"I was watching the ghost of a vampire eat one of those historical society assholes." I fluttered my lips. "Hand to Jesus, cousin. She showed up, the leader of the pack acted like he was seeing his long-lost mother, she ate an old lady from the inside out, and everybody else ran hell for leather. They were digging for something out there. The leader tried to talk to the ghost, too. 'We'll make you whole again,' he said. He knew who she was, and he knew to be afraid of her. Did you get my text? I don't think that guy's exactly what he seems to be. I think… I don't know, that he's possessed by a vampire, or he's a vampire in disguise, or something."

I filled Roderick in on the whole story, in the right order this time, and when I was done he nodded. "*Joyriding*," he said. "It is an unusual power. It is probably what Herman has—well, whatever vampire now controls Herman. Normally they inhabit the flesh of the victim for a short time, leaving their body behind. There are stories, though: the cautionary bedtime tales of the dead. They say a joyrider leaves her body behind, unprotected, and that if that body is destroyed the rider is stuck in the flesh of their victim. In some versions the vampire's spirit retains its powers. In some versions, it loses them, forced to live out their victim's natural life. If he used, as you call it, the hoodoo, I guess the former must be true. It is reputed the vampire's powers put stresses on the mortal's body. It degrades faster than it otherwise would—much faster. Soon it fails. The joyrider must return to his own body or find another victim into which he can jump before it is too late."

I nodded at him. "So if whatever vampire jumped into Herman subsequently, you know, got waxed—well, his *body* got taken out of the picture somehow— and he got stuck there, but being stuck there started causing an already-frail body to start going downhill…" I trailed off and picked up again. "And if he needed to stay in that body to keep control of this little cult he's started so they can find *something* they need to 'restore' this vampire *ghost*…"

Roderick nodded at me. "A vampire's ghost. We live in a most unusual world, Cousin."

"So, the obvious question is, is that ghost…"

Roderick met my eyes. "The Rhinemaiden? It would seem obvious enough."

"But why's she a ghost, then? When I drained Dmitri, he knew about a vampire they brought back from the dead, just like all those zombies on Z-Day, not a *ghost*."

Roderick smiled just slightly. "When the zombies rose from their graves, were they made whole?"

I thought back to that first night, years ago—so many years, and I could feel every night of them in my bones, but at the same time it felt like last week—and the first zombies I saw stagger around the streets of my quiet little suburban neighborhood. Those not-faces, the caved in pits of flesh, the eyeless sockets, the lips eaten away by time and worse: that was as far as I could imagine from "whole." Their faces were so awful the news had to blur them out when they showed them on television, and grody-as-hell zombies show up on television all the goddamn *time* in fiction. "No," I said. "No, they were rotten and desiccated. They just stood up the way they were and went about doing their thing."

"Which was?" Roderick had the tone of a teacher leading me patiently to an answer he already knew and it grated on me like steel wool.

Then it dawned on me. "They were hungry. They were only hungry, nothing else."

"Exactly, Cousin." Roderick smiled more broadly. "The elder vampires did their magic to bring back the dead, but they did not do the magic to *restore* them. It is that story—*The Monkey's Paw*—all over again. When the mortal dead answered the call, they came back in what was left of their original bodies. So did she: but she was a vampire. When we are killed, there *is no body*, only ash. They got back the spirit, and it is hungry, but there is no body for it to inhabit."

There was a thread there—a vampire who could hop bodies, perhaps stuck in the one he was now using, and a vampire with no body at all—but I pushed it aside. It was one of those symmetries I would just have to think about later.

"And Old Shoe?" Roderick clucked his tongue. "I suspect this was all too much for him. He hesitated, sent you his text of resignation from the field of battle, and the demon captured him as a hostage. We will undoubtedly hear a ransom demand."

"I never should have brought him here," I said.

"Cousin," Roderick said, and his eyes softened, "Do not pretend Old Shoe is some innocent waif in your charge. Do not let his childish face fool you. He is as much a monster as any of us." My cousin shrugged mildly: *que sera, sera*: what will be, will be. "This is not generally the life of one who thinks of others *first*, as I believe you once said to Jennifer, though with other words. Shit, as they say, happens. In the meantime, we must assume whatever he knows is now compromised."

I was quiet for a few moments and then said, "Some of us are more monster than others of us, and some of us are never monsters at all no matter how ugly we get." It sounded silly and oversimplified once I said it, just a bumper sticker philosophy I could say in response. I was feeling something I didn't quite know how to express, though. Now, with some time to reflect, I know what I was feeling then: disappointment. Vampires feel plenty of things—anger, hatred, fear, lust (of a sort)—but we don't often feel disappointment because of what it requires to be felt: preceding *hope*.

I was afraid, by then, that I needed people in my life: mortals, other vampires, persons who weren't just like me, persons who could be trouble and cause feelings and find a crack in my armor plating every now and then. I knew if I relied on others I would wrestle the animal inside more and more over time. It feeds on the inevitable disappointment that comes from dashed hopes and errors in judgment and personal failures and unrequited affection and all the other stumbles coming from giving over a little of our psychological real estate to another. I also feared that struggle—with my feelings and with the animal inside—was the price required not to turn into an elder myself.

I drew a breath at long last. Roderick was still standing there. His face was turned towards the shore of the Inter Coastal Waterway, where he dived in and I ran across, but his eyes were cut to the corners to look at me while I ran through it all in my head. "You're damned right," I said. "To hell with a bunch of pretending any of us is a saint. So, what do you think of this ambush thing?" I nodded at Jennifer and the technopagans, who were still ahead of us but starting to notice how far back my cousin and I were falling.

Roderick smiled a little and turned towards me. "I think the elders got a nasty shock. But I think they also probably sent their weakest forces against the technopagans. There are clearly more of them than we anticipated. Or there *were*. But the elders did not survive this long by being reckless and losing fights. They will move, now. They are under too much pressure from too many corners. The Rhinemaiden is acting without guidance and they are desperate to contain her. We are harrying them. Their havens are under attack. The locals undoubtedly notice too much by now. Eventually not even fear will keep the mortals acquiescent—and the tourist season is just weeks away. The elders must pull the trigger on *something*, as they say."

I nodded at him. "My thoughts exactly. And they're probably hoping this fight was scary enough to get the technopagans to hole up for a hot second, and maybe Old Shoe's…" I hesitated. "…Maybe Old Shoe's abduction would make us stop and question ourselves, giving the elders just a little bit of breathing room."

He nodded at me. "Perhaps."

"So," I said, "Let's just assume from this point forward that Old Shoe is already dead." I shrugged. "Let's just take him out of the equation entirely. If they haven't already killed him, just because, we know they will as soon as they think they've extracted all his useful information."

Roderick nodded, standing a little straighter. "Oh *good*," he said.

I arched one eyebrow.

"I was afraid I might have to convince you to set it aside and move on," he said, ducking his head a little. "I apologize. I should have had more faith in your professionalism."

"*You* think *I'm* getting soft," I said with a grimace. "You've got a fucking boyfriend." Roderick and I were stopped, standing in the middle of the street just yards from where the night started: the road we walked to get back to the motel we were using as home base ran through the golf course abutting the Waterway. Right there, on a narrow strip of green between the asphalt and the Waterway, were the chunks of turf I tore out with my own boots not two hours before. We both turned our eyes up, looking at the stars, letting the humans get farther and farther ahead of us with each second.

"I say again, 'boyfriend' is rather a strong term for the connection Dan and I share. That is beside the point, however, which is that I never left the world. Not like you did, Cousin," Roderick said. His tone was very even. He wasn't being snide or cruel, just honest. He met my gaze with steady eyes and behind them were more sorrows, more psychic scars, than I would have guessed. "You all but died to mundane society. I did not. I wonder sometimes how it is for you, having left the world and come back to it. I sometimes fear your feelings will be… delicate; or that you will be confused." He laughed suddenly. "I mean no offense."

I smiled a little. "None taken. But I'm fine. Trust me."

Roderick held up a fist, as though to punch me straight-on, not with a Wild West roundhouse but like one of those guys in a kung fu movie who punches straight out like a robot arm. "Bump me," he said.

I arched both eyebrows at him. "What?"

"Fist bump me," he said.

I stared blankly at his hand.

Roderick sighed. "Never mind."

"Give me Jennifer's number," I said as I pulled out my phone.

"Cousin," Roderick said, eyes narrowing. "Are you about to give your number to a mere mortal?"

I gave him a look. "Just give me the fucking number," I said.

He did, and I started texting with painful slowness.

"Oh, for the sakes of all the gods," Roderick said, and started texting. "It will kill me dead to stand here and watch you peck out a message."

"Then shut your damn eyes," I growled.

OLD SHOE, I typed, but then I stopped. What *was* he, exactly? GONE. R AND I FELL BEHIND BUT WILL MEET YOU AT BASE.

I sent the text. A thought occurred to me, and I sent another: THIS IS WITHROW.

Seconds passed, and then this: SEE YOU BACK AT HQ. IF THEY HAVE HIM WE NEED TO RELOCATE. A few more seconds passed and I got another: I AM PLEASANTLY SURPRISED YOU KNOW HOW TO TEXT.

I frowned deep, my face creasing like wadded up newspaper. I was about sick to death of people thinking I didn't know how to live in the here and now, no matter how true it sometimes is. I texted back, I'LL BET NONE OF YOU ASSHOLES KNEW I COULD WALK ON WATER, EITHER, BUT I CAN DO THAT, TOO.

Then I harrumphed, put the phone in the inner pocket of my big black trench coat, and turned to Roderick. "Fuck all y'all," I said out of nowhere. His eyebrows and the corners of his mouth lifted a bit in amused surprise. I took two steps back, blurred into motion, and ran straight across one corner of the golf course with more huge chunks of turf flying up behind me, right out into the dark and silent country roads of Sunset Beach in the middle of winter, past the technopagans—moving so slow they were just a tableau as I shot by—past a trailer park as dark and silent as a Mayan ruin, past the Dollar General with a big sign that read SEASONAL HOURS, past the self-storage where a few thousand lives were boxed up for winter. I ran all the way back to the motel without ever slowing down or missing a step.

I could hear Roderick laughing at my back, a few yards behind me, the whole way. By the time we got to the motel and walked onto the second floor balcony, with Dog and Smiles just about falling all over themselves coming up the stairs behind us, I was able to laugh about it, too.

"Getting old is for the birds," I said to Roderick. I eased down onto the cement and dangled my legs over the edge, my arms through the old painted metal bars of the handrail, sitting like a kid. "Everybody starts treating you like a child, like you've never been anything but very young or very old your whole damned life."

Roderick smiled but his eyes were serious when he replied. He was easing slowly into position next to me, cross-legged, elbows on his knees. "That is why we got out when we could," he said. "That is why we chose this, why we get up every night and feed on the living when we must: so we can stay young and strong and vital past what mortality allows. Yes?"

"But the world keeps changing," I said. "There's always something new to learn and even if you learn it, the parts of the world that know how old you really are—you, for instance, and Jennifer, and all y'all—all act like you never learned anything the whole time. It doesn't seem to matter that I'll look the age I *was*, forever. I've become an old man in your minds."

Roderick nodded once, eyes on Dog. He stroked Dog's fur and the St. Bernard settled onto his haunches on Roderick's other side. "Only because you work so hard to cultivate that impression, Cousin." He smiled at me. "But, I know what you mean. It is frustrating to escape death only to discover one must work doubly hard to keep pace with *life*."

I wondered again about Roderick's turning. No one knew who his maker was. He wouldn't talk about it when we first met as vampires, years ago, when I found out the baby cousin saw in a single Christmas picture in 1950 was now a vampire. I burned that photo when I got it in the mail because I didn't know how his daddy found me and I knew Agatha, my maker, would kill any relation who did. She killed my whole family after I was turned—my parents, my siblings. I barely remember them now. I didn't want to doom an unmet, hardly even known uncle and cousin, too.

I thought about asking him, right then, in that moment, on that balcony, if that was what he hoped for when he got the Big Flush: was *he* trying to escape death? Did he actually find it difficult to keep pace with life? He looked young, he was good looking, he was well off, and Roderick was a hippie after the age of flower power. His father died right before he was made a vampire, leaving him everything. Roderick was crazy as a batch of catfish cookies, sure, but there were plenty of people who would have traded places with him back then. The part of me that was once 19 and hated myself from head to toe sure would've. It seemed hard to imagine someone in his position—then or now—having trouble feeling like he was staying current. Roderick was as current as anyone I'd ever met.

It occurred to me, as I looked at my cousin, and as *he* looked out at the night, at the landscape of the coast, at this wind-blasted little town, *that* must be why he became a vampire. Roderick didn't want to escape his life: he wanted to extend it. Most vampires, I think, become this to get away from who we were. Roderick wanted to stay who he was—who he still is: the fearless explorer, forever young and forever capable. All vampires are addicted to life in a really obvious, blood-red, thirst-quenching way. Roderick is addicted to *living*. Whereas most of us become scared of it over time, Roderick seemed to love living more than ever.

Roderick said, without looking at me, and as though he could hear what I thought, "Cousin, there are those who look at me and the future for which I preserved myself and think, *there goes the luckiest bastard on land*. They are wrong, however. It is not happy coincidence I am suited to the now. I have worked to make myself suited to it, and I have worked to make it suited to me. Do not go passively into the unknown of tomorrow. Anticipate what you can, and treat the unanticipated like a garden plot uncovered in spring: weed out what offends and cultivate what nourishes."

I stared at him for a few seconds before I drew a breath. "Well," I said to change the subject, "Let's learn a lesson from that. Let's not let the elders trick us into thinking they don't know how to live in the now or anticipate things." I nodded at the parking lot, at the water beyond, at the island comprising most of Sunset Beach well beyond it. "They knew enough to look *up*, apparently, because they took a pot shot at that model airplane Jennifer's pretending is Xi."

I realized we hadn't thought to look for him—for *it*—when we came back. I stood, walked up and down the balcony in each direction, and looked into the stairwell at the other end from where we'd come up. There he was, sitting in a corner of the stairwell, hidden in the shadows. A tiny red light blinked every eight seconds. I wasn't sure a human would even see it.

"Well I'll be damned," I said to Roderick as I carried him back.

Roderick, nodded. "Probably," he said.

When Jennifer and her crew walked up ten minutes later, Roderick was sitting cross-legged on the balcony of the motel with Xi's drone body resting in his lap, caressing the molded plastic frame and telling him what a good boy he was.

"Don't pet Xi," Jennifer said as she walked up. Her voice was hard but her eyes were amused or something very close to it. "He's not a pet. He's a person."

"He is wounded," Roderick said. "I thought about trying to fix his rotors but, let us have no polite fictions: I am neither healer nor engineer." Roderick stood in one smooth motion, coming to his feet and lifting Xi's frame in his hands to offer him to Dan.

"So what's next?" Jennifer looked back and forth between Roderick and me. "I mean, other than reporting our van stolen and getting a rental." She smirked a little.

Roderick looked towards me for a moment. "They have now seen more of our capabilities. We need to bring other forces to bear, ones they cannot expect or counteract. I believe the time has come for you to call in *the others*."

Jennifer arched one eyebrow, just as Spock as all hell.

I sighed a little. "Not yet," I said to Roderick, without any explanation for Jennifer. "Anyway, what's next for me is that I'm going to talk to Deputy Crew Cut. Again."

Now Roderick arched an eyebrow. "You wish to do so alone." He didn't ask it.

"I do," I said. I looked to Jennifer. "Like you said, y'all have to do some regrouping. The last time I went to talk to this guy, I didn't have anything other than bluster in my pocket. Now I think I might know some real shit. I'm hoping I can get him talking."

Jennifer let out a long breath through her nose: not quite a sigh, not quite an endorsement. "If this guy is a human, maybe a human should talk to him. You said he's a magic user, right? Maybe we could approach him as peers."

I shook my head. "I considered that earlier, but now I think this is something I need to do. I feel it in my gut. I was the one who saw what he saw. I was the one who felt what he felt. We've got some trauma in common, and that can be powerful. Let me try one more time."

I walked down the steps and pulled out my phone, standing beside my car. I needed to make a call as I drove.

I didn't want to say so, but Roderick was right: I needed the others.

Beth and Marty walked with the technopagans, and in the silence before I unlocked my Firebird's driver door we all looked up at the sound of rushing air. Hundreds of birds began landing all around us, alighting on the asphalt, all staring in silence at Beth.

"Ding," she said. Her voice was high and light. "Soup's done."

Two perched together a moment in her outstretched hands, the GPS transmitter held in their beaks, and dropped it. She turned and offered it to Jennifer like this happened every day.

Hell, I thought, *maybe it does.*

I could feel something snap in the air, like a rubber band twanging, and the birds all looked around in confusion. Half of them didn't even get along with each other in the wild but here they were all bunched up in one place that didn't look much like home. With a cacophony of wings and squawks, they burst back into the air as individuals again, winging it this way and that before they got their bearings and headed off more or less for the waterway.

Sheila took the transmitter from Jennifer and started doing stuff with that tablet of hers. After maybe 30 seconds she looked back and forth at a couple of different apps, flipping between them, then sighed. "They're gone," she said.

"Gone?" I can't even count how many of us said it at once.

Sheila nodded. "The data is as clear as can be. They're performing a mass exodus of the island."

"To where?" This time it was Jennifer, Roderick, and me, speaking in unison.

"I don't know," Sheila said. "We were mapping the *island* for supernatural factors. Now there aren't any." She hunched over the tablet again. "Actually… let me monitor this for a bit. It may just need some fine tuning."

I waved it off. Magic and technology were frustrating enough individually. Combining them seemed to make them get worse, not better. "I'll be back," I said. "Then we relocate. Y'all do what you do."

They stood in the parking lot, and on the balcony, and watched me go.

Chapter 11

Keep looking, keep looking for somewhere to be.
--Jethro Tull, "Witch's Promise"

"*I am an invisible man*," I said, which is the first line of the novel you might guess it would be, and also what Lorraine insisted I should say were I ever to need to call on her explicitly for help. I've dropped in now and again on the rituals of the Book People, which is how those witches refer to themselves, off and on for years now. For lack of a better description, I'll just say they use books to create magic, and I didn't used to think it was real magic but I know better now. I'm not quite sure what they think of me, and neither do they seem to be. It's easier when a mortal is afraid of me. It keeps things simple. The Book People are decidedly *not* afraid of me, but they don't quite seem comfortable, either, and that makes me uncomfortable, too, and I suspect that's how *they* prefer it. I think at this point I can say with confidence a witch prefers uncertainty in many circumstances because that gap between perception and knowledge is exactly where the magic lies.

Lorraine let out a long breath. "Wow," she said. "You actually used it."

"It's a bad time, isn't it?" I drew a breath. "You're in the middle of something." I tried not to sound too hopeful. I didn't like having to play this card.

"No," Lorraine said, hurriedly. "What do you need from us?"

"It's complicated. It involves a road trip, and a lot of danger, and I'm not yet totally sure what I need." I had no idea how I was going to get Jennifer's buy-in on this. I knew the technopagans and the Book People knew each other somehow, and the latter didn't think tremendously highly of the former, or saw them as immature, or something. There seemed to be a rivalry there, but the nature of it was opaque to me.

"Where?"

"An hour north of Myrtle Beach," I said. "Little town on the coast."

There was silence on the other end, Lorraine holding her breath as she calculated what this would cost in the currency of witches. The Book People didn't take money for their favors. Their legal tender was reciprocal favors or, sometimes, information: ungodly expensive to those of us who live behind secrets. The technopagans accepted cash on the barrel but the Book People insisted on barter. They seemed to think less of anyone who put a monetary price on their work, too. As an artist I can respect both sides of that argument, but I'd a lot rather pay someone in money than secrets.

"Two questions," Lorraine said.

"Go for it."

There was a smile in her tone. "I don't mean I have two questions for you about this… situation. I mean our price is two questions, put to you, which you must honestly answer without obfuscation, deception or misdirection, and at sufficient length to satisfy our curiosity."

An answer caught in my throat. Two questions, put together by people for whom words were magic? Hanging out with the Book People always raised the hair on the back of my neck because I could tell they were dangerous, as dangerous as I am and maybe more so. I could put my fist through a brick wall, sure, but the Book People could *talk* it apart with a few well-chosen lines from a novel they read thirty years ago. The book people don't just read between the lines. They look into the space between words, the hesitation between syllables, the whitespace at the end of a verse, like an astronomer searching the dark between distant stars, and they see *power* there. Answering a question they had time to work on? Answering *two*? It was a hell of a price.

"Two from the whole group or two from each individual member?"

Another smile in her voice as Lorraine replied. "Two from the group, but…" She chuckled. "You should be glad you clarified it. Give me an address."

"Not so fast," I said. "I can't do two questions. That's too much. One question, sure."

"For that, we help but we stay here." Lorraine was all business. "Those are the terms. Take it or leave it, and no hard feelings either way."

I made a growling noise as I turned a corner and pulled into the parking lot of Crew Cut's motel. "Okay," I said. "Remote support it is."

"What do you need?"

"I need to convince someone to get on my side in a fight, and to trust me with information. And he's another magic user." I gave her the run down on the guy's motel room.

"Incredibly crude," Lorraine said when I finished describing the cages of living animals—if you could call that "living"—and the map covered in algae. I went on at length about the general stench of the place. I could hear the disgust, the disapproval of one craftsperson assessing another's work and finding it lacking. "Undoubtedly effective, but he's using the energy of other creatures. He ought to be able to raise the energy himself."

"Well, he's scared," I said. "He's got plenty of good reason for it, too. He's all alone out here and he's up against things far more powerful than he is."

Lorraine let out a long breath through her nose. "OK. How much time do we have?"

I looked up at the front of the motel as I parked. "About a minute?"

"Jesus, you don't exactly plan ahead, do you?"

"Sorry," I said, "Next time I'll make an appointment. Listen, I'm in a *situation* here."

Lorraine sighed. "I'll make some calls. Give us… five minutes. When the time comes, when you want him to say yes, use the phrase…" I could hear her breathing as she did something. "*A man cannot handle pitch and escape defilement.*"

I blinked, pulled the phone away from my head, glared at it, put it back to my ear. "You have got to be fucking kidding me. I'm supposed to just drop that in? Where'd you get that? Some Bible passage?"

"Mark Twain," Lorraine said. "But he was quoting when *he* said it."

"And, what, now it's magic?"

"It *will be*." She sounded a little exasperated with me. (I suppose she had every right to be, but in the long view, this was probably the least reason I've ever given them to regret knowing me.) Then, like any mechanic talking shop to a client who doesn't really understand, she went on. "Part of the power in it, of course, is that *he* was such a powerful persuasive speaker, and when he wrote that he was being a little ironic considering his own speech patterns. Of course pitch is an historic product of North Carolina, where we are, so there's a connection to the environment there and *anyway*, give us five minutes and you should be good to go. I will call on you at another time when we have formulated our question."

"It's going to be—for *reasons*—a little hard to spin that particular phrase to my advantage in this upcoming conversation."

"Not my problem," she said. "You're a smart guy. I'm sure you'll figure it out." It struck me suddenly that she sounded just like a mother telling her child they have to clean up their own mess even if she *did* bring them the dustpan and broom.

I chewed my lower lip for a second. Maybe I should have agreed to the second question, but it was too late now. Lorraine, when a deal is done, is done dealing. "Alright," I said. Then: "And thank you." And then: "I really mean that."

Lorraine was smiling again, but I didn't know if it was with me, or at me, or at my expense. "You'd better," she said.

I killed five minutes—and then another five—looking at the Internet on my phone. The modern world is remarkable and I have no fucking clue how anyone gets anything done.

Eventually I got out of my Firebird, Smiles beside me, and we clack-clack-clack-clacked our way up the cement stairs of the ratty old motel. I could smell the livestock from here. It had only been a couple of nights, but Crew Cut hadn't kept the place clean. He was probably too busy digging at the behest of his fake-ass not-vampire cult leader.

I was still struggling with exactly what I was going to say when I got to his door. I stood there, raised my knuckles to rap on it, lowered them again, and turned to pet Smiles for a moment. He didn't pant or wag his tail, but sometimes the most comforting thing in the world—in addition to being the most distressing—is to pretend he's just a normal dog all the same.

As the seconds passed, I realized something changed: there had been no light coming from the other side of the peephole in Crew Cut's door. Now there was.

He heard me coming, and had been watching out the peephole while I stood there debating what to do. *Awkward.*

The door opened a quarter of an inch—the chain was latched, bless his heart—and he spoke to me from the other side of the gap. I considered it a very safe bet he was armed, but probably not with a gun. He was likely holding a sharpened stake made out of a mop handle or some shit. "Why are you here?"

I looked at that gap in the door, and at the cages beyond it, lined up all around the room. I looked at the sliver I could see of the big map he kept in the tank. I drew a breath to speak, let it out in a long flutter of my lips with a sound like a great fart, and drew another. "Because I need your help," I said. "And because you need the help of *somebody*, and I don't see any other candidates around. So we might as well work together on this, whatever it is." He started to say something but I kept talking right over him. "You don't have to trust me. You don't have to *like* me. Some days I'm not even sure the people who like me actually like me. You don't have to think I'm a nice vampire, and you don't have to pretend you don't plan on knocking me off eventually, too. That's all for another night, Deputy. Right now you have a ghost problem, and I have a vampire problem, and it happens they apparently overlap. So let's finally get it all out there in the open and help each other for five minutes, like the civilized people we both probably used to be."

There was a long silence from the other side of the door. I knew what he was doing: weighing the pros and cons, the risks and rewards. He was wondering how good an idea it would be—or how bad—to make nice with an enemy just long enough to defeat something worse. He was wondering if he could—aw *fuck* the Book People and their word games—handle pitch and escape defilement.

"How do you know about the ghost?"

I blinked. "I was hiding behind a dune. Tonight. When you were digging."

"Tell me what's wrong with… the guy in charge."

"I think you just tried not to say *my cult leader*, Deputy." I snickered a little. It was a dangerous gambit, going for a tease, but you never know what makes some people feel comfortable with you.

"Oh, rich, especially coming from a fucking vampire."

"We're not *all* blood cultists in the sway of a fake demon."

"Fake?" That seemed to get his attention.

"Long story," I said. "My cousin thinks it's actually a case of Tulpas Gone Wild."

"I thought the same thing for a while," Crew Cut said after a moment. I could hear him scratching his own neck. (We get an ear—and an eye, and a nose, and a taste—for necks.) "But I actually think maybe they summoned the real deal."

"I wouldn't know," I said. "I just want to destroy it. And them. And then go back to my quiet little house and watch reruns and pay the neighborhood kids to mow my lawn and take my dog for long walks and maybe play a hand of solitaire once in a while. *Forever.*" I licked my lips. "Deputy, this is supposed to be *my* state. I, myself, killed off the last generation of vampires in charge and I did it for that exact reason: so I could be left alone. I don't want to take over the world. I'm not even especially interested in *saving* it. But these vampires and their pet evil spirit are bad news for everybody and especially for my remaining *me time.* I'm saying all this in hopes it will convince you I don't want to make you a slave again. I don't want to stop your one-man crusade, either. Actually, I admire you for breaking free. I'm assuming that's what happened anyway: that you were enthralled by a vampire in Charlotte—and believe me, there are reasons why I have about a *million* questions around that but *not right now*—and eventually you got free and vowed revenge. I like that. I'm big on righteous revenge-seeking. But right now you're worried that," and I paused to draw a breath, "*A man cannot handle pitch and escape defilement.*"

I was going to finish the thought—something about how he could trust me, or it was worth the risk, I don't know, whatever came out when I get to babbling like that—but I stopped. When I said those words—the words Lorraine gave me—I felt power unwind all around me. I felt like I threw open the curtains on a window and fresh air blew in. I felt like I cranked the last turn of a jack in the box but when the lid swung open a thousand white doves flew out.

I felt *magic* happen.

The feeling of the universe opening a birthday present shot through me, out of me, and across the threshold of Crew Cut's door, over his room, a wave of something positive in a place where there had only been fear. The animals in cages stirred, and I heard sounds from them: mewling, sick sounds, sounds of creatures on the brink who longed to be pushed over the edge, to let go, to be free of suffering, but suddenly wanted to live again.

Deputy Crew Cut drew a sharp breath, like something panged him, as though someone pressed a knife to his back or kissed him by surprise.

I didn't hear her or see her, but I could *feel* Lorraine saying, somewhere in my head, *Now, you only have a few moments.*

"But I am here to tell you, Deputy," I said all of a sudden, "That if you want revenge for the sake of revenge, *that* is what will taint you forever. If what you want is redemption, you need to seek *justice* and you need others around to help remind you of the distinction between the two. I'm not exactly perfect, or even marginally good, and I don't pretend I'm redeeming myself, but I am trying to be better: better than I was before, better than I was when I didn't know a single soul who smiled to see me walk through the door. You will be better—*better*—if we work together than if you get trapped in evil of your own making no matter how satisfying that might seem."

I stopped and drew a breath. In the silence beyond the door, I could hear Deputy Crew Cut's heart pounding like it had been buried alive and was trying to get out. For my part, I was feeling total euphoria: like a shaft of sunlight was shining right out my ass. For that one moment, I felt genuinely good again.

"*Fuck*," I said aloud. "I mean, what else can I say? You can try to kill me later, Deputy. I've got all the time in the world. Right now, we can do something good for everyone and we can do it together." I paused, feeling high as a Georgia pine. "Shit, this is a *gas*."

Crew Cut unlatched the chain and opened the door to look at me with narrowed eyes. "What the hell is going on with you?"

I held out my hand as though to shake. "I don't have any fucking clue," I said. "Now shake my hand and let's be friends for a little while. Please." I could have tried to put some hoodoo behind it, of course, but in that moment I knew I shouldn't. Maybe it would have worked really well in the wake of the Book People's magic, maybe not, but that… goodness? No, maybe not goodness so much as *camaraderie*: that sudden rush of camaraderie with the whole human race just wouldn't let me. I wanted Crew Cut to like me. I wanted *everyone* to like me. *That* was certainly a novel feeling.

Crew Cut looked deep into these old eyes of mine. I don't know if he saw anything in particular there other than the bafflement I was feeling, but he reached out and took my hand and pumped it up and down. "Okay," he said. "For now." He hesitated again, then stepped to the side and held the door wider. "Come on in and let's talk. I'm tired of being the only one in this."

Something nagged at the back of my mind about that, but I was feeling way too good to care.

We sat down in Crew Cut's jumble of a room. He sat on the end of the bed, which was covered in linens twisted and braided like he spent all night doing twirls. I sat on the one chair tucked in the corner, moved aside and covered in papers and maps and pop magic books about demons and angels and shit. Probably not a word of it was worth a damn. Roderick was probably right: if Ross was a product of the beliefs about him, he was probably more accurately described and constrained by Dungeons & Dragons than by a book some crystal-licker tossed off about their sleep paralysis bullshit.

I set the books on the floor in a pile—which immediately fell over—and eased into the chair. "So here's what I know: they tried to bring a dead vampire back to life, and when they did, it worked. But they also got all the zombies from Z-Day, like, years ago, and the vampire came back uncontrollable in some way. And now it sounds like what they got back was actually her ghost, because she didn't have a body to inhabit anymore."

Crew Cut nodded at me. "That's right. But it's more complicated than that. She's not just uncontrollable. They brought her back and she was more of a monster than they could imagine. She still feeds, but..." He shrugged, searching for words.

"Like I saw on the beach," I said. "She consumes a person from inside. She does to them basically what happens to us when we get waxed."

"They think she needs to do it—to consume people?—to become permanent, like maybe if she does it enough times she'll have a full-time body again, but I..." Crew Cut looked at the carpet for a minute. "In my old life, I saw people sometimes who were cruel just for fun. I saw people who let a momentary impulse drive them to make a spectacle of pain." His eyes flicked outside, towards the world beyond, for a moment. "I saw how she made a show out of killing Gwen. I think The Mistress does it for pleasure," he said. "And she *loves* doing it to vampires. They—and I—think that's because she gets more, I dunno, *juice* from a vampire, you know?" He gestured with his hands as he spoke and I nodded. "And here's the thing: the older, the better."

"Okay," I said, "Let's come back to this older-the-better thing. So she can't manifest full-time, I take it?"

He nodded. "That's what they thought in Charlotte. They didn't know why, but she can't stick around for long when she manifests. It's like it wears her out. But, vacuum out a human, or a vampire, and it *seems like* next time she appears she can stick around longer."

I thought of that flash of gray profile I saw dash in front of my car the night this all started, and how it was gone right away. I wondered if she had just come from feeding on a weak human or if she was running low on gas. "So, obviously they want to stop her from feeding on *them*," I said. "I mean, they wanted her back, but they ain't volunteering to be the Tinker Toys she uses to put herself back together."

"Originally they thought they had a way to give her back *her* body. Now they don't want her back anymore," Crew Cut said. "Ross promised them they would get her back in a controllable form: that she would be a slave, basically. He promised them no mind, no agency, just a hungry vampire ready to be pointed at a problem and fired like a gun. They got the opposite: an appetite with no body, no ability to be controlled, and it wants to destroy them rather than work for them."

"How did they think they could get her body back?" I shook my head. "That's, I mean…" I wrinkled my brow. "If there's an especially big gotcha to being a vampire, it's that: once we're dust, we're *dust*." There are vampires, of course, who look to that old Bible passage about dust-to-dust, ashes-to-ashes, and they see the judgment of an angry god in what happens to us when we die. Me? I say if God's so eager to be pissed off at somebody he ought to start with the bastard in the mirror.

"So," Crew Cut said, shuffling around a little as he dug into the topic. Lorraine's magic worked: he was spilling everything now. "When she died, it wasn't back during the big revolt. It was years later. She was on the run for decades, moving around, staying out of sight. She was one of the best at that part of surviving the revolution. I think the rest of them considered her kind of a mentor in that regard. But eventually a bunch of you guys, the young ones, found her hiding out here. This was in the 1940's, when Sunset Beach was just a village. It wasn't a vacation destination yet. Hell, nobody was even sure exactly where the state line ran through the island because nobody had a reason to *care*. This was a rock with a couple of huts on it. The war was on, and people had to keep their lights off at night. Nobody much was around. It was the perfect place for her to set up shop and meet with her right hand man."

"Who was that?" I figured it was Herman, the cult leader, the one I thought was a vampire trapped in a human body, but I wanted to see how much Crew Cut knew.

"I don't know," he said. "What I *do* know is it was a Nazi officer in a U-boat. Imagine that: U-boats operating right there on the coast of North Carolina."

I smiled a little. "Oh, it happened. A *lot*. North Carolina saw more U-boat action than any other Atlantic state. That's *why* the lights had to be off all the time. It was hidden from the public until later. But rumors traveled, and eventually they were more or less honest about it," I shrugged. "We used to hear about it even way up in the mountains. But, go on."

"They caught her out here, having a meeting with that U-boat officer," Crew Cut said. "I'm guessing it was a hell of a fight, but they managed to destroy her. The henchman got away, apparently with her ashes. Later he came back with a bunch of them and they buried those ashes on the spot as a memorial to her greatness or something." Crew Cut shrugged. He had no time for considering a vampire to be a great anything. "Ross told them if they found the ash canister he could show them how to bring her body back and use it to bind her. If she makes—well, whatever it is she's doing when she sucks down a person…" Crew Cut shook his head. The metaphysics were too much for him. "Anyway, I *think* they're worried she's doing something that will make it impossible to control her."

I held up a finger to stop him. "You've been out on that beach. The wind is crazy. Ain't nobody gathering up any ashes out there while they run away from a fight." In my mind's eye I saw nothing but a puff of grease gray dust blowing away the moment a vampire got dropped. The parking lot where Jennifer was ambushed was clean of all but the clothes when I got there, and they weren't even exposed to the heavier winds on the beach.

He shrugged. "That's the story, though."

I shook my head. "Then it's bullshit. They've got something else they're looking for. And they don't care about controlling her at this point. They're just scared she'll kill 'em all before they can put her down." I thought for a second. "Put her *back* down, I guess."

"Why do you say that?" Crew Cut knit his brow.

"Hunch," I said. "But it would go a ways towards explaining why my crew's managed to kill so many of them and they've only killed one of us: they're distracted, big-time, about as big-time as it gets, and the quickest explanation for that is they're scared shitless of something a lot worse than a couple of whippersnappers and their magical mortal friends." I looked back at him. "They've all pulled out, by the way. They've gone somewhere else to hide. We thought we were going to force them to move, show themselves, try to relocate their secret weapon, whatever, but it sounds now like it isn't *us* they're trying to get away from. I'd hoped we were going to make them regroup someplace convenient we could just set on fire and watch the show, but maybe instead they're hunkering down and…" I shook my head at myself. "And what? I don't get how going to ground helps them right now. I mean, why leave Herman out there on his own? Unless he's a patsy—you know, bait to keep her busy while they get farther away."

Crew Cut nodded. "I know Herman knows something about all this, but I don't know how much. I figure he's a thrall. Maybe for the *other* elders. Sometimes he has that aura of elitism they can have. It tends to rub off on people."

"'Other' elders?" I raised both eyebrows.

"The ones out here are, as far as I can tell, maybe kind of a splinter faction? I don't know. There are elders in Charlotte who are pissed off these guys are out here. That's what I can tell from what they said around me, anyway."

I drew a breath and sighed. "So you were a thrall of the elders in Charlotte?"

Crew Cut flinched. "Yes," he said, though it took some time.

I nodded. "And you betrayed them."

"I saved myself, and…" He trailed off.

"There's no crime in that, certainly," I said.

Crew Cut looked at me with dark eyes. "Try telling them that."

I shrugged. "Maybe one day I will." I could tell I'd pushed it too far, though, so I switched back to the topic at hand. "Why would Herman be leading the effort to restore The Rhinemaiden—what you called The Mistress—if he works for ones who are pissed off this is all happening?"

Crew Cut shrugged at me. "Nothing they're doing is working. They haven't found whatever they're looking for. They haven't mounted a successful defense or counterattack against you. They haven't managed to control The Mistress. It kind of feels to me like someone is sabotaging things from the inside. He's a prime candidate."

I chuckled. "Like the way the guy at the FBI who was charged with finding Woodward & Bernstein's informant *was* the informant?"

"Exactly," Crew Cut said.

I shook my head. "No, he's way freakier than that," I said. "And I bet he knows where the elders—the *local* elders—went."

Crew Cut shrugged again. "Sad story, bro: I don't know where *he* is. Herman calls meetings but nobody gets to know where he's staying. He wants us to know as little about each other as possible. He operates the 'historical society' like a terror cell."

"Okay," I said, putting my hand out. "Hold up. How did he get everyone on board? You don't show up for a historical society interest meeting and find out it's a secret blood cult and just say you're okay with it."

"He's got this crazy story about there being pirate treasure, and about there being dark forces," Crew Cut said. "And remember what I said about no one being exactly sure where the state line is? North and *South* Carolina are going to draw it once and for all next year. Herman's got everybody wrapped up in this bunk about the state line being finalized and how we need to find this pirate treasure before it's located in South Carolina because then something bad happens. He tries to be pretty vague about it, and he seems to just convince the others to go along with it. Trust me, man, you can be pretty smart and still get coerced by enough dollar signs. Just ask Bernie Madoff."

I humphed. "Still seems far-fetched."

"Regardless, I figure that gig is up now. After what we saw tonight—well, I don't think there's any coming back from seeing someone get eaten from the inside out. They've probably scattered. Something like that speaks even louder than the promise of doubloons."

"I sure do wish we could put our hands on him," I said. "I'd love to ask him where the other elders are."

"'Other' elders?" Crew Cut parroted my words back to me.

I gave him the run-on sentence summary: vampire possesses person, normal body gets taken out, possessing vampire is stuck jumping from one failing frame to another for eternity or as long as they can stand it anyway.

"That's *crazy*," Crew Cut finally said.

I shrugged. "That's elders for you. They'll do anything to survive. Including eating their own, or bringing their own back from the dead, no matter how many times their magic never gets them much of anywhere. It's what we do: we survive."

We made a plan to meet up the next night. I hoped by then the technopagans would have their car situation worked out and, if we were super lucky, know where the hell the local elders *went*.

When I went outside and got in my car, holding the seat forward so Smiles could climb into the back, I realized something: Smiles stared directly at Crew Cut the entire time.

Crew Cut never once looked at my dog.

I thought again about his origins, and how he broke free, and if when Crew Cut thought of my dog he considered Smiles to be another unwilling slave.

I went to bed that morning a little early. I didn't *sleep*, of course, because we don't really get a choice about that. I can't lie down for a nap. I can't fall asleep early or wake up late. When the sun rises, my eyes close and I go away. When the sun sets, I open them and I'm back again.

That morning I decided to settle in early and do some thinking. I had a good hour before sunrise, but I wanted to spend some time alone. Something about Deputy Crew Cut's story was bothering me—it didn't seem to hold together quite right—and something about *him* was bothering me. Sure, I had magic on my side, but he'd been too friendly too quickly when we spoke. I couldn't help feeling like he must surely be sizing me up as his next target. It's what I would do: use him to help me and then dispatch him at the first convenient moment.

In fact, I already knew that was exactly what I was planning to do.

Earlier that night we all packed up and moved, to another run-down motel just a little further up the road. It was technically closed for the off-season but the owner lived in a modest room in the back. Some hoodoo put him of a mind to open early and exclusively for us. Outside on the balcony I could hear murmuring voices. I recognized them as Roderick's, and Dan's, and they were having the quiet sort of talk two people have when they're on their way to more than conversation. I could hear the words but I didn't even process them. I knew what they were saying: Roderick was apologizing for how they grew apart, and Dan was saying he was scared of everything that was happening.

Five minutes and a shared cigarette later, I heard them retire to Roderick's room next door. Sure, the technopagans were useful as hell, and brave, and I was growing to admire them almost as much as they worried me, but Roderick was going a hell of a long way to maintain their friendship.

It honestly never occurred to me—not before overhearing those gentle words of real fondness—that Roderick might take Dan's hand and lead him to bed out of genuine affection, or honest lust, or even the very human need just to be held for a little while.

So I lay in my bathtub, pillows under my head, a hellhound crunching kibble from a bowl nearby, and tried *not* to listen to my cousin get fucked in the room next door. I passed the time until sunrise wondering instead if he was the weirdo, or was I: him for having that sort of relationship, or me for spending decades avoiding one?

Chapter 12

I don't want my fangs too long.
--Ghost B.C., "If You Have Ghosts"

Two blinks later, it was the next night. I didn't feel the day pass, but I could tell the time had changed.

"I am Roderick," I heard my cousin say from the balcony as I lay in the dark of my motel room's bathtub. I sometimes think vampires are especially suited to picking out voices. When I ponder it, I'm likewise led to wonder where many of our powers came from. I wonder how we got our start. I wonder why we have the weaknesses we have, and why the strengths, and why not some other mix of one or the other.

There are legends, of course, but nobody believes them. We're supposed to live forever but none of us knows anyone who actually has. Oh sure, every now and then you hear a story about someone turning up claiming to be Cleopatra or Claudius or Sun Tzu, but they're always fakes. Somebody else will turn up their driver's license photo from 1972 and we all have a big laugh at their expense. That sort of thing is one of the frequent cautionary tales of the vampire world: don't get too big for your britches, because nothing lasts forever.

Personally, I always assume those con-artist vampires just get bored and decide to throw a Hail Mary to pass the time. Unlife can eventually become as dreary as life. We're just as prone to fading away as anyone else aged beyond their useful years. Some people decide to spice things up while they have the chance. Even getting caught in a scam is more interesting than being forgotten.

"I'm Deputy Rudyard," I heard Crew Cut say outside.

Okay, now that got my melancholy ass out of the bathtub.

I stood, pulled on my trench coat and walked out through the little room to the dark balcony beyond. Smiles had spent the day against the door of the bathroom, standing guard over me while I slept as he always does, and now he fell into silent lockstep with me.

Roderick looked like he'd already showered, styled himself and dressed for combat: the same white pleather pants and white plastic jacket he wore the time he and I went after a bunch of the Transylvanian's brood in a bar in Asheville. Jennifer was by his right shoulder, arms crossed. Dog was sprawled on the bed in Roderick's motel room, snoring to beat the band.

"Cousin Roderick," I called, and the three of them started subtly and turned to look at me. Crew Cut looked just slightly surprised.

"Cousin?"

"Cousin." Roderick and I said it in unison. He smiled; I didn't. I had less than zero desire for Crew Cut to know where we were. I didn't know how he'd found us, but I was guessing either he pulled some cop strings or he used his magic map, or maybe both.

The look on Crew Cut's face told me he felt like he'd won a round. I wasn't sure what game we were playing, but it felt like cat and mouse. I was not okay with that—not at all. Mostly I wasn't okay with it because I'm accustomed to feeling like the cat.

"Deputy Rudyard's been filling us in on the situation," Jennifer said.

I arched both eyebrows. "He has?"

"Yes," Jennifer said, "And I don't like what we're hearing." The corners of Jennifer's mouth tugged down. "It's confusing, to be honest," she said. She pulled out the tablet computer they'd been using the night before. "And I don't like what the surveillance sigil-grid is telling us, either. I have to assume we fucked it up."

I frowned. "Why?"

"Because according to this, there were vampires running around inside various beach houses *all day*." She shrugged. "Well, all morning, at least. Then the grid shut down, like someone or something turned it off. But before then, the *morning* part of that is what doesn't make sense." She pointed at Roderick and me. "I mean, you guys just fall over at sunrise, right?"

Roderick and I glanced at one another, and I looked back at Jennifer. "Yeah," I said. "You must have a bad reading."

Jennifer sighed and shook her head. "Maybe they..." She trailed off. "I don't know, maybe they have some kind of decoy signal? The thing is, when we saw it happening this morning, we set up a small version over this motel."

She gestured around us. "To test it out, you know? We know you guys should show up, so I estimated this would be a good way to validate our method using some known-good data. The thing is, it worked exactly as expected. It showed us four vampires, immobile, in this motel. Period."

"Thralls?" Roderick looked at the humans for a moment. "Perhaps they fed their thralls a great deal of blood for one reason or another and the thralls set off a false positive?"

"No," Jennifer said. "That's another thing we tested for by doing it here: you've both got dogs you feed your own blood, right?"

I shifted my weight to lean against the railing and nodded down at Smiles, sitting by my side with his back turned to the group so he could watch behind me. "Yeah. Not a lot at once, but for many years." I shrugged a little.

Jennifer nodded back. "Your dogs don't show up on the map. So whatever was moving around inside a few beach houses all morning wasn't a bunch of thralls. They were vampires, or the magic wasn't working right."

This wasn't something it sounded like we could settle once and for all right here on the spot. I shrugged. "Either way, can we use your map to find out where they went?"

She shook her head. "No. They must have detected the surveillance magic and jammed it somehow. Maybe they figured out what Xi was doing in their airspace last night."

I ran a hand through my floppy, curly hair, mussed from sleeping, pushing it off my forehead. "Okay," I said. "So how do we find them?"

Jennifer shifted her weight. "If we had the corpse of one, or an article of clothing." She looked at me. "Maybe they went somewhere in such a hurry they didn't bother to pack? We could go search some of the houses on the island and look for something to use as a tracker for a sympathetic compass. Or there might still be clothing debris back at the coffee shop parking lot."

I scratched my goatee. "That could take a while."

Roderick tapped his thumbnail against his front teeth. "I have an idea," he said. His voice was quiet, his expression neutral, but then he smiled. "Yes." He produced his phone and dialed. I heard a woman answer, and I recognized her voice. "Hello, Beatrice," Roderick said to her. "Yes, it is a pleasure to speak to you, as well. I wonder: would you mind answering what is perhaps a delicate question?" The other end of the line was quiet. "It would help us to deal with the problem we have so recently discussed."

Okay, I heard her say, even though she was anything but.

"I need you to tell me the name of the seediest, least reputable real estate agent in the area. The one to whom I would go if, for instance, I had a meth lab I needed to relocate on short notice. The one who asks no questions and is always slightly damp to the touch."

Deputy Crew Cut arched one eyebrow. Jennifer chuckled. I did the same.

Dirk, I heard Beatrice say without hesitation There was a long pause, and then: *That fucker would sell crack cocaine at a Girl Scout Cookie stand.*

Roderick reached into his jacket and produced a slim pad of paper and a tiny pencil, like from a mini-golf place. He wrote the name and address. "Thank you, Beatrice," he purred. "I will never forget this."

She hung up without saying goodbye.

As she did, there was the subtle buzz of a device set to vibrate. Sheila looked down at the tablet in her hand and looked back up. "The sigil is back online, and we've got a signal on the island again. Way down the shore from the houses. Well over the line into South Carolina."

"I thought you said it didn't work anymore," I said to Jennifer.

"It didn't," Jennifer replied.

Marty, looking over Sheila's shoulder, read off the GPS coordinates: a string of numbers with absolutely no meaning to me. I didn't need to know the points they described, though. I already knew where it had to be.

Crew Cut and I looked at each other. "The dig site," I said.

"Or something near it," he replied.

"Okay," I announced to the others. "We need to go check this out—all of us, loaded for bear —sorry, Cousin, but we don't have time for your idea with this shady real estate guy. We need to get out there on the beach and put a stop to all of this, right now."

Beth and Marty stood a little straighter. They were ready to get this over with, whatever it was, and go home.

Jennifer looked around. Her people were nervous, I could smell it, but they had all survived their last encounter and they were with her. She nodded at me.

"Okay," she said. "But we have to know this is a trap, right? They want us to see that signal."

I shrugged. "It's all we've got without a lot of work and wasted time."

Roderick zipped up the front of his jacket. "What of the Rhinemaiden?" He looked between Jennifer and me. "What do we do to end her?"

I shrugged. "We can't do anything about her until we have more info, and that vampire—whoever they are—is the only shot we've got at more info right now. Once we know where she is…" I waved a hand around. "We'll ask the magic people to deal with that." I nodded at Jennifer. "Or we'll figure out a way to do it ourselves."

"Why not just walk away from that?" Jennifer sounded sincere. "Sure, let's throw down with these elders again, fine, but the Rhinemaiden? She isn't physical. If you prevent them from restoring her, she stays a spirit. I mean, so the town is haunted? So what?"

I shook my head at her. "It's not as simple as a story kids might use to scare each other. This town is haunted by something so freaky it will raise curiosity. It will cause people to look into the supernatural. Ghost hunter TV shows will come here and catch something on tape. People will start believing in the supernatural again. That's the best case scenario and I can't afford that. I like it when people think about things using modern materialism. The worst case is she does in fact turn solid again, for good, and then this town has an ancient vampire in it more powerful than anything we've seen before."

"Also, because vampires made it happen and Withrow feels we are his responsibility." Roderick smiled when he said it, then he looked back at the rest of us. "Let us away," he murmured. A set of keys with a great big Cadillac logo on them dangled from his tiny hand. "I'll drive," he said. "I can seat at least five more. Six if you're friendly."

I drove in front, with Roderick behind me in his gigantic early '70s Cadillac Coupe de Ville. It looks about fifty feet long and is painted gold with sparkles. It's the opposite of camouflage. It's a car that says, "Notice me, motherfucker, *or else.*"

All the technopagans and Dog packed into Roderick's Caddie, with Beth, Marty, and Crew Cut taking up the three extra seats in my Pontiac. Crew Cut and Marty tried to squeeze Smiles between them, but in the end he kind of wound up on top of them and halfway on top of Beth in the front, too.

There was a car abandoned in the other lane of the great big bridge into town. Its emergency flashers were going, but they were dim and blinked languidly, like the car disapproved of being awakened.

We drove past To Kill A Sunrise. The neon lights were off, though it was time for the place to be open, and the front door was hanging ajar. It was a deep and inky dark inside.

I parked the Firebird at the end of one of the long streets running the length of the residential portion of Sunset Beach. There were a bunch of signs with NO PARKING all over the place but considering every house was dark and every streetlight around us was off, I didn't figure we were too likely to get towed. There was a paved pathway from there to the far southern end of the beach for regular people. Beyond that was the half mile of sand to the dig site and then, after that, the place where the Intercoastal Waterway reconnected to the Atlantic Ocean.

Once we were out of the cars and standing under starlight I asked if anyone needed flashlights to see. Jennifer shook her head.

"We come prepared," she said as she opened a backpack she'd brought with her and passed around sunglasses to all the mortals. They each put on a pair, then Jennifer said aloud, "*Lux.*" I could feel something hum in the air, and the others all looked around for a second and nodded at her.

"You made night vision sunglasses?" Crew Cut seemed impressed. "You've got to tell me how."

"Sorry," Dan said with something sharp in his voice. "Proprietary information." Jennifer shrugged at him.

Crew Cut looked taken a bit aback.

Roderick pasted to those NO PARKING signs another round of photocopies of his doodles, his series of bad things happening to Ross.

"Okay, you have to tell me," I said.

Roderick smiled to himself. "Is that a request from a cousin and friend, or is that an order from the boss of all the vampires of North Carolina?"

"Yes," I said, frowning.

"Tulpas," Dan said, and he clapped his hands together once. "Tulpas! Thoughtforms! Modify the thoughts about the subject and the subject is modified accordingly."

Roderick smiled more widely. "Make the subject a mockery and he may lose some of his power."

"You're softening him up by making fun of him?"

"Softening him," Roderick said to me, "In the minds of those who might encounter him. It won't do anything to him *right now* but it might over time."

"Okay," I sighed. "Moving right along, let's get going. The dig site is a few minutes walk south from here."

Sheila had the pad open, the night vision glasses pushed up and propped on top of her head. "The signal is still there, and seems to be more or less stationary," she said.

I harumphed. Roderick looked at me and I shrugged. "I don't like it," I said. "They knew we were trying to surveil them. Why come back here? It's too easy."

Beth opened her mouth and said, "You know, 'surveil' is a hybrid word-" but Marty put a hand on her arm.

Roderick ignored her and said to me, "Yes, but it is worth checking out. Perhaps one of them is desperate. One of them alone cannot present a real challenge to all of us, surely."

I clicked my cheeks. Smiles went from sitting behind me to standing beside me. Dog was glued to Roderick's side.

Beth looked around and whistled—a sharp chirp—and a bird seemed to land on demand.

"No," I said, knowing what she had in mind. "It would be nice to send a big flock of birds to check it out before we get there, but they'll be obvious as hell. We're just going to have to sneak up on them."

We set out, stomping down the path to the beach with all the stealth of a small herd of bison trying to cross the goddamn prairie.

The tide was heading back out, leaving the sand a wide, almost bright-white strip between the shadows of the nature preserve and the vast inkwell that is the ocean at night. The sky was gloriously clear, and the stars and a giant full moon were out in force. I think at this point I've forgotten how dim the stars look to human eyes. To a vampire, they are exceptionally bright and there are a clean gazillion of them. In the cities, we're as prone to having them washed out by light pollution as anyone. In the middle of nowhere, with the nearest lights the glow of a few hotels way out on the north end of North Myrtle Beach, well away from us, the stars were like something out of a movie. At one point I actually called for us to stop just so I could stand there and stare at them.

Nobody seemed to mind.

The water rippled in the silver light of the skies above, like mercury from an old thermometer spilled across the floor of the world. The water sounded as distant as it felt, even though it was right there, and the silence of the world around us was profound. We were not on a beach in a modern little town. We were in the caves of the ancients, looking up for the first time.

"That is the water that is winning," Roderick said, sticking his chin in the direction of the surface of the sea, the moon reflected on it.

"Huh?" I didn't look at him when I spoke.

"All the water in the world is trying to get to the moon," Roderick said. "That is the source of the tides, is it not? All of it, even the water in the blood in our veins: it stretches for the sky, in response to the strange magnetism of that mysterious sentinel. None of it ever wins. None of it ever makes it. But that water, the water with the moon in the mirror it makes of itself, is the water that *is winning*."

"Are there vampire astronomers?" Dan whispered it, and he seemed to be addressing it to Roderick. In my peripheral vision I could see the boy pull the glasses down his nose so he could look at the stars with just his human eyes.

"I know a vampire scientist in Seattle," my cousin replied. His voice was equally low, like he was talking in church. I wondered if perhaps he kind of was: if he was feeling the same awe I did. On the other hand, I'm not sure it's even possible for Roderick to feel *smaller* than something given how confident he always is. "But he is a necrologist. I have met no astronomers."

"How many are there?" Beth asked.

"G…" Marty started to speak, but his voice caught. "Given forty seven minutes I could count with precision one quarter of the sky, then make an estimate based on light density." He sounded like he was in heaven.

"Alright," I whispered. "Let's get moving again."

I hope I've never got forty seven minutes to listen to a man count under his breath.

The smell of vampire was very faint when it hit me, and the Atlantic was whipping hard that night, but Roderick and Beth and Marty all stopped walking when they caught it, too, so I knew it wasn't just my imagination. I put up a hand and we all stopped. The dig site wasn't quite in view, but I figured we must be getting close.

"Two hundred yards," Sheila whispered. She was shielding the screen of her tablet with her other arm. "Slightly to the right of where we're headed." Sheila showed us on her tablet where the vampire was.

I nodded, and we began walking more slowly. "Tell me if it moves," I said.

With nothing but the sound of splashing waves, the howl of the wind, and the call of the occasional night bird, we crossed half the remaining distance. I signaled to the others, and the technopagans and Crew Cut and Beth and Marty hung back a little bit, letting Roderick and me get ahead. I figured we had a far better chance of sneaking up on another vampire than any bunch of humans, no matter how clever.

We got close enough to the dig site to see it, but there didn't seem to be much of anyone there: just the abandoned lights, not powered on, and the massive maw of the hole the historical society dug out at Herman's command, its edges smoothed now by a day of Atlantic wind running over the top of it. Behind it, though, were two Beach Patrol four-wheel ATV's and, slumped on the sand next to them, two dead Beach Patrol officers. They looked like their necks had been slashed with a knife, but of course lots of vampires deface the corpses of our victims so as to obfuscate why they died. *Poor bastards*, I thought. *They should have abandoned ship with everybody else.*

Roderick nodded to the right, at the massive dune overlooking the scene, and I nodded. The mailbox, where I'd perched the night before, was just visible in the starlight at the very peak of the dune. The mailbox, sticking out of the sand in a place with no houses in sight, was even more surreal from down there on the beach. It was easy to imagine some mail carrier making her quiet rounds, walking up the side of the dune with great effort, and sticking a letter inside without so much as looking up. The mailbox was so bizarre it felt mundane, and in that respect I knew exactly how it felt. I think the same can sometimes be said of how I relate to the neighborhood where I live or the people who are my friends.

It looked like the only way to the top would be to cross the bottom of the dune and go around the back, ultimately ascending from the other side the same way I did. I didn't like that we just walked right up to the same place I so effectively spied on just the night before. I didn't like how hidden someone could be up there.

My dislike was immediately confirmed.

"Where are your friends? Tell them to come join us," I heard Herman say from above.

So much for sneaking up on him.

"They're shy," I replied. No need being subtle now, so I started snapping my fingers and clapping one fist against the other palm, like a tough from an episode of *Happy Days*. "C'mon down and maybe we can introduce you to 'em."

Herman appeared at the top of the dune. In his hand was one of the notebooks from the mailbox. "Do you know what people write in these things?" He gestured with the notebook itself.

"No, but I suggest you write 'goodbye,'" I said.

"Great," he said, his voice dripping with sarcasm. "A tough guy. Oh, Withrow, I'm *so* scared." I could practically hear the rusty squeak of the decrepit old bastard rolling his eyes. "Do you think I came here to fight you? In *this* body?" He snorted aloud. "I can barely *breathe* sometimes. Admittedly, I have been pretty hard on this one, but it's a wonder he was alive at all when I moved in. I barely made it up here." He took some wheezing breaths and cleared his throat. "Now shut up and listen to me."

Roderick and I exchanged a glance. My cousin shrugged at me. "Okay," I said. "Impress me with your big last-stand speech."

He held up the notebook again. "They—the humans, the *tourists*," but it sounded like he'd just said the worst cuss he could possibly manage, "They come here and write *poems*. They have their children scrawl decidedly un-precocious little essays about how they love the beach and they love Jesus and thank their sad little god for making this place." He slapped the notebook shut and dropped it from the edge so that it fluttered to the wet sand like a dead seagull. "Never mind that humans made this place. Most of the island is artificial. It was created to sell *real estate*." Again, disgust dripped from every sound his mouth made.

"Okay," I said. After a pause, I added, "I have to say, I don't quite see where you're going with this. I mean, they're sentimentalists. Big fucking deal if they want to waste their lives feeling twee little things about places."

"And yet you fight on their side," Herman said. He crossed his arms. The breathing still wasn't easy for him. He sounded like he'd more than worn himself out getting up there. He sounded halfway to a coronary. I wondered again if his possession ability made bodies break down faster than normal. "Why is that?"

"I don't fight on their side," I said. "I fight on my side. If some of them choose to fight with me, well, I compliment them on their good taste."

"Bullshit," Herman said. The accent had come back in the moment of vehemence. He sounded fresh off the boat from Germany. "Gah, you cannot even be honest with yourself."

"I do have to agree with him on that, Cousin," Roderick said. He was idly dusting an imaginary speck of something from the front of his white plastic jacket. "You clearly do in fact fight on behalf of others than yourself." My look of shut-the-hell-up just made Roderick smile. "Why deny it? But do not worry, I will not insult you with the term 'humanitarian.'" He winked at me then mouthed in silence, *This is a trap*.

I looked back at Herman. "You're the U-boat officer, right?"

"A long time ago," he said. "Lifetimes ago. I see no reason to hide that."

"But you were destroyed in the battle. Here. On this site." Roderick put his hands in his pockets as he spoke. "At the last moment, you leapt into a nearby human and used them to escape. You have been leaping from one to another ever since. That is why you are digging here. You think whatever method the others wish to use to bring back The Rhinemaiden can instead be used to bring back *you*."

"Of course," Herman said. "I should think that much is obvious."

"How'd you plan to do it?" I pointed at the hole. "Is there really a canister of ash down there? Can you really use that to restore a vampire's body? It just seems…" I gave an apologetic shrug with one arm. "It seems pretty far-fetched."

"Ross says it can be done with blood," Herman replied. "He says a vampire's ashes, in the right ritual space, in the place where they were destroyed, when the stars in the heavens attain the correct configuration, can be used to reconstitute that vampire if those ashes are drenched with blood in sufficient quantities—or of sufficient power." Even from here, in the light of the stars, I could see the flash of his eyes. He drew from his shirt pocket a little glass vial, like a test tube, and with a vampire's sight I could see it contained something dark and malleable: ash, no doubt, and probably *his*.

"I know this may seem obvious," I said, "And I'm flattered you think my blood is powerful, but let's be realistic. You are not killing anybody in that rickety old body no matter how much you want to resurrect yourself." I looked sideways at Roderick. "Do you hear what I just said? 'Resurrect yourself?' Do you hear the things shit like this makes me say? Jesus."

"Oh," Herman said holding up the vial. "These are not mine. They are my mistress'. I have given up finding my ashes. I was told they were here, but I think that must be untrue."

I scrunched my eyebrows close together. "How'd you get her ashes? If she really died out here, I mean, I don't know man, there's a bit of a breeze."

"She foresaw her own death," he said simply. "She was gifted with a vision. When she realized she would be destroyed, she set aside some of her own blood in a vial in her stronghold."

Roderick made a small 'ah' sound. "Where it stayed intact until her death, at which point it turned into a vial of ash." He chuckled. "Clever. But why wait until now to do the ritual?"

Herman grinned. "The stars were not right," he said. "When they were, the first time, the ritual was fouled. Too little blood."

I snorted. "Yeah, right. You assholes? You're all on the Liz Bathory diet. There's no shortage of blood around when you fucks are in town." I gestured at him, at the hole, at the sky full of stars supposedly now "right," then I looked back at him. "Besides, she's had plenty of blood and then some, right? She's been turning people to slag left and right." I gestured back the way we came, towards the houses, towards the little cinder block bar, towards the planetarium closed for winter. "Look around, man. This island's practically a ghost town in its own right. She's chugged down just about everyone alive at this point. That's why it's so fucking dead around here. And what's it gotten her? A big fat goose egg, that's what. What makes you think this is going to go differently?"

Herman smiled again. "I'm no mage," he said. "I just report what Ross told us."

"He is a demon," Roderick said. His voice was utterly cold. "He lies. It is his only imperative."

Herman ignored him. "As I said, this ash is not mine. It's that of my mistress. And though I am forced to make do with the frail failings of mere mortal flesh, exhausted by decades of sunlight and weakness, my blood is still quite powerful. Surely I owe her this service after all my failures to serve myself." With surprising alacrity he yanked the cork out of the test tube with his teeth and his other hand produced a knife.

Roderick and I both immediately sank our feet into the sand and shot forward in a blur, aiming to stop him, but we were too far away. We scrabbled at the near face of the dune, too steep for us to climb, sand tearing away in our hands in great chunks, as Herman drove the knife deep into his own neck and then tore it back out. Smiles and Dog hadn't even managed to catch up to us. Roderick and I were going hell for leather trying to get up the face of that dune and making zero progress.

A great, red gout of the blood of a living body—tainted by the clotted black ichor of the vampire possessing it—pumped from the wound in an obscene spurt of fluid. The mixed smells, the aroma of human blood and the stench of another vampire, hit my senses like a brick to the face. With his last strength, Herman pressed the test tube to his own wound and cried out, "Mistress! I restore you to life in gratitude and eternal service! *Destroy these thine enemies!*"

Though there wasn't a cloud in the sky, a bolt of lightning struck the sand where Herman stood above us. There was a boom of thunder, and a roar of wind, and I could smell ozone in the air.

Screams rose up from all around us: the screams of a monster freed at last and behind that the gibberish cries of its countless victims protesting from the beyond-realm they now inhabited. Strange light erupted from the sand all around us: blue and yellow, unnatural in their hues, like the unfocussed glow of a computer screen in the next room, but bright as a floodlight. I felt someone push past me with tremendous strength but Roderick was still beside me, shielding his face with his arms.

"Jennifer!" Roderick screamed over the howl of the wind, but I wasn't sure he could be heard ten feet away, much less three hundred.

On the other hand, they could probably tell some shit was going down.

Chapter 13

You said your body was young but your mind was very old.
--The Chemical Brothers, "Setting Sun"

Roderick and I backpedaled from the dune in the blinding glare of the not-blue light shooting out of it in great rays. The glow got brighter and brighter, and when we got a few yards, Roderick and I both decided to all-out run for it. Each of us scooped up his respective dog, still bounding towards us in relative slow motion, and took off back towards the technopagans. We could see them ahead of us, many yards away, expressions of shock just beginning to form on their faces.

I glanced back in time to watch as the dune—mailbox, notebooks, and all—exploded in a great pulse of light and energy and wind. Imagine a smoke bomb going off in a Batman cartoon: a little sound and a huge great whorl of gas concealing his escape. Now imagine that happening to a dune the size of a large house.

Grains of sand shot in all directions, sharp as needles, and the sound of the explosion—a boom followed by a hiss and then the patter of rainfall as sand sprinkled back down to the ground from high above—was so loud as to about knock us over. Even in slow motion, the audio distorted by our speed, it was a gargantuan boom that rattled the fangs in my skull.

Looking back in front, I realized who had pushed past. His body clearly failing, burning it down to its last embers with a final push of his vampiric strength in that clattering, wobbling, all too mortal frame, Herman was barreling towards the technopagans with his arms out.

Maybe he could smell the magic on them, or maybe he just wanted someone younger to try to jump into so he could have his cake and eat it, too, sacrificing himself to resurrect his maker and yet still surviving in his own right. I will never know exactly what went through Herman's mind. I saw the sound wash over the technopagans, each of them rocking backwards. Jennifer was about to fall prone, and Herman was running right for her.

It occurred to me to wonder if he could produce fangs when he inhabited a mortal body or if he was going to attack her throat with the dentures of a 70 year old man?

Herman dove forward, his mouth hinging open, the mixed blood supplies of his host and himself pumping out the wound in his neck in ever-weaker streams with each pound of his feet. Jennifer's throat was bared in horrible slow motion as she fell backwards. But in that moment, Ramon—the quiet one, the one who had the sunlamp the first night we'd seen the technopagans here, the one who when I met them told me he was studying at Durham Tech in hopes of transferring to NC State and majoring in electrical engineering—happened through the sheer bad luck of Brownian motion to fall into the gap between Herman and Jennifer, shielding her with his body.

Herman landed on top of them, twisted Ramon's head to face him as though for a kiss, and then, to my horrified fascination, buried Ramon's mouth in the folds of waddle he'd stabbed open atop the dune moments before. As blood shot obscenely across Ramon's face, and into his mouth, Herman's body kicked wildly at the sand once, twice, and died. Roderick and I carried our dogs towards them as fast as we possibly could.

We dropped out of super speed as we ran up and everyone else tumbled to the ground around us. Smiles and Dog both leapt from our arms and ran over to the now obviously deceased Herman and Ramon struggling to get out from under him. Smiles was silent but alert, his head down, his ears back, the sort of pose I see him take when he thinks he might be about to fight something.

Dog walked right up and started sniffing Ramon, then Herman, then back to Ramon, up and down his face and torso. I noticed he sniffed all the way out Ramon's right arm to his fingertips, then all the way back up.

"Are you alright?" Roderick said words that sounded normal but his tone was hostile. He was ready to kill Ramon on the spot if he didn't get an answer he liked.

He didn't get a chance. Ramon shoved Herman's corpse off of himself with a show of strength well beyond what Ramon could have produced himself. There was fire in his eyes as he leapt to his feet and shot around us towards the Beach Patrol ATVs.

Roderick and I looked at each other as we both spun back up to super speed to chase him.

My cousin's eyes positively gleamed.

Waaaaaaaait, I heard Jennifer shouting at us as she started to stand. I wasn't sure whether she was speaking to us or to Ramon. I also realized we still had no idea what was the name of the vampire whose spirit was now driving Ramon around. All we knew was that the last living part of that vampire was some small amount of blood, passed from one victim to the next for, what, seventy years? And that one small part of the monster, that tiny volume of blood, was apparently enough to keep his psyche alive and transport it from one mortal vessel to another.

Jesus, I thought to myself. *Is this what we are? Are we so indestructible we only need a little blood to live forever? Are we so determined to survive we don't even need bodies to do it?*

I always thought of my transformation into a vampire, to some degree, the ultimate attempt at preserving who *and what* I thought of as *me,* body and all. I thought the body was the most important part of that, too. After all, what's a soul but a lie we tell ourselves to make us feel like we're more special than a rock? Who I am, I always believed, is *what* I am.

The monster that leapt into Ramon by the forced feeding of a little putrescent blood didn't even seem to have retained *that* anymore.

Ramon's body was young and strong, and the critter inside it was taking full advantage. He was moving fast, and though he wasn't as fast as Roderick or I, he had a head start. Ramon leapt onto one of the Beach Patrol ATVs with obviously supernatural grace and a feral grin, gunned it to life, and spun away in a sharp turn to go back up the beach towards town as fast as it would go. Without a moment's hesitation he ran right over the corpse of one of the cops who rode it there in the first place. The four-wheeler's fat tires dug into the wet sand and Ramon shot forward as fast as its engine would take him.

Roderick whistled and I clicked my cheeks, and Dog and Smiles spun up beside us as all four of us took off on foot after the ATV. Behind us was some commotion.

I glanced back and saw Jennifer and Crew Cut both moving faster than human speed and both headed for the other ATV. Crew Cut beat her to it, jumping onto the driver's seat, but Jennifer straight-up side-tackled him, slamming into his upper arm with her own dropped shoulder. Crew Cut tumbled off the ATV's other side and rolled onto the sand as Jennifer took the driver's seat away from him. I clapped my hands once and laughed, a loud sharp shot in the howling wind of the beach at night, and Roderick cackled beside me at my delight.

"Yes, Cousin!" Roderick called as we ran, our dogs beside us, "Finally, *finally*, a proper hunt!"

The sound of the ATV started to catch up to us, which I didn't think it should really be able to do, and as it went past I saw Jennifer driving the ATV, Crew Cut clinging to it behind her, and sparks shooting out of the engine. *Of course*, I thought, *A vehicle is just another kind of technology, and that's Jennifer's specialty.* Whatever witching she'd done to the ATV, it was throwing off smoke, too, and it looked like maybe it was shaking all over as she rode hell for leather after Ramon. She shot past Roderick and the dogs and me, fast as we were going, and practically left fire in her tracks as she tore ass up the beach in pursuit of Ramon.

"Naturally, Cousin," Roderick said conversationally as we ran, "There is the small matter of whether the one we called Herman was successful in resurrecting his maker."

Right on cue, lightning struck again, behind us, back where we'd been standing. Then it struck again. Then it struck a third time and this time the light stayed on: not just a flash from one bolt, but as though someone had turned on a spotlight aimed at the sky. I looked back and sure enough, where once had been the dune with its local landmark mailbox, there was now a giant crater of sand. Light poured out of it—blue-silver light, blindingly bright, utterly unnatural, clearly not the light of the sun but rather the light of the moon brightened a thousand times—and emerging from that light, walking at a normal pace, was a figure I clearly recognized, even in silhouette.

It was Herman's maker, and this time she was absolutely as solid as you or I.

Sheila and Dan were still standing there, both trying to tug the other to run faster as they beat a path back in our direction. As they moved, molasses slow, I saw Sheila draw a symbol in the air and just like that they faded from view.

"Things are about to get really super complicated for your boyfriend," I said to Roderick, both of us still running. "But I think maybe he's got some magic to protect himself."

"I told you 'boyfriend' is too strong a term, Cousin." He looked annoyed as all hell, too.

Jennifer and Crew Cut surged ahead, but the ATV Jennifer was pushing past its normal maximum was clearly suffering for it. Smoke absolutely billowed from its underside and occasionally little jets of flame shot out of the motor. It wasn't going to last much longer, but Jennifer had gotten so close to Ramon it didn't matter. She was maybe six or seven feet from him and slightly to his left, with Roderick and me running maybe six feet behind them, but slightly to Ramon's other side. Dog and Smiles were behind us, in turn, churning up huge clods of wet sand as they tore into it, tongues hanging out to the sides.

The failing and scattered lights of Sunset Beach glowed maybe a half mile away, but getting bigger all the time.

Jennifer gunned the motor again, and it made god-awful noises: a high-pitched metallic shriek came from it, and the sound of combustion was sufficiently jerky it sounded like there was something getting into the fuel that shouldn't be. The engine was literally tearing itself apart to get the speeds Jennifer was demanding from it.

I saw Crew Cut's mouth move in Jennifer's ear, and she nodded. With one final surge, she pushed the ATV up beside Ramon. He looked over, tried to veer away, but Jennifer and Crew Cut simultaneously leapt from their vehicle—which immediately produced a giant cloud of black smoke and flipped over—to tackle Ramon off of his. The ATV he was driving went shooting away from him as the three of them rolled end-over-end into the sand in a tangle of arms and legs and the guttural howls of the thing riding Ramon's flesh.

Roderick and I ran up as Crew Cut twisted Ramon's arms behind his back and Jennifer grabbed Ramon's jaw.

"Come out of him right now!" Her voice was a hoarse growl, and I thought of that old advice you always hear about walking around in the woods: never get between a mother bear and her cub. Jennifer's eyes were at once as full of malice and affection as two eyes can ever be. Ramon was one of her people, and she had lost one too many of her people already.

Ramon didn't try to twist away. Instead he bore into her with his own gaze and said, hoodoo in full effect, "*Release me at once and kill yourself.*"

My heart sang: I learned years ago Jennifer is immune to the hoodoo.

She didn't just tell him no. Instead Jennifer reared back and walloped Ramon across the jaw with the back of one hand, literally trying to slap some sense into him. "I said come the fuck out!" Jennifer hit him again, and then again. "I call on every power," she said, and her voice dropped and the shape of her mouth changed. I could see, as Roderick and I stood there a few feet away, that Jennifer was at this moment doing that witch business and doing it hard. "*I call on the untamed and untamable power of the ocean before me,*" she said, and her voice gained new dimensions, unearthly echoes, the depths of power resonating from within her and yawning before us like the sort of water so deep it doesn't know light *exists*. "*May it rip from Ramon the thing inside him and take it to the grave it has so long escaped.*" With one hand she struck him again, but this time with her fist, as sure and hard as a prizefighter scoring a knockout. I saw his lip burst and blood shoot out from Ramon's face.

Despite our being at least twenty feet from the edge of the water, the tide so far out it exposed many tens of yards of sand not normally seen by beachgoers, I could hear the roar of the water as a wave started to crest. Driven forwards, drawn further in than it should have been, a breaker about waist high slammed into all of us where we stood, knocking Roderick and me and our dogs aside. It washed over Ramon as Jennifer and Crew Cut held him under it together for a moment before being dragged off their feet themselves, and the five of us were pushed inland, then tugged back and dumped on the sand where we started, all in one rapid arc.

As the water ran back into the sea, revealing Ramon's drenched body, I saw blood—human and vampire—stream from him in a great gush. Ramon bled from the mouth, from the nose, from the ears, even from the eyes, as the vampiric essence within him was ripped free by Jennifer's magic and sucked into the ocean on the back the wave receding from us. Ramon produced a gurgling scream, the sound of a human throat being shredded by its own effort, and his neck muscles bulged as though he were straining to stay in his own skin. The sound of his screaming didn't wind down, it just kept going, making my skin crawl all over. I stood back up and ran over, clapping my hands on his shoulders.

"*Let go of him,*" I shouted, putting all I could into my own hoodoo, and with a shudder, a grotesque mockery of a lover's climactic convulsion, Ramon's whole body shook once, then twice, then a third time. The blood stopped shooting out of him and the last of the giant wave Jennifer summoned carried off with it the last of that vampire. Whatever—whoever—had ridden Herman and Ramon washed away into the sea. Ramon's scream died somewhere in his throat and he fell forward, face first, into the sand. He was still bleeding and he'd lost a lot of blood already. His skin was white and starting to turn gray. His lips were already blue.

Jennifer stood beside us now, and reached down to feel at Ramon's neck. "He's alive," she said. We were all back at normal speed, and the ocean crashed heavily at its usual pitch instead of the deep and distended bass chords it played during our whole ridiculous chase.

Roderick stood, wiped seawater and sand from his plastic jacket, and said, "So is she."

We turned and looked, and half a mile down the beach from us, still backlit from the unnaturally argent light from the crater, there was that figure of a woman walking toward us at a casual pace.

Jennifer was standing back with the technopagans the whole time Herman spoke to Roderick and me. She looked down the beach where Roderick indicated and said, "Who the hell is that?"

"The Rhinemaiden," I said without looking away from the resurrected vampire's approach. "Herman—whatever his name really was—succeeded in bringing her back."

Like a film skipping a few frames, abruptly the silhouette of the Rhinemaiden was closer one moment than it had been the next.

"*Shit,*" Roderick and I said at the same time.

In another blink, she was closer still.

"*Jumpstart,*" Roderick said. "That's what we call short-distance teleportation in Seattle. She has multiple Last Gasp abilities." He blinked slowly and said to me, "Cousin, I suspect her power is the ability to absorb the abilities of others."

I stood and started to back away, Smiles walking warily alongside me, glancing backwards, but with a third blink of the eye the Rhinemaiden was standing in the midst of us.

A few feet back, standing with their eyes open but catatonic, were Beth, and Marty Macintosh, and Dan, and Sheila.

The Rhinemaiden was not physically imposing. She was maybe five foot seven, Caucasian, with long dark hair and features like you see in old portraits of nobility: thin, a long and narrow nose, lips like a slim line across her face, and cheekbones you could use to hang laundry out to dry. I was surprised she wore clothing, but in fact she was dressed in a fashion I immediately recognized as the sort of off-the-rack Georgiana-ish frock women wore all the time at the end of World War Two: a hemline just below the knee, a cinched waist, and short puffy sleeves hanging off a high-collared neckline. She looked cruel in the face, but dressed for a garden party seventy years gone. If this was the boundless, irrational appetite the elders had summoned back from the beyond when she still had no body, now she seemed to be restored to her previous self *exactly as she was when destroyed*. She didn't look mindless. She looked calculating. She glanced between us with the piercing, frost-wreathed, and indifferent gaze of a thousand year old housecat.

The voice that came out of her was not verbalized. It was in my head, and apparently in all our heads. She spoke directly to our minds, without need of words. *Which of you destroyed my servant.* It was a question, but it was stated so flatly it sounded like a statement. She didn't sound angry. She didn't sound *anything*. What she sounded was old—unfathomably ancient, old beyond words, old beyond my ability to envision one lifespan no matter how supernatural somebody got. The way she addressed us was the way one addresses a particularly disinteresting carpet stain: we were there, but we weren't really her top priority, but maybe also she should go ahead and clean us up while she was around. Receiving a communication from her also had a certain clumsiness to it, like maybe she was having to blow the dust off the concept of *words*.

I guess Roderick must have thought something back to her, because they looked at one another for a moment. The Rhinemaiden started to open her mouth and needle-teeth—gods, I can't even call them fangs, they were like a row of icicles, with another behind *them*, and another behind them, her face transforming around them as she bared them at him—but Jennifer spoke.

"I did," she said. "I summoned magic to undo his possession of my friend."

The Rhinemaiden turned to regard Jennifer with narrowed eyes, that horrible mouth hanging open. Her mind-voice rang in my head as she caressed the ridiculous shark-jaws jutting out of her too-wide lips with her tongue, like a snake tasting the air. Her whole face was twisted into a grotesque, like something right out of a stop-motion animated movie. Watching the skin flex around her deformed skull, and watching the skull deform itself, was like watching the devil work clay with his own hands. *Magic? And who gave a serf permission to use our powers against us?*

Though he was lying there in the sand looking more dead by the second, Ramon sprang into action. I don't know how he did it. I don't know how his body *worked* with that little blood in it. I could tell—some innate sense we have—that, had I known the right ritual, I could have turned him into a vampire right there on the spot without taking a drop. He was running on fumes *at best*. But when The Rhinemaiden threatened Jennifer—the leader of his coven, the extraordinary genius who walked into his house and told everyone she was in charge now, thank you very much—he came up off that sand with his fists balled and the fires of hell in his eyes and he went right at The Rhinemaiden, ready for war.

Ramon's hands caught her by the front of the dress and he tried to head butt her, a straight-on frontal attack, but he didn't get as far as hitting her. Instead, those stomach-churning jaws cranked open and Ramon stuck his head—his whole head, all the way to the neck—right inside her mouth, carried by his own momentum.

The Rhinemaiden's jaws snapped shut on him. Just a little blood flew in all directions, and with a crunch and a snap, Ramon's headless corpse fell straight down to the ground at her feet.

I started screaming, I don't mind one bit being the one to say it, because something about the Rhinemaiden told every cell in my body to *get the fuck away*. Years before, when I walked into the street to fight zombies that arose in my neighborhood, I was shocked when they instinctively strove to escape me. It was like they knew, even in their mindless and senseless state, there was a hierarchy of the monstrous and I was above them on it.

When I watched The Rhinemaiden kill Ramon, I knew exactly how they felt.

I knew why my maker, Agatha, and the vampires who were her contemporaries, *had* to rebel against the ancients who made them.

I knew the fear they must have felt when they were commanded by horrors like this, and I knew just as surely the hatred that fear fostered in them.

Kneel, I heard The Rhinemaiden command in my mind.

Jennifer produced a dagger from somewhere on her and hand to Jesus I could *smell* magic on that knife. Roderick bared his teeth. Crew Cut let out a battle cry, a meaningless yell from deep inside. Smiles started to lunge, and Dog shook his enormous flanks to do the same. Beth and Marty still stood there staring at nothing. I punched one fist into the other hand, hearing my own heart pump black blood through my dead body, and figured if this was how I was going to die, at least I had my boots on and my fangs out. I was not going to goddamn -

The Rhinemaiden waved a hand, and all went dark, and that was the end of thinking I could fight her with my fists and a little moxie.

CHAPTER 14

Chin up, buttercup / When your number's up
--The Darkest of the Hillside Thickets, "Cultists On Board"

My eyes snapped open, and my senses told me it was almost sunrise—but not quite.

In movies, whenever somebody wakes up from being knocked out, you get that blurry vision thing that slowly resolves into the faces of the hero's enemies leering at the camera. That doesn't happen with vampires. With vampires, you're awake or you're asleep, period. There doesn't seem to be a transition period. In that sense, I know intellectually that days happen, and I can sense their approach, but their passage is just a blink from my perspective.

In the same way, there seemed to be only a blink between The Rhinemaiden waving her hand at me in the middle of the night on the sand of Sunset Beach and it being hours later, almost morning but not quite.

We were in what looked like a misshapen movie theater—one that had seen better days. Everything was 1970's rust-red-and-burnt-orange, and the pattern on the carpet was just a bad case of vertigo: lines and circles and paisley all over the floor like the pattern delivery truck hit a bump in the road as it drove past. Even the walls were carpeted, though they were solid colors.

The ceiling was high and domed, and there were thick black curtains draped all over it. In the center of the room stood an apparatus covered in lenses and eyes, like an ebony alien mantis the size of a golden retriever. The chairs were arranged around it in three rows. The apparatus was on a raised stage, so a presenter could walk around it in a circle and speak if they wanted. The sign on the machine read: STAR PROJECTOR COURTESY OF ASTRONOMY LIVE! C. 2002.

We were in the small planetarium in Sunset Beach, the one that did light shows in summer and had a glass domed roof for lectures at night.

Ah, I thought. *A big glass room. Hell of a way to execute vampires.*

We—Roderick, Jennifer, Crew Cut, Dan, Sheila, Marty, Beth, and me—were arranged in an arc in front of and beneath the raised platform, facing it. We were on those shitty old auditorium seats you've surely been forced to suffer for the duration of someone's high school talent show.

I resolved right then and there I would not die in an uncomfortable chair.

There were three chairs on the platform, bigger and plusher, like they had been pulled from the lobby. They were just as old as everything else in the place—covered in mildew stains humans probably wouldn't notice, fraying at the seams and long since missing some stuffing—but I guessed they were as close to a throne as these assholes could manage.

Seated on the one in the middle was The Rhinemaiden. She was looking at us, one at a time, and when she got to me I could feel the same sort of probe I sometimes felt from Roderick. Whereas his invasive mind is like a gentle pressure, hers was like a drill. She was in my mind, reading it, sifting it, sorting it, and I couldn't do a damned thing to stop her. I tried to shut her out by force of will, but it was like trying to arm-wrestle a strongman while covered in butter. It was pointless. I couldn't get a grip on the part of her that was in my head.

I tried to strain at the chains being used to bind my hands behind me, but I couldn't make them budge. Maybe they had been magic-ified somehow, but maybe I just couldn't get good leverage. The elder vampires of Sunset Beach used the same chain on Smiles, binding his front paws together with an extension of the chain they used to bind my wrists and hands. Too short a length of chain to allow either of us to move linked us to each other through a gap in the arm rest.

I gritted my teeth as I strained, and I could see Roderick doing the same thing but with much more composure. He didn't blink or look away from The Rhinemaiden. He merely flexed his spindly arms to no effect.

Whereas Roderick seemed composed, Marty was visibly frightened. He looked to Roderick, who didn't look back, then to me. I shook my head slightly side to side: *don't bother fighting. Not right now. Save your strength.* I didn't know what strength I thought Marty would have, but it seemed like the thing to try to convey.

Jennifer's eyes fluttered open but sharpened in a heartbeat. She looked around the planetarium, lids narrowed, assessing. She didn't bother to try to overcome her bonds. She just took in the room and what was around us.

Beth was staring at the thick, dark curtains over the glass-domed roof as though she could see the stars beyond them.

Dan and Sheila, when they awakened, turned slightly pale but stayed quiet.

Seated on The Rhinemaiden's right was Ross, blue-silver skin shining in the dim globe lights and that too-perfect smile on his face. It was a kind smile, a generous smile, the smile of a judge who knows you're about to be sentenced to death and is frankly glad to see you go but doesn't want to seem like he's being too much of a dick about it. I hated him so much I thought my spleen might cut its way out and take a flying leap at him.

On The Rhinemaiden's other side was someone it took me just a second to recognize, but of course that was also the case a couple of nights before: Old Shoe, but still in his "Brodie" form, recognizable only by how generic and forgettable he was. He wore a different popped-collar polo shirt and a different pair of beige cargo shorts and a different pair of boat shoes, but it was like flipping pages in a Sears Roebuck catalog and seeing the same model wearing only marginally different outfits. Somebody could stick him in one of those find-the-one-that's-different visual puzzle things, where there are like a thousand panda bears and you have to find the skunk or whatever, and you'd never spot him in a million years.

Around them, down at floor level with the rest of us, were maybe half a dozen other vampires. One of them, I noticed, was one of the three card players from To Kill A Sunrise.

Another was the woman who tended the bar.

So it wasn't just that the elders or The Rhinemaiden ate or scared off almost all the people in town: they were desperate enough to start converting *en masse* any locals unlucky enough to be left. *At least we made them feel the hurt before they caught up to us*, I thought.

The others were an assortment: a guy dressed in hunting camouflage. A woman dressed in kind of a plain-Jane modesty dress: black and high-collared, with tall lace-up boots that disappeared under her long skirt, like a schoolmarm from the early 20th century. A dude who looked like he probably drove a big-rig for a living.

"So when did you go over to the other side?" I was looking at The Rhinemaiden when I spoke, but Old Shoe knew I was talking to him. "Or were you always one of them?" He was sitting by her, right there on the dais, and there wasn't a chain around *his* wrists. Old Shoe was nobody's prisoner. He was a defector.

"I'm sorry, Withrow," Old Shoe said. "I never signed on to be a hero."

I looked at him now. "What *did* you sign on for? What did they offer you?"

"They can fix me," Old Shoe said. His voice was very soft, and his hands were fidgeting with one another in his lap. He wouldn't look at me, or at any of us.

"I didn't know you were broken."

"Don't patronize me," he said, and this time Old Shoe's voice was stronger. "I'm a monster, Withrow. *You made me live in the sewers.*"

Now I looked at him. "N-"

I stopped.

I was going to say no, to deny what he just said. But it was true. I told him to stay out of sight. I told him he was a danger to the rest of us. The Bobs told him the same thing, and I could have pointed at them and claimed it was their fault, but I could have changed the rule, too.

That he was a danger to us, that having someone who looked like Old Shoe—face half-peeled away, skull split open, burns across a third of his flesh, a hand he couldn't use, a foot that turned the wrong direction, everything about him screaming he was walking, talking road kill—didn't change the fact it hurt to be shoved literally underground and told to stay there. Sure, it turned him into our resident gossipmonger. It made him a useful spy. It granted him a unique role in the community of vampires living in the very specific realm of Raleigh, North Carolina.

It also made him more alone than any of us could have imagined.

"I'm sorry," I said.

Old Shoe looked up and blinked at me.

"I'm not going to defend myself," I said. "I'm just sorry."

In five minutes you will die. The mind-voice of The Rhinemaiden spoke to all of us. *The curtains open on a timer. We have set them to open at a specific time of our choosing. When they do, the sun will be up. You will perish.*

Roderick and I looked at each other in confusion. I said aloud, "But the sun comes up before then. We'll be asleep."

"Lady Beatriz has a number of unusual abilities," Ross said. I followed his gaze and he and Roderick were staring at one another. I wondered which of them was trying to hoodoo the other, and which of them would win. "One of those is the ability to extend a vampire's—or many vampires'—wakefulness beyond dawn."

"Well," I said aloud, looking back at The Rhinemaiden—Lady Beatriz, I guessed—and harrumphed. "Touch *her*."

"I wouldn't recommend that," Ross said mildly. He smiled that death-sentence smile again. "She has rather an unfortunate effect on vampires who come into physical contact with her."

"*Osmosis*," Roderick said. "It is another of the Last Gasp powers. Are there any she does not have?"

"I think perhaps your generation have misunderstood the nature of your condition," Ross said to us. "You seem to think each of you has some special gift only available to you once certain preconditions of a mystical nature have been met. That is not how your maturation works."

"Fucking great," I said to the room. "We're about to have vampirism mansplained by a demon."

Ross went on without missing a beat. "In actuality, that event you consider so momentous, when the world of the living no longer knows you, is just the beginning of your maturation, not its conclusion. Vampires of sufficiently strong blood and experience are able to call upon a vast array of the powers you think are one-of-a-kind. To her, each of your powers is just…" He paused, searching for the right term. "Vampirism 101." Ross shrugged lightly—lithely—and I hated him all over again. He still wasn't inspiring the sort of lust or attraction he did before, but he was radiating a kind of calm certainty I felt in my bones was not natural. He wanted us to chill out.

I smiled to myself: he was trying to keep us acquiescent by the use of his powers.

That meant he was *afraid*.

Ross went on blathering about how Lady Beatriz this, and Lady Beatriz that, and she could make an angel pole dance on the head of a pin, and blah blah fucking blah. While he did, I looked around the room and realized none of the vampires other than Old Shoe had spoken. They were barely even looking at us. They were looking at each other, or the floor, or the raised platform where The Rhinemaiden sat, but not actually at her.

She was staring at us, but she wasn't using that power of hers to speak to us. She was letting Ross kill time so none of us would try anything.

Something about this didn't add up. Something about the whole thing of coming out here to the beach, and doing this whole charade with the historical society, and knowing how to resurrect The Rhinemaiden's body but not *doing it*, and Herman trying to make it look like he killed himself to bring her back so he could run away, and Crew Cut being right under their noses but not going after him—it just didn't make *sense*. And now The Rhinemaiden was stalling, and the vampires were cowed, and that meant there was a chance things could still go wrong for them.

If they did, that would almost certainly mean they went right for us.

I don't know what I was hoping *for*, to be honest. I couldn't move, my dog couldn't move, my cousin couldn't move, and I doubted any of our powers would work on The Rhinemaiden. If our powers worked on any of her minions she would probably just override them somehow. Ross had made it clear The Rhinemaiden was all that and a bag of chips when it came to mystic firepower. We were screwed on that front.

But everyone here was still scared, and I was pretty sure I was starting to figure out why.

"Herman was trying to destroy you for good," I said to The Rhinemaiden, interrupting whatever campaign speech Ross was in the middle of making on her behalf. I looked right at her as I said it. "He knew all along how to bring you back. He told me he was trying to get *his* body back instead, but I don't think that's true. He didn't have a hope of getting his body back. The ash he turned into was blown away seventy years ago. I think he was trying to figure out how to keep you from going *too* ape-shit crazy while his people tried to deal with *me*. He was getting mortals involved in something secretive so he could feed them to you without lots of *other* people knowing where they were or what they were doing, just to cover his own tracks. Mortal blood wouldn't be strong enough to restore you fully but it might keep you occupied. That would buy them time so they could focus their efforts on bringing you back, bodily, but *only* to kill you again and get rid of you forever." I wasn't totally sure what I was saying, but it kind of *felt* right when I said it. "It would explain why I never quite seemed to be the focus of their attention even though we were actively killing them. It would explain why we thought they would have all kinds of traps laid for us, plans within plans, but in fact they did nothing but react."

"Cousin," Roderick said mildly, "Of course they had some other priority. Not everything is about you."

I didn't take the time to give him a shut-up look. I just kept yammering. "In fact, I wonder, now that I'm talking about it, if maybe he didn't betray you that night on the beach, all those decades ago. I mean, sure, he would tell everybody else it was a group of rebel vampires who sprang a trap on you, fine, whatever. But what if that wasn't it at all?" I licked my lips. "What if what *actually* happened is that the elders knew they'd already lost to the rebels, and the best thing to do was to go ahead and hurry on over to the side of if-you-can't-beat-'em-join-'em. Like, the rebels kind of drew an arbitrary line: the old don't-trust-anyone-over-thirty thing the hippies used to say. They drew their boundaries of "young" and "old" and started fighting, but that left some vampires on the young-ish side of *old*, right? And maybe even some sort of in limbo in the middle, not really trusted by either side. And maybe some of them went along with the elders because it was better, to them, to be a living slave to something powerful than the distrusted outsiders among a bunch of know-nothing kids in the throes of rebellious fervor.

I licked my lips and drew a breath too fast for anyone to interrupt. "Then, eventually, some of *them* would figure out they were on the wrong side after all and maybe y'all should just surrender and let the other guys declare victory. But they knew the *really* ancient vampires like *you* would never understand, would never give in, and so some of them decided to rearrange circumstances in favor of their argument. You know, set the ship on fire so there's no choice but to abandon it. Herman was basically a suicide bomber: he would get you out there on the beach and they would spring some trap on you that would destroy *both* of you. But he, of course, would have someone else around into whom he could jump to get away." I made a little hmph noise. "Probably sunlight. Yeah. Get you on an eastern-facing beach and keep you there until the sun came up and fried both of you, but he has a mortal on hand he can use to get the hell away at the last possible second, and then boom, he's stuck in mortal bodies for the rest of his days but it beats being dead." I laughed suddenly. "You fought the rebellion so hard, and so single-mindedly, you drove your own closest allies to gin up *an entirely different rebellion*." I looked around. "And then they had to spend, what, months? Weeks? The whole winter, anyway, trying to figure out exactly where you died because it's been so many years the beach itself has changed: erosion and 'renourishing' and a million footsteps by tourists stomping down to that mailbox full of messages for the ever-after. It all changed the shape of the beach and they couldn't be sure where it happened anymore. All that blood, all the sacrifices, all those rituals, the maps in the secret rooms in the houses they rented: they weren't trying to find some artifact. They were trying to identify the right spot to bring you back. They wanted to be sure they were in the correct location when they brought you back so they could kill you again. And you know that."

Roderick's eyes narrowed. "That would explain why *this* particular display of hubris: bringing us to a place that can be exposed to the sun, after sunrise, and forcing your 'followers' to be here also. You wish to prove you are not afraid of having it happen a second time. You need to show them you can annex the plans they had for you and use them yourself."

I looked around at the others. "And that's why nobody came running from Charlotte to help you when my cousin and I started knocking you off. They're the ones who wanted her back. You didn't tell them you were coming out here to try to give her a material form again, because you didn't want them to help *her* against *you*. You aren't the elders I'm trying to find and fight. You're the elders who are trying to double-cross the ones I'm trying to fight. I just happened to get in the way of your double-cross. Shit, we might've even been allies if you'd just fucking told me."

"There aren't any of them—of us—left," the bartender from To Kill A Sunrise said. "Herman was the last of the visitors. All of us were locals until..." She looked at her watch. "Recently."

"And now," Roderick said, smiling the smile I imagine he produces before murdering someone, "You have no idea what to do, because she is back, and you cannot oppose her, and you fear she already knows all of this and is going to make slow work of her revenge even if none of it was especially your idea."

I looked at Old Shoe, who stopped fidgeting and listened with the attention of one who knows his fate is already sealed but has no idea what it actually will be. "You know they can't actually fix you, right?" I shrugged as best I could in my chains. "Ross lies. That's his whole deal. He'll probably offer you magic that makes you look 'normal' for longer than you can do on your own, but I bet the price is awful. I bet it requires something you find really distasteful, like you can only drink the blood of, I don't know, babies, or puppies, or something like that, so you decide it isn't worth it and you're back at square one all over again—only worse, because now *no one* trusts you."

Ross arched one silver eyebrow.

Old Shoe's face fell. So, I guess I was right about that.

I spoke to the rest of the vampires in the room, the ones standing around not looking at me and not looking at The Rhinemaiden and not looking at Ross. "I bet y'all wish things had gone differently, don't you? I bet y'all wish there were more of you left, that you'd been stronger, that you'd been better at fighting. Maybe all of you together could have taken her on and won. If only you'd known she had that vial of blood tucked away, ready to resurrect her in case something bad happened. If only some of your best fighters were still in the world and here to be your champions. If only someone really strong were here and could save you." I hoped to whatever dark powers might answer the prayers of a vampire that somebody in the room would take the hint.

Beth looked up from her lap—she had not spoken and had not looked around—and said, "Before we die, I wish to make a phone call."

You will die in ninety seconds. The Rhinemaiden's mindvoice was emotionless and matter of fact. *The curtains will open and you will see the sun a final time.*

Out of the corner of my eye, I could just barely see that Sheila's hands were fidgeting behind her.

"Under the medieval rules of hostageship," Beth said to no one in particular, "Hostages were encouraged to communicate in order to remind those who cared for them of the importance of compliance or cooperation."

"If there's a hell," I said aloud, "I will be waiting there for every last one of you sad bastards when you arrive." I looked around at everyone else, all the vampires who were now stuck serving the monster they were created to destroy.

"If her victory tonight teaches you anything, it's this: death isn't the end, even for those of us who think we're immortal. I *swear* I will come back to you, one way or another, and you will all regret this."

The Rhinemaiden stood from her overstuffed chair and projected, with something like a hint of relish, *Sixty seconds.* She adjusted the collar of her dress absently and began to step down from the raised platform. *Follow, slaves,* she thought to the others. *The time has come for us to go. The truck is waiting. The rest of you will be given the privilege of being awake to count out your final moments.* So they were going to go climb into a truck and get driven somewhere safe, just like that, the end.

What a bunch of bastards.

Ross moved with her, still smiling that hanging-judge smile. Old Shoe looked like he wasn't sure exactly what to do, or where to go, but he stood and started to walk behind them.

I fought down a rising bit of panic I hadn't felt since I was very young and—like all young vampires—tried to stay awake past sunrise. I felt that internal clock tick over, like an alarm going off, and I knew the sun was rising outside. Normally, at that moment, my eyes would slam shut and I would be dead for a few hours. Not this time. Not that morning. Instead, I felt a little like I was floating. Wakefulness persisted past the point when it should have, and my heart made a fist in the middle of my chest.

"Give the lady her fucking *phone call!*" Jennifer said aloud. I thought it was incongruous but she seemed really insistent, and then I felt that spark of something underneath, the magic the technopagans do, and I heard aloud—like there were an old speakerphone in the middle of the room—the sound of a phone dialing.

RRRRRRRRING

The Rhinemaiden stopped walking, and everyone seemed to freeze in place.

RRRRRRRRRING

Slowly, the Rhinemaiden started to turn to look at Jennifer.

The phone picked up.

"Beth?" The voice on the other end was Seth's.

"Baby," Beth said, her voice dreamy and far away, "I'm in a lot of trouble."

The eyes of *many* other vampires in the room—and Ross', too—went wide in recognition. After all, Ross didn't really make them forget Seth existed. He just made them think Seth was gone.

"Just tell me where you are," Seth said. I couldn't believe he wasn't asleep yet, but of course, we were on the coast and he was to the north and west of us in Raleigh. The sun comes up in Raleigh a full sixty seconds later. "I'll come get you."

Who is that?

Sheila finished whatever she was doing, and with a roar like an animal she stood up and tore apart like paper the zip ties holding her wrists together. Blood shot out of her hands and wrists in all directions, tiny hot flecks of burning red like puddle-splash from a passing car spraying across us in both directions, and with wild eyes she shouted, "*Corrosion!*" Another ripple of magic washed across the room, and I heard the sizzle as the blood ate away at everything it touched.

Where it touched my clothes, piping streams of smoke shot out.

Where it touched my skin, pain like molten metal being poured over me erupted from my flesh and I couldn't contain the involuntary yelp of agony. Beside me, Smiles produced a gut-wrenching howl and tried to get away.

Where it touched my chair, I felt the metal buckle underneath my weight.

Where it touched the chains binding me, I felt them fall away.

Then a lot of things happened all at once.

Roderick and I both spun up to super-speed at the same time. His arms flexed like a thin longbow underneath that white jacket—now smoking and looking like it might melt away altogether from the gout of Sheila's blood across it—and he struggled to shred the chains.

Mine had taken a direct hit and so I felt them give a little when I tore with all my strength.

Smiles snapped the chain holding him to me and started to leap for Ross.

Crew Cut screamed but couldn't get his restraints off. He looked like his shoulders might rip themselves out of the sockets if he pulled any harder, the veins in his neck bulging, the blood rushing to his face.

Marty closed his eyes and prepared to die.

Beth stared into the middle distance, that dreamy look on her face, her mouth moving as slowly as all hell as she tried to tell Seth she loved him.

Dan, in freeze-frame as he rolled out of the chair he had been in, was turned to dive into the row behind us.

Jennifer, slow as molasses, shouted, "*Fast fucking forward,*" and was suddenly moving as quickly as Roderick or I.

Old Shoe, damn his traitorous hide, was physically leaping for The Rhinemaiden, catching her off-guard.

Sheila was standing, arms outstretched, head held high, eyes locked open to gaze at something near the ceiling, and at the pace I was moving I could hear the pops and bursts as the blood in her veins started to eat at her own flesh, combusting against the air.

The technopagans might have been electronics fetishists—like the Book People said one time, they were kids who liked to bring their toys to the dinner table—but they were also the real deal. They used *magic*, and that all comes down to power, doesn't it? The Rhinemaiden asked who dared to use *our* powers against her. Crew Cut used the blood of the living to hide himself from his former masters, and from the vampires here who didn't even know to look for him in the first place. The vampires of Sunset Beach used blood upon blood, buckets of it, to try to find the location The Rhinemaiden died.

In the end, blood is the magic we *all* know, even you, the person reading this. It's the thing we all recognize is powerful and necessary. It's the thing the bravest among us shed to save another.

Blood is the sacrifice that gets results every time.

Jennifer was up and running, and as Smiles leapt through the air for The Rhinemaiden, and Ross tried to speak, and my chair fell to pieces underneath me as I stood, and Dan also achieved super speed and dove for cover, and Old Shoe got a hand on one of The Rhinemaiden's arms with terror in his eyes, and Dog grabbed Roderick's chains in his teeth and pulled, and Roderick's eyes turned blood red as he screamed, and Jennifer executed a perfect parkour jump onto the edge of the dais, and up, shouting *light as a feather* as she did so—

Jennifer grabbed onto one of the curtains by the edge, and pulled, hanging from it as she shouted *heavy as stone* so that the curtain began to peel away and sunlight began to pour down the side of the far wall and spill into the room

Sheila's body began to erupt like a water balloon full of fire and light

I turned to Ross, looked him right in the eye, and flipped him two birds with the last moment of my eternal unlife.

I heard the glass of a window shatter as Jennifer's weight pulled down not just the curtain but the whole framework holding the glass dome in place above us.

In the corner of my eye I saw dust drifting lazily in the light—sunlight, golden and pure and terrible as anything I have ever seen in my whole life, worse than all the blood I've taken and all the lives I've ended and all the suffering I've caused or cut short—and I knew it was over, that this was the end, that I was absolutely going to die but by all the demons in Hell and whatever ones escaped it I was sure as shit going to take every last one of these bastards with me –

There was the sound of a chime, like someone struck a gong underwater.

There was a hand on my shoulder.

Everything turned grayscale around me.

"Withrow," Seth said beside me. "Come on. We need to walk home."

I turned and looked at him, and looked all around us. Roderick was standing, with Dog by his side. Smiles was growling at the tableau version of Ross, grimacing at me in the space between two moments.

Beth was standing beside Seth.

Marty was blinking at everything around him.

Dan was frozen on the other side of some chairs.

Jennifer was hanging mid-air, paused perfectly as she executed an acrobatic spin to wrap herself in the curtain she had grabbed at the peak of her jump. Rays of sunlight stuck through the roof all around her, into the room, like beams of half-solid lumber smashing their way through the glass.

"Why are we not dead?" I said it aloud, but I knew the answer: Seth, and his power to stop time. He used it in Raleigh, awake in the last minute of local night, and walked here on borrowed time. He hunted until he found us—found Beth—and now he was going to walk us all back home in that not-time he had in such plentiful supply, in which everything was gray and we were safe.

"Thank you," I said to Seth. "Oh, Jesus fucking Christ, thank you." I took his hand and pumped it up and down, and I won't lie to you. I felt a great big drop of blood well up and roll like a tear down the front of my face.

He smiled a little. "No sweat. Come on."

"What about Dan?" Roderick said this with pursed lips, not quite ungrateful but not willing to let his boyfriend—not-boyfriend, whatever—die here with the others without at least *asking*.

"They have helped us many times here," Beth said to Seth.

Seth shrugged and walked over to him, put his hand on his shoulder, and the kid turned pink and fell to the floor screaming.

It took some explaining, but eventually he came and stood with us.

"Now Jennifer," I said to Seth, looking up at her, frozen in mid-air.

He looked at me with his brow wrinkled up. "How do we get to her up there?"

I reached up and clapped my right hand on my own left shoulder. "Hop on," I said. "We'll form a human ladder." I paused. "Well, technically a vampiric ladder, I guess."

Seth looked at me like I'd had a stroke and spoken in tongues, but thirty seconds later I was taking little steps one direction, then another, while Roderick urged me to remain steady and Beth silently gripped *him* with her legs around his shoulders, and Seth stood on tip-toe on *her* to reach up and touch Jennifer.

She moved again, like a movie un-paused, and landed screaming in Seth's outstretched arms. Some of the glass around her moved with her, but I noticed it froze again in mid-air just a few feet away.

"Huh," I said, and looked at Roderick. "Okay, that is creepy as all hell."

"This gives me an idea," Roderick said, and he and Dan started picking up the shattered, gray, frozen remains of the chairs in which we were seated before, and then The Rhinemaiden's makeshift throne, and threw them as hard as they could at the dome overhead.

The objects all re-froze in mid-air, inches from the falling curtains and the windows beyond.

I turned to look at the dais, where The Rhinemaiden was frozen and Old Shoe was gripping her, frozen as well, just starting a grapple there was no way he would win.

"I can't save him," Seth said. "He's touching her. If I put him on borrowed time, it'll affect her, too."

I was silent for a long moment and then I shook my head. "I didn't want you to save him. I wanted one last look before he dies." I turned around and surveyed the scene. "Okay. *Now* we walk home," I said.

"No," Jennifer said. "Not yet." She walked up to Sheila, who was frozen still in time, the blood in her veins turning to fire, a look of eternal anger and eternal pain on her features.

"If I unfreeze her," Seth said, but he trailed off.

"I know. She dies." Jennifer reached up and scratched her own nose.

"And so do we. But if we leave her," I said, gesturing around, "Maybe she injures these assholes enough they can't get away in the split-second they'll have before the light hits them."

"She saved us," Jennifer said. "She spilled her own blood to free us all."

"Yes," Roderick said.

Dan asked, very quietly, "May we touch her?"

Seth nodded. "Just me—I can't."

So that's how four vampires and two witches gathered in a circle and gave Sheila a group hug in the time between her last moments alive. Each of us thanked her, some with words, some with promises, some with a nod of the head.

Jennifer pulled out her phone and took a picture. "Now we walk home."

The last time I stood in sunlight was January 10th, 1947.

It was a Friday. At least, I think it was. It *felt* like a Friday. Agatha told me to spend my last day doing things I loved, so that morning I got up early, ate a big breakfast at a diner in downtown Asheville, and went to the movies. I know, movies on the morning on my last day in the sun, but I've always loved going to the movies. I went to see *The Ghost of Frankenstein*. It was old already, then, so it played in the mornings in a low-rent theater downtown. (In later decades, that theater became a porn palace and, last I knew, an evangelical church featuring snake handling.)

That afternoon, emerging blinking into the sunlight, I was so determined to be rid of daylight and life and the world in general that I tried to find other ways to hide from the sun: I went to the library. I went and had lunch in a big, dark restaurant I couldn't really afford. I went to a department store and got measured for a suit I didn't intend to buy.

In the late afternoon, with barely two hours of day left, I realized I was about to lose my chance to paint in sunlight. I would never again get the most natural light possible for my work. I ran ten blocks back to my apartment, about to have a heart attack the whole damned way, and I dragged an easel and my oils and a couple of brushes out onto the roof of the appliance store over which I had my shitty studio apartment. I painted fast, imprecisely, getting my colors muddled with each other. I spent the last hour-forty-five minutes of my last day on Earth painting my city—back then it was more of a town—nestled in a bowl of blazing pink and orange light, like it had been set in a fire growing cold.

The wind was terrible that day, and it was threatening snow, but the weather never delivered. I sat up there, my hands shaking from the cold, my mouth and face wrapped in a scarf, my hair blown all over like that of a madman, trying like hell to work the oils before they dried in the wind, and in the end I had one of the most impressionistic pieces I've ever done.

When the last of the light died, I wasn't quite finished. There was one corner undone. But the light was gone, and I couldn't see a damned thing, so I set my brush down and sat back and sighed through my scarf.

An hour later, I was dying in the bathtub of a hotel room, with Agatha chanting by my side.

Nearly seventy years later, I stood in the lobby of a run-down observatory about to be destroyed by the explosive demise of a half-dozen vampires.

I hesitated in the gray darkness of the lobby. I knew, intellectually, that Seth walked here through this frozen not-light, this gray expanse suspended between moments. That didn't make it easy to step into it.

"Come along, Cousin," Roderick said from beside me, and he took the sleeve of my trench coat and pulled so we stepped into it together.

I didn't explode.

Neither did he.

I looked around. Things in that suspended state weren't exactly sun-drenched. They were more like a brighter shade of gray. Still, I knew—I *knew*—I was doing something that was supposed to kill me.

"There," Roderick said. "That was not so terrible, was it?"

I could have chosen a lot of reactions: shouting at him, laughing at him, making a wisecrack of my own in response. Instead I looked him right in the eye and said, very softly, "Thank you."

Roderick closed his eyes, bowed his head forward just a moment in acknowledgement, and walked outside.

It took us the equivalent of two days of our perceived time to walk all the way back to Raleigh, stepping between cars and walking the emergency lane along the side of the Interstate. At first we pointed out all the birds frozen in mid-flight and the bugs half-smashed on windshields and the accident someone was just about to have, but eventually even those marvels got old and we grew quiet. Even Jennifer stopped asking questions eventually. Jennifer and Dan never needed to take a piss or eat or *anything*. Seth said he'd never done this with mortals, so he didn't know that. He just figured they would have to starve for a couple of days but it beat the alternative.

Dog and Smiles sniffed everything we walked past, at first, but they gave up when they realized nothing in the wide gray world smelled like anything at all.

The whole way home I thought about how precious little I actually *know* about the kind of creature I am. But then, who really knows themselves?

"I should warn you," Seth said when he dropped Jennifer and Dan off outside Dan's apartment. "You're going to be dropped back into normal time when I get… a certain distance away. When that happens, all the delayed time is going to hit you. You'll be exhausted and starving and you'll need to…" He gestured vaguely at his torso.

"Got it," Jennifer said.

Dan and Roderick exchanged a look, and squeezed each other's hands just once.

I turned to Jennifer, on the spur of the moment, and said without preamble, "Revenge is not enough."

She blinked at me.

I stared her right in the eye, and I didn't use the hoodoo, and it wasn't just because I knew it wouldn't work on her. I wanted to persuade her as a friend, as a compatriot, not as a supernatural being. "Revenge will poison you, and you are too good for that. If you want to keep fighting, I want to fight by your side, but you have to fight *for* something. It isn't enough to drive a stake through the heart of the past. We have to fight to make something good happen in the future."

Jennifer didn't nod, and she didn't agree, but she didn't disagree, either. So I walked away.

Seth took Marty and Roderick and me to my house in Raleigh. We wound our way there through the beginnings of morning rush hour. I saw Ken Watanabe from the neighborhood association's executive board, just about to turn out onto the main road on his way to work.

Marty and Roderick walked inside after saying their thanks and goodbyes.

"You're welcome to stay here with me during the day," I said to Seth. Beth was hanging beside him, going with him to her place or his. It was deeply strange, indescribably surreal, to know full well our enemies were all still back there in Sunset Beach, in that ratty old hotel-turned-science-lab, waiting between moments for time to resume and for the frozen sunrise to end them forever.

I thought of that bartender, who hadn't even been a vampire a week before when I questioned her about Crew Cut's whereabouts. The local vampires didn't even think he was worth going after when one of them knew exactly where he was. Nothing mattered to them except trying to bring back The Rhinemaiden so they could kill her again. I almost felt sorry for them, but not quite. They were a bunch of right bastards. They'd emptied out a whole town. In a town like that, where the permanent residents are few to none, would anyone even notice they were gone? The rental management companies could make deposits to accounts, and those balances would build up over time, and mortgage payments would get auto-deducted, and the whole town might run on autopilot for who knew how long? Years, probably.

I held out my hand to Seth, and he took it, and we shook. "Thank you," I said.

"You're welcome." He shrugged a little.

"I'm sorry you got dragged back into things. I didn't mean for that to happen."

"I know," Seth replied.

"I won't blame you if you make yourself scarce now." I nodded at the gray world around us, frozen still. The two days of perceived time as we all walked back from Sunset Beach didn't result in us all bonding over rounds of campfire songs or anything. Rather, we all grew quiet and withdrawn, retreating into our own heads for most of the trip.

Seth sucked his teeth for a second and shook his head. "Nah," he said, looking at his boots. "Nah." He looked up again and smiled. "See you around, Boss."

"See you around."

I shut my door, walked inside, and joined Roderick and Marty upstairs in my bedroom with the blacked out windows and the triple-layered curtains and the plywood nailed over the glass.

"Cousin," Roderick said, though his eyes were on Marty. "What happens next?"

Outside, I heard a bird chirp. My house went from gray on gray to beige on beige. The time freeze ended. Sunrise was less than a minute away for Raleigh.

I slipped off my big black trench coat, kicked off my boots, and untucked my shirt so I could properly relax. "We've been running around for years—hell, our whole lives—while a war waited for us. So let's go finish it." I glanced at myself in the mirror of my dressing table. My hair was a mess. I looked back at Roderick. "We're going to Charlotte."

Roderick smiled. "Yes," he said, but it was more like a sigh of pleasure than a spoken word.

My phone started ringing, and I made a little sound when I looked at who was calling: Agatha, my maker.

I swiped it with my fingers and put the phone to my ear. "Hello?"

Agatha employs a small army of "staff," most of them being foot soldiers and hired thugs. She's a big wig in the power structure in Atlanta, and across the whole Southeast, and by then I knew she maintained whatever authority she had as much through fear and intimidation as through anything more like loyalty or kind regard. Decades ago I was her best muscle, the guy she sent in to knock heads until she got her way. These days she has a whole bunch of vampires to do that for her. Sometimes I wonder if the reason she let me cut the apron strings wasn't that I was too strong to control but that she just didn't need me anymore. I was such small potatoes compared to whatever she had going on, what did I matter?

I expected the person on the other end of the call to be one of her servants, but it was Agatha herself. Her voice was rich and mellow and smooth, just like always, and it sounded like it could talk the sweet out of sugar. She also sounded *angry*. "What exactly did you just do?"

"Huh?" That's me, the picture of eloquence.

"Something big just happened. *Tell me what you did.*" It was the hoodoo, and for all that I am good with the hoodoo, I remind you Agatha is the one who taught *me*. Hers is good enough to work over the phone, from hundreds of miles away.

I opened my mouth to speak.

The sun came up.

My eyes slammed shut, and I slept like the dead.

Epilogue 1

"You didn't think that would hurt me, did you?" Ross' voice was deep and smooth, like the sort of clear mountain spring in which careless children drown.

Roderick stopped a few feet from the doorway to Seth's bar. He looked at his watch: half-past midnight. He had a lot to get done before he drove back to Asheville. He didn't have time for this shit, and the watch-check was calculated to communicate exactly that. "Oh, Ross. Still trying to go for the dramatic entrances? What do you think this is, a rerun of *Dark Shadows*?" Roderick turned and smirked from behind reflective glasses.

Three weeks had passed. Roderick studied the demon's face for signs of scarring, of lingering damage from the silver dollars he pressed to its face. Ross looked exactly as he always looked. Roderick blinked and looked more closely, sliding the glasses down his nose with a wiggle of his ears. Yes, exactly the same—*almost*. Not quite. There were changes. The demon had needed to *heal*.

"Very cute," Ross said. He pursed his lips a little, just slightly pouty, the sort of petulant expression that begged to be kissed or slapped.

"I know I am, and thank you, but you are not my type." Roderick turned to walk inside, but Ross reached out and grabbed Roderick's twig-thin upper arm in his comparatively massive hand.

"You don't get to walk away from me, leech." Ross growled it, angry, deadly serious.

People walked past. The part of downtown Raleigh where Seth's bar stood was once called the warehouse district. Back then, it folded up at night, slightly embarrassed by its major tenants: a few porn stores, a gay bar, a lot of whores. In the last ten years it became trendy and flourished. Now there were people all around. There were million-dollar condos to mark the grave of the last porn store to disappear. The people who lived there liked to pretend the neighborhood owed them something for showing up to save it. As far as Roderick could tell, real estate was just a more-wicked relative of the porn trade. They both sold mostly fantasies, but nobody ever went bankrupt buying porn.

No one glanced at the man and the boy having a tiff on the street. Noticing that sort of thing might lead to a 911 call, and 911 calls were bad for property values.

"I know what you're up to, Roderick, and it won't work." Ross hissed it, like the words themselves pissed him off.

Roderick smiled. "I do believe you are afraid of me. Even more so than before."

"I fear no material being." Ross smiled back, but it took effort to do so.

"And yet you grab my arm, and you clamp down like you are a little concerned I might be able to pull away. You hate me, Ross. You hate me so much you cannot express it. But you cannot remember *why*. You have a fascination with me, yet *you cannot remember why*. Is that not interesting?"

Ross blinked a few times in rapid succession but said nothing.

"I know *why*," Roderick said. "I could even explain it to you. But it would not work. Just like you do not remember the *other* deputy, you will not remember what I tell you."

Ross tightened his grip on Roderick's upper arm and, for a long time, said nothing. They simply stared at one another. Roderick cocked his head to one side but didn't try to push into Ross' mind. He was mad—he knew that about himself—but he wasn't *crazy*.

Eventually, Ross licked his lips. "Tell me."

"Ah," Roderick breathed. He lifted one hand and put a fingertip to Ross' chin, tracing the divot in its center, that movie-star dimple so loved in the monochrome heroes of old. "So you admit this fascination? This desire to understand?"

Ross tightened his grip again. "Tell. Me."

So Roderick did.

Thirty seconds later Ross was standing there, blinking, looking a little confused as to where he was or why. Roderick watched the look of comprehension and fear on Ross' face fade, like an old film reel burning up, as the things Roderick said simply melted away again.

"Oh, and," Roderick said as he peeled Ross' fingers off his upper arm, one by one, "Hands off the merchandise."

EPILOGUE 2

We held a funeral for Old Shoe. It didn't seem right *not* to. Roderick asked why I wanted to memorialize a traitor, so I reminded him Old Shoe kind of tried to un-traitor at the last second. It didn't save him, and I haven't let myself answer the question of whether it would have saved him in the long run even if it saved him right then. I might have killed him anyway, and I'll never know for sure.

Seth and Beth and Roderick and I got together at Seth's bar. I bought a casket and had it delivered there, and even though it was empty we talked over it like it had him inside. That's the thing about a funeral: honoring the dead doesn't actually figure too much into them. If there's a body on display, most of the people there just want to see how they looked in the end. If there's no body, they want to see how everyone else dressed. Funerals are rituals for the living. They're a way survivors can grant themselves permission to say goodbye.

I'm not judging, mind you. I like closure as much as the next guy, even if I'm avoiding it as hard as I can.

I told a couple of funny stories about Old Shoe, times he cracked wise or came up with a particularly useful bit of gossip. Beth talked about how he used to come around her club after hours, when even the dancers were gone home for the night, and play cards. Seth told about sneaking into the sewers one night and sneaking up and surprising Old Shoe, kind of beating him at his own game for once. Seth looked like he wished he could blush when he told that story, like he felt dumb admitting he did something so youthful, and we

223

all kind of laughed. Seth still looks like he's maybe 20. I figure adding a zero would just be the beginning of a more accurate count.

Roderick didn't have a single thing to say, but he watched and smiled and chuckled as appropriate, and so as usual my cousin played the role of the living in our drama of the undead.

When we were done telling a few stories, Seth asked what was next.

I shrugged. "I don't know," I said. "I've never had a funeral for a vampire before."

"Where are we burying him?" Roderick asked.

"I always met him out at a specific graveyard," I said. "I figured we could have a little procession, take him out there."

Seth looked at me. "The corporate memorial garden place? Out on Glenwood?"

I shrugged. "I know. It's a hell of a walk."

"Walk?" Roderick arched an eyebrow.

"Well, I ain't exactly going to tie a casket to the roof of the Firebird," I said. I looked meaningfully at Seth.

He sighed a little. "This better not become a habit."

There was a sound like a gong, far underwater, and everything turned gray.

I hefted the empty casket onto my left shoulder. "I'll carry him."

"No," Beth said. "We all carry him. He tried to save all of us."

So we all carried him, in his empty casket, out into a street full of frozen cars, and frozen people, and frozen time. We walked in silence, past all those frozen lives, between frozen moments. We went to the farthest, oldest corner of Raleigh's biggest, most generic graveyard: not the section where they bury people now with memorial plaques low enough to the ground they can mow right over them, but to the part that was once a church cemetery, where the dead were too old for there to be any living left to know them. We dug a grave and put Old Shoe's casket in it, covered it back up, and walked back to Seth's bar through that eternally still gap between instants.

The people on the sidewalk, the people in the frozen cars we wove between, none of them noticed us. They *couldn't*. From their perspective we never passed. We disappeared from the stream of time, into our own not-moment, and I tried hard not to think just how on-the-nose it was.

I like to think Seth's power to take us out of the world is the exception, not an exaggeration of the way things always already are. I've realized something, though. Making it be that way—making it be that I'm a part of the world of the living, that we all are, and that we don't disappear into our own legends of ourselves and pull the world shut behind us—is something we have to do ourselves. We can't be passive forever. In the end, life is lived by those who show up.

About the Author

Michael G. Williams is a native of the mountains of western North Carolina. He is a brother in St. Anthony Hall and Mu Beta Psi and believes strongly in the power of found families. Michael lives in Durham with his two cats and more and better friends than he probably deserves.

Michael earned a BA in Performance Studies at UNC Chapel Hill and works as an engineer. He has been a successful participant in National Novel Writing Month for many years and encourages anyone interested in writing to jump headlong into the deep end of insanity for thirty days. More information can be found at www.nanowrimo.org.

For more information on this work and others by Michael G. Williams, visit www.michaelgwilliams-author.com. For information on Michael's open-source marketing, visit The *Perishables* Project at www.the*Perishables*project.com.

ALSO BY MICHAEL G. WILLIAMS

Perishables (The Withrow Chronicles #1)
Tooth & Nail (The Withrow Chronicles #2)
Deal with the Devil (The Withrow Chronicles #3)
"COMPLICATIONS"
"The Several Monsters of Sainte-Sara-La-Noire"
(Theme-Thology: Invasion, HDWPbooks.com)
"Daddy Used to Drink Too Much"
(Wrapped in Red: Thirteen Tales of Vampiric Horror, Sekhmet Press)
"A Shrine to Santa Muerte Behind the Reference Desk"
(Wrapped in White: Thirteen Tales of Spectres, Ghosts & Spirits, Sekhmet Press)
"Stories I Tell to Girls"
(Wrapped in Black: Thirteen Tales of Witches & the Occult, Sekhmet Press)

CONNECT WITH MICHAEL VIA THE FOLLOWING SITES:

www.the*Perishables*project.com
@*Perishables*Book on Twitter
www.facebook.com/*Perishables*.novel
Amazon Author Central
GoodReads

Character Tumblrs:
rodericksurrett.tumblr.com
withrowsurrett.tumblr.com

Visit www.the*Perishables*project.com for information on Michael's novels and short stories and for doodles he's drawn of Roderick's and Dog's superhero identities.